What others are saying about *The Gi*

The Girls
of October

JOSH HANCOCK

Burning Bulb

PUBLISHING

The Girls of October
By **Josh Hancock**

Burning Bulb Publishing
P.O. Box 4721
Bridgeport, WV 26330-4721
United States of America
www.BurningBulbPublishing.com

Cover designed by Gary Lee Vincent with the following licensed elements from Fotolia: the victim © ivanfff.

First Edition.

Paperback Edition ISBN: 978-0692412442

Printed in the United States of America

ACKNOWLEDGMENTS

Thank you to the following individuals who without their insight and contributions *The Girls of October* would not have been written: Brittney Aresta, Leah Darnell, Ethan Harkin, Peter Razavi, and Hanna Scheuerman. A special thank you to my parents, Larry and Terry Hancock, who always supported my writing and who let me watch all the horror movies I could get my hands on as a kid. I am also forever indebted to my wife, Angeline, who rescued this book in every conceivable way. She is my motivation and inspiration in all things, and I dedicate this book to her.

.

The following documents originally appeared in Eugene Stone's 'zine "The Black Notebook," Volumes I-IV. I have added Beverly Dreger's essay on *Halloween*, plus several additional articles relevant to her story.

--Lauren Reid, Professor of American Literature, Woodhurst State

"THE BLACK NOTEBOOK": VOLUME I

"Fairy tales do not give the child his first idea of bogey. What fairy tales give the child is his first clear idea of the possible defeat of bogey. The baby has known the dragon intimately ever since he had an imagination…"

--G.K. Chesterton, *Tremendous Trifles*

From "Stone Cold Horror" by Gustavo Carrillo (originally published in *Monsters & Mayhem*, Jan. 1984) p. 3-4:

Monsters & Mayhem scribe Gustavo Carrillo talks to maverick director Eugene Stone about his first full-length feature, *Squatters*, a psychedelic splatter film starring Burt Temple and Amy Walsh. Stone also opens up about his side project, a 'zine about Beverly Dreger and the Woodhurst Murders of 1981, and what it's like to be known as the man who once hated *Halloween*...

M&M: What can audiences expect from *Squatters*?

STONE: It's a nasty little flick! Greg Locke, who wrote *The Return of the Prowler*, penned the script and really belted it out of the park. It's got deranged hillbillies, vampire squid, a cop with a prosthetic face, and a pair of deformed twins looking for revenge. The perfect movie to take your mother to!

M&M: After your two horror shorts, "Crankers" and "The Werewolf Strain," why did you choose *Squatters* as your first feature film?

STONE: For all the script's blood and guts, it was also really funny. We watched stuff like *An American Werewolf in London* and *Motel Hell* and tried to capture the same spirit. And the practical effects are killer. There's a death scene involving a claw hammer and a rototiller that took us three nights to shoot...

M&M: What can you tell us about your true crime 'zine "The Black Notebook," and how fans can get a hold of it?

STONE: "The Black Notebook" is about more than just the murders at Woodhurst State. It starts from the moment Beverly Dreger was born in 1960, and goes all the way through the murders and beyond. The police haven't caught her yet, so I don't know when it will be finished, but my plan is for the 'zine to come in three or four volumes, with the first one hitting record stores on Halloween of this year.

M&M: Why devote an entire 'zine series to the Beverly Dreger story?

STONE: Like most of the country, I was drawn to this case from the start. But I actually knew Beverly. We both went to Woodhurst and I was living on campus when the murders happened. It was like California during Manson, or New York City during Son of Sam. Everything changed and you saw the world for what it really was. I started writing "Crankers," about evil flower children living in the woods, just days after all those bodies were discovered.

M&M: How well did you know Beverly?

STONE: We met only once, at an off-campus party. But we had this silly feud going in the school paper over *Halloween*. See, I was kind of an asshole at the time. I enjoyed classic films like *Nosferatu*, *Dracula*, and *Frankenstein*, but I considered *Halloween* low-brow and cheap. Of course, I don't think that now! But, as you already know, Beverly had a certain affinity with that picture, and we got into a written spat over it. Now here I am, directing a slasher on a shoestring budget and trying to unravel her life story!

M&M: Can you tell us about the format of the 'zine, and why you chose this platform to tell the story of the Woodhurst Murders?

STONE: I've gathered newspaper articles, essays, stories, screenplays, police reports—a boatload of stuff—and arranged them in a way that allows readers to decode the mind of a suspected killer. The end result will be like a true crime scrapbook, revealing new information with every turn of the page and without my obnoxious voice intruding on the process.

M&M: Are you worried about the consequences of some of your research methods?

STONE: Truthfully, no, not really. I've never been one to do things by the book. And some of the stuff gets sent to me anonymously—letters, transcripts, medical reports, things like that. "The Black Notebook" is indie publishing at its finest, stripped-down and raw. Copyrights and legalities be damned!

Stay tuned to the pages of *Monsters & Mayhem* for more gory details on Eugene Stone's *Squatters*, and be sure to look for "The Black Notebook" at your local record shop or bookstore this Halloween...

JOHNSON - Johnson Memorial Hospital is moving patients into different rooms after a fire broke out in the maternity ward on the night of October 28th.

A hospital spokesman reports that several mothers and their babies were evacuated from the floor after a fire ignited under the oxygen hood of a newborn infant. Women in labor were also moved to another area in the hospital.

"Fortunately, our staff was able to extinguish the fire before the baby could be severely burned," said the spokesman.

As Johnson County police officers evacuated the floor and began interviewing hospital staff, county fire officials arrived to investigate the incident.

"We are hoping to determine the exact cause of the fire," said Division Chief Michael Bell of the Johnson Fire Department. "The goal is to make sure something like this never happens again."

The baby, named Beverly, was ten hours old. She was wearing an oxygen hood, a clear plastic canopy placed over a baby's head to supply additional oxygen and humidity, when the gas ignited.

Beverly was taken to Johnson County Medical Center, where hospital officials said she was in stable condition with first-degree burns on her scalp.

From *The Girl Who Loved Halloween: The Strange Case of Beverly Dreger* by Raymond Sutcliffe (Gauntlet Publications: 1983), p. 20:

In the days after her birth, Beverly Dreger witnessed bizarre behavior from her parents, especially from her mother.

Alberta Graysmith, a nurse and hospice caregiver at the medical center where Beverly was transferred after the accident, shudders as she remembers meeting Jack and Susan Dreger for the first time.

"They were an odd-looking couple," says Alberta. "She was a big woman with long black hair and this witchy-looking charm around her neck. He was tall, thin as a wishbone, with grease-stained hands and all these tattoos of eagles and mermaids.

"They sat apart in their room, with the baby in a crib against the wall. Neither of them had a clue what to do. I had to show them how to carry her, how to feed and nurse her—everything."

Alberta lights a cigarette with shaky fingers. "And then things got a little weird," she says.

The night after the fire, Alberta entered Susan Dreger's room to find the new mother in a rage. "We needed to show her how to change the baby's dressing, but the woman refused to let us take her. She began cursing, sticking her tongue out at us, clutching the child in one hand and waving her charm around with the other. When we did manage to take the baby, the mother started having a panic attack, and her husband had to slap her across the face.

"I walked out of the room with the child," Alberta says, "and I didn't want to take her back."

But three days later the Dregers left the hospital with Beverly, returning to their modest home in South Hill, a small town about four hours south of Chicago.

"New mothers can be overly protective," Alberta says now. "But this was unlike anything I had ever seen. I thought she was a witch. I thought she might have been on drugs. I had no idea."

When the murders at Woodhurst State first hit the headlines, Alberta refused to follow the story. She avoided the first book, A.P. Bullock's trashy *Shattered Mirror, Shattered Lives*, when she saw the neon-tinged paperback in the supermarket. If Beverly's face appeared on television, the nurse would change the channel.

"I felt guilty," Alberta says. "As a caregiver, you always want to do your best to help someone.

"I didn't want to face whatever she might have done. I knew her when she was a baby, when she was innocent and pure. And I didn't want to know her any other way."

From *Shattered Mirror, Shattered Lives* by A.P. Bullock (True Crime House: 1982), p. 10-12:

Rumors began flying around South Hill as soon as the Dregers brought the burned infant home. Small-town gossipers believed the child was born of black magic and the occult, her mother was a witch, her father a moody loner. The little white-and-yellow village house on Wichita Road became the subject of sleazy speculation…

But Deborah Clark, who lived next door to the Dregers for many years, had far more realistic concerns. "Susan didn't care for the child the way a mother should," Deborah says. "She was a cocktail waitress at Sparky's, this real dingy bar in town, and after work they'd all gather at their house and drink and play weird music. I had to call the cops on them a few times. It just wasn't a safe place for Beverly to be."

Deborah recalls one alarming incident in 1963, when Beverly was 3-years-old. On a summer afternoon she found the child sitting alone on the front stoop of the Dreger house. "It makes me sad saying this, but Beverly was always by herself," Deborah says.

But as Deborah walked over to see if the child needed help, she saw something that chilled her blood. "Beverly was playing with a book of matches, tearing them out one by one and throwing them on the ground. I ran over and snatched them out of her hand, and she burst into tears."

At that moment the front screen door crashed open. As Deborah stood there helplessly, Jack Dreger scooped his wailing daughter into his arms. "He was very embarrassed," Deborah remembers. "He said that he only left her for a second. But when I showed him the matches and explained to him what I saw, he looked horrified. He thanked me, and then he hurried into the house with Beverly and closed the door. Jack was a tough guy, kind of gruff, but he closed the door *gently*. I don't know why I remember that, but I do.

"Frankly, with all the awful things that happened later, I always felt me and Jack were slotted for the same fate in life," Deborah says. "We suffered a lot in this world, and there wasn't a damn thing either of us could do about it."

JOHNSON - Authorities in Johnson County have located the body of a 10-year-old girl after the child had been missing for over a week, officials said.

Natalie Stubson's body was found along the side of Highway 33 late on Saturday night, according to a press release from the Johnson County Police Department.

A local man in the search party discovered the body. It had been partially wrapped in a blanket and placed in a shallow ditch.

"It looked to me like she had been there a while," the man told WLS-TV Chicago. "The blanket was dirty and covered in leaves."

Natalie was reported missing last Thursday at about 9:30 a.m. when her parents realized she was not in her bedroom. Investigators initially thought that the girl had run away, but none of her clothes or belongings was missing from the house, reported WLS-TV.

Detectives believe that Natalie was abducted from her room and killed sometime afterward. Yet the press release indicated that there were no signs of forced entry in the house and all the windows were securely locked.

Investigators did not discuss whether they had any suspects in the case, or what evidence was found at the residence. They are awaiting the autopsy results to determine the exact cause of the child's death.

"Once we get the results, we will know a lot more about what happened to Natalie," said Det. Hank Baldwin of the JCPD. "We are determined to get justice for this poor little girl."

CHICAGO - A 911 recording reveals the terrifying moments that a group of friends experienced when the hostess of a Halloween party became violent and claimed a demonic spirit had taken over her house.

Susan Dreger, 34 and a resident of South Hill, was taken to the hospital after a game of Ouija board caused her to curse at her guests and physically assault one of them. Her co-worker, Stacy Miller, 39, told South Hill Police that "something went screwy during the game" and that Mrs. Dreger believed she had summoned the spirit of the "bogeyman" or the devil himself, according to the police report.

Photos of the residence taken by police show a living room in disarray, with beer cans, records and cassette tapes, and tarot cards scattered all over the floor. One photo shows a large burn mark in the center of the carpet, while another shows the Ouija board thrown in the corner of the room.

"I thought she was just drunk, but then she started acting like she was really possessed," Miller said, who works with Mrs. Dreger at a cocktail bar in South Hill. Miller added that Mrs. Dreger exhibited muscle spasms, claimed to hear a non-human voice, and screamed obscenities at anyone who came close to her.

According to the police report, partygoers at the residence were playing with the "talking board" after a night of food and drinks. The game became frightening when Mrs. Dreger, who has always been interested in true crime and the occult, began reciting an incantation that scared some of the revelers away.

"She was trying to cast a protective circle around the spirit of Natalie Stubson," said a guest who fled the party when things started to get strange. "I thought I saw something—a puff of green smoke or something—and then I just got the hell out of there."

Natalie Stubson was the 10-year-old girl who vanished from her bedroom last summer in the middle of the night. Her body was found in August in a shallow ditch off the side of a highway. Her murder has not yet been solved.

During the game, Mrs. Dreger said that she felt a painful weight on her shoulders, like someone was trying to push her onto the floor. When her husband and friends tried to intervene, she swore at them and struck a female guest across the face with her open palm.

On the 911 recording, Jack Dreger, 31, told the operator, "I don't know what's happening. My wife is threatening to hurt her friends. Please hurry."

According to witnesses, Mrs. Dreger did not want her guests interfering with the board game, which some associate with demonic possession and cult practices. "Susan felt she had started something bad, and she was the only one who could fix it," Miller said. "She had this freaky-looking knife that she called her ritual dagger. And she was swinging the knife, stabbing the air with it. It was terrifying."

The 911 call also recorded several background noises during the altercation, including moaning sounds and a woman screaming.

Police arrived at the residence to find Susan Dreger wielding the knife and struggling with an unseen force. As police restrained the woman and paramedics arrived, Mr. Dreger took his sleeping 4-year-old daughter out of the house and to a neighbor's house.

"Thankfully, she slept through most of this," Mr. Dreger said.

The police report indicates that Mrs. Dreger was intoxicated and may have been suffering from alcohol-related psychosis. She was taken to the nearest hospital for tests.

Stacy Miller remained at the residence until after the police had left, cleaning up the mess and helping Mr. Dreger return his daughter to bed.

"I've known Susan for many years, and she's a kook sometimes, but what happened here tonight was beyond her control," Miller said.

"She was trying to summon an angel, but the devil showed up instead."

ROSENDALE - The Rosendale Library hosted its 12th annual pumpkin weigh-off this weekend in an event that offered fun for the entire family.

With a pumpkin that weighed over 500 pounds, Reggie DeLapp of Johnson County was certain he would win the first-place prize.

"I thought she might break the scale," the 35-year-old farmer said, "but the mice had other plans."

As it turned out, on the morning of the contest DeLapp woke up to find a large hole burrowed deep into the bottom of the giant gourd. His plans of winning the weigh-off were crushed.

"The critters dig tunnels right under the netting. I didn't set any traps, but I won't be so nice to the mice next year," DeLapp joked.

Ken Pembrey arrived at the weigh-off with the hopes of beating the record set by Doc Maveport of Rosendale, who won first prize last season with an impressive entry that weighed 752 pounds. Pembrey's pumpkin, which weighed over 800 pounds, was enough to beat last season's results, but it didn't win him this year's competition.

The winner was amateur grower Leland Wesson from Franklin Grove, who amazed the crowd with a 1,005-pound behemoth that ushered in the Halloween season with style. The victory awarded Wesson, 28, a free weekend stay at the Rosendale Cottage and a gift certificate to Last Chapter Books in Franklin Grove.

For a young grower new to pumpkin weigh-offs, the victory was an emotional one for Wesson. "I'm honored to represent Franklin Grove and all of Johnson County," he said.

Orange gourds of much smaller sizes also played a starring role in the day's festivities. On the patio outside the library, people of all ages lined up their pumpkins for the 12th annual pumpkin-carving contest.

Marisa Redsun, who took home the first-place ribbon, used a chisel and a melon baller to design a spiderweb into her pumpkin. "It took a lot of trial and error," she said. "I must've gone through five pumpkins or more."

Other winning pumpkin designs included a haunted mansion, a scary ghost, and a silhouetted cat.

The third-place winner featured a candlelit diorama of a small figure being chased by a monster made out of toothpicks and flecks of red candy. Susan Dreger, who crafted the ghoulish pumpkin with her 5-year-old daughter, said she was inspired by ancient tales that center on the famous holiday.

"On Halloween, instead of trick-or-treating, we carve pumpkins and read folk legends from the American past," Dreger said, pulling her daughter close. "It's become a family tradition."

Excerpt from letter mailed on Nov. 17, 1966, from Susan Dreger to Stacy Miller:

...two years later and people still give me that *look*. Especially the people at work, the ones who came to the party. A look of disgust. Of horror. They think I'm a freak. And after you read this letter, you'll probably think the same thing...

That night, I allowed something into my house. Something with flaky, burned skin and blood-webbed eyes. Something that nests in the back of my closet, smelling noxious and foul—like sewer gas.

You saw the circular burn on the carpet. That was the sign of his homecoming. The mark of his arrival.

He comes out at night now, when I'm alone, undressing for bed or drifting away in the bath. He taunts me, closing doors, clicking his toenails across the floor, breathing his foul breath into my ear. Sometimes he tugs on my hair or pinches my fat. Sometimes he whispers my name. He tells me to do things, to *sacrifice*...

SOUTH HILL - A mother has been arrested after police say she stood over her young daughter with a knife while the child was asleep.

Susan Dreger, 38, was booked on child endangerment charges. Her daughter remains in the custody of the child's father, who called the police to report the incident.

After receiving the call, officers went to the Dreger residence in South Hill. When they arrived, Jack Dreger, 35, was in the kitchen, consoling his daughter. They found Susan Dreger in another part of the house and arrested her.

Police say the child, age 8, had no injuries but was visibly upset. According to the police report, the girl woke up from a nap to see her mother looming over her with a knife.

Police say the child's scream brought her father into the room, where he wrestled the weapon away from his wife.

WLS-TV Chicago spoke to a neighbor who has lived next to the Dregers for three years. "The mother acts crazy sometimes," she said, "but her husband doesn't want her locked up in some looney bin. It's a terrible situation because there's a child involved."

According to police, Jack Dreger will seek medical treatment for his wife, who he said has suffered from psychiatric problems for most of her adult life. It is not clear what charges, if any, would be filed.

Police would not say why Susan Dreger was standing over her daughter with a knife or what her intentions were, only that the mother has a history of mental illness and altercations with medical staff at a behavioral health center in Franklin Grove.

"It's like someone cut the wires in her brain," the neighbor said. "There's no other explanation for why a mother would want to risk hurting her daughter like that."

From the mental state examination of Susan Dreger (Crestwood Behavioral Health Center, Franklin Grove, 1968):

Susan Dreger is a 38-year-old woman with a husband and an 8-year-old daughter. Diagnosed with borderline personality disorder, Susan has symptoms that include mood swings, impulsive behavior, and impaired reality-testing. Susan has exhibited passive-aggressive rage behavior in the past, especially when challenged about the care of her daughter. Last week, she endangered the child by holding a knife over her while she slept. Susan suspects her husband has plans to file for divorce due to her psychiatric condition.

During her last stay at Crestwood in October of 1963, Susan got in an argument with another female patient and threw a glass ashtray at the patient. During the altercation, Susan also slapped the face of a member of the Crestwood staff. Susan's family background is deeply rooted in physical abuse, which explains at least some of her violent behavior. Susan's mother died of a cranial brain tumor when Susan was twelve. Susan was raised by her father, a carpenter who beat his daughter and who was obsessed with "necromancy, superstition, and spiritual investigations." A lifelong smoker, her father died from lung cancer when Susan was in her early twenties. He left behind for Susan his collection of "mystical" objects and trinkets, including books on witchcraft and sorcery, prayer cards, and a "ritual" knife that Susan believes is infused with "anti-demonic power."

During this examination, Susan exhibited signs of depression and feelings of melancholy. Her shoulders sagged and she picked at her skin. Though generally clear, her words were sluggish and thick. She expressed anger at her husband for "dumping" her at Crestwood and said that she missed her daughter. When asked to describe her most frequent mood, Susan wrote, "Like my head's going to explode."

The abuse that Susan suffered as a child, combined with her father's unusual interests and her mother's death, has contributed to the depressive disorder that she is experiencing today. While Susan often describes her daughter with feelings of joy, she has committed acts of physical aggression on the child that reveal signs of borderline personality disorder. These acts have been reported to the police. Knowledge of these factors will help doctors to determine the future management of Susan's illness...

"Beverly Dreger's Shocking Childhood Revelations" by Lara Hanley (originally published in *The National Buzz*, Dec. 1981, p. 4-5):

As early as the fifth grade, Beverly Dreger loved scary movies and gross-out Edgar Allan Poe stories like "The Tell-Tale Heart" and "The Murders in the Rue Morgue." But an interview with a source close to the Dreger family reveals even more details about the alleged killer's disturbing childhood.

Today, 21-year-old Beverly Dreger remains a fugitive, having fled the college campus where three students were found stabbed to death in October of this year. The subject of an exhaustive manhunt that has now lasted over a month, she remains the sole suspect in that murder investigation.

The BUZZ can now reveal the inner workings of Beverly's mind when she was a child and what might have led to those ghastly events at Woodhurst State.

According to the source, little Beverly had a fascination with fire and drew pictures of hooded figures dressed in black. She had dreams about talking skeletons, masked killers, and "bogeymen" with burning red eyes.

Other examples of the girl's chilling behavior include throwing a dish at her mother and building plastic monster models and setting them ablaze.

"Because Beverly was burned as an infant, she has an obsession with fire," the source said. "She is fascinated by its beauty, but drawn to its destructive power."

But there's more—the source provided The BUZZ the full text of a creepy retelling of an urban legend that Beverly wrote in the winter of 1971, when she was just 11-years-old.

"Beverly's drawings and stories reveal a truly damaged psyche," the source explained, "and her combative relationship with her crazy mother only made it worse."

As police continue to piece together the gruesome puzzle that Beverly Dreger allegedly left behind at Woodhurst State, the image of a little girl haunted by her own monstrous imagination serves as a disturbing reminder that children are not always what they seem.

"Beverly was tormented by a mother who loved and hated her equally, and by her own macabre creations," the source said. "The real world played second fiddle to her sick, homicidal fantasies."

"The Girl Came Out of the Fog," written by Beverly Dreger when she was 11-years-old:

John waited for his girlfriend Cindy outside the movie theater. After a few minutes, she came out of the fog in the park. She ran into his arms.

They kissed. Then they bought their tickets for the show, which was about a scary disease that killed people. When the movie ended, Cindy took John's hand. They left the theater and walked through the park.

"Don't be scared. It was only a movie," John said.

"I am not scared," Cindy said, but she asked him to hold her hand tight. When they reached the end of the park, he stepped away. He got down on one knee and took a small box from his coat pocket. He had been waiting for this moment for a long time.

"Cindy," John said, "will you marry me?"

John opened the box. Cindy saw a beautiful diamond ring inside. Her smile was bigger than John had ever seen.

"Yes!" Cindy practically shouted. John put the ring on her finger. It fit nicely. As John talked about their future, they walked the rest of the way out of the park.

The big yellow house where Cindy lived with her parents was on Chamberlain Road. When they got to the road, Cindy let go of John's hand.

"I will walk the rest of the way from here," Cindy said.

"But shouldn't we tell your parents the good news?" John asked.

Cindy looked sad. John thought she was crying. "They are probably asleep. I will tell them tomorrow," Cindy said. She kissed John and said, "I love you." Then she walked onto Chamberlain Road and disappeared into the dark.

John turned around and started to walk back through the park. He lived in a house near the movie theater. But then he stopped.

"Cindy is going to be my wife," he thought. "I should not let her walk alone late at night."

John ran back to Chamberlain Road, looking for Cindy. The night was dark and John was getting scared. "I should go to Cindy's house. I need to make sure she got home safely."

Cindy lived at the end of the road. John ran all the way there and rang the doorbell. Mr. Belgrave answered the door.

"Come in, John," he said.

Mr. Belgrave took John into the living room. "I am sorry to come over like this," John said. "I wanted to make sure Cindy got home safely. Did she tell you our good news?"

Mr. Belgrave looked unhappy. "Excuse me?"

"After our date tonight, I asked Cindy to marry me and she said yes," John said.

Mr. Belgrave sat down in a big chair by the fireplace. "That's impossible. Cindy died this afternoon from a terrible disease," he said.

John fell onto the floor and Mr. Belgrave had to help him stand up. John was shaking all over. "I don't understand," he said.

"Would you like to see her?" Mr. Belgrave asked.

They walked to a room down the hall. Mrs. Belgrave was sitting in the room next to the bed. Her face was covered in a black veil. Cindy was on the bed with her eyes closed. Her skin was blue and her lips were gray.

John walked to the bed with tears in his eyes. He reached for Cindy's hand. He wanted to hold it one last time. Then he noticed something on her finger.

It was the diamond ring he had given her. It was shining in the moonlight coming through the window.

FRANKLIN GROVE - A South Hill auto mechanic is reporting a frightening story about something that happened at the Byrd Movie Theater in Franklin Grove on Saturday night.

Jack Dreger, 38, took his young daughter to an evening showing of *Frankenstein*, part of the Byrd's Halloween film festival. The 11-year-old girl likes painting monster models in her spare time, but what she saw after the movie may have her rethinking her hobby.

As she exited the building with her father, the child spotted a suspicious man standing in the field at the edge of the highway.

"It looked like he was wearing a mask," the girl said.

The girl pointed out the figure to her father, but Mr. Dreger had his glasses tucked in his shirt pocket. He couldn't see anyone standing in the field.

But his daughter kept her eyes on the man. A moment later, she saw the figure remove what she thought was a knife from the inside of his jacket.

She screamed.

"It was an awful sound to hear your child scream like that," said Mr. Dreger. "We ran back to the theater as quickly as we could."

Mr. Dreger found the theater manager, Christine Bixby, who immediately called Franklin Grove police.

"Two officers arrived and spoke with the little girl," said Bixby. "The poor thing was terrified."

Bixby watched as officers searched around the theater and field with a flashlight. She saw one of the officers talking to a man at the edge of the highway, but she was too far away to hear anything.

"The police said the man was a transient," Bixby said. "Hobos sometimes camp near the highway, hoping to catch a ride."

No police report was filed, but the father said the officers found a pocketknife on the man, much smaller than the knife his daughter described. Mr. Dreger said the the man was not wearing a mask.

"After seeing the movie, my kid thought the man was a monster, a bogeyman," the father said. "I had to break the news to her that monsters don't exist."

Bixby plans to ask city officials about the possibility of installing better lighting throughout the theater parking lot and adjacent field. "It can get kind of spooky at night," she said, "especially if you've just seen a scary movie."

Franklin Grove Police said the transient man did nothing illegal, so he was not arrested. His name was not released to the public.

SOUTH HILL - South Hill Grammar School had been gearing up for the exciting day for the past three months: the seventh-grade science fair, an annual event in which 25 seventh-graders displayed their research on topics that included rock candy, photosynthesis, and volcanoes.

The school held the fair on a Saturday in the gymnasium. The students devoted the morning to transporting their physical projects to their assigned tables, setting up their tri-fold posterboards, and practicing their speeches. After a break for lunch, parents, teachers, and members of the community were welcomed inside the gym to interact with the students and experience their projects first-hand.

"It's their moment to shine," said science teacher Sandy Briggs. "The kids have been working on their projects since September. Now is their chance to show the community how much they've learned and grown as students.

"We don't assign the topics," Briggs added. "The students get to choose, which gives them the opportunity to research something that they are truly interested in. Or maybe it's a subject that has simply piqued their curiosity and they want to know more."

Curiosity has never been a problem for seventh-grader Beverly Dreger, who has always had an interest in fire dynamics.

"At first I wanted to build some kind of fire simulator," Beverly said on the morning of the fair, "but my dad thought it would be too dangerous. I decided to make my own sparklers instead."

Briggs requires that the students formulate a question that their subsequent research and project will answer. Beverly Dreger, who has seen a few fireworks displays in her lifetime, was always interested in how all those roman candles and crackling pinwheels worked. "We see the big explosions in the sky, but we don't exactly know how they happen," she said.

Beverly's father drove her to a chemical supply company to buy the chemicals she would need for her project. Beverly also checked out chemistry books from the library. "My research taught me a lot about fire safety," she said. "When I tested the sparklers at home, I always kept a bucket of water nearby to drop them in."

Beverly explained that she used old wire hangers to dip into the sparkler mixture. Under her father's watchful eye, she experimented with different sparkler colors, including strontium nitrate in the mix for red sparklers and barium nitrate for green sparklers.

"They look best at night," Beverly said, "and I'm not allowed to light any of them at the science fair." For these reasons, the energetic 12-year-old took pictures of her sparklers lighting up the night sky, and then attached the photos to her tri-fold poster.

These posters play an important role in the learning objectives of the assignment and the overall look of the fair. "When an audience approaches your table, you have to be ready to present your findings," said Briggs. "The poster can guide the students along as they talk."

Community members act as judges, asking questions of the young scientists and filling out a survey for each project. Top projects received a certificate of achievement, but Briggs emphasized that the awards were not the focus of the fair. "It's more about taking pride in your work and developing an appreciation for the scientific method," the teacher said.

Beverly Dreger received high praise from her judges as she demonstrated how to mix the ingredients to make colored fire. She guided her audience through a photo exhibition and a step-by-step graphic that she designed and illustrated.

"I'll never look at fire in the same way again. It's energy, life, history, and danger, all rolled into one," Beverly said.

From "Johnson County Crime Blotter Roundup" compiled by Bradley Ruffalo (originally published in *The South Hill Gazette*, Sept.-Oct. 1972, p. 8):

FRANKLIN GROVE

Obscene phone calls. On Sept. 15, a woman called deputies to report a series of obscene phone calls that she received at her residence in the 1300 block of Sumpter Road in Franklin Grove. The woman said the caller was breathing heavily into the phone and made crude remarks that indicated he was watching her from somewhere near the house. Police are investigating the incident.

Peeping Tom. On Sept. 15, Johnson County police officers responded to calls from several residents in the 1330 block of Heatherdale Lane in Franklin Grove. Witnesses said they spotted a figure walking in between houses and looking into windows. The suspect was identified as a tall, bulky male wearing dark clothes and a mask that covered his face. Police arrived on the scene and found the suspect in the process of scaling a fence. A chase ensued but the man was able to escape. In their search of the area police found a knife, but are uncertain if the weapon belonged to their suspect. The investigation is ongoing.

ROSENDALE

Suspicious man. On Sept. 21, during a girls' softball game at Rosendale Park, police answered a call about a suspicious man standing behind the fence at the far northeast end of the field. When officers arrived and searched the area, the man was gone.

Harassing phone calls. On Sept. 22, police officers responded to a call from the 1200 block of Richmond Road. A woman at the residence played for police the recorded phone messages left on her reel-to-reel machine by an unknown person. The messages were lewd and violent in nature. Police secured the reels and are investigating the incident.

Electricity outage. On the evening of Oct. 10, a woman placed a phone call to police after spotting an unfamiliar man standing at the far edge of her driveway on the outside of a locked gate. The man was lit up by the driveway lights and the caller could see him clearly. As the woman gave a description to dispatch, the power went out in her home. Police responded promptly but could not locate the man.

He is described as tall and barrel-chested, wearing dark clothes and gloves. Police are still investigating the cause of the power outage.

SOUTH HILL

Barroom trouble. On Sept. 24, police responded to an emergency call from Sparky's Bar and Lounge at 355 Tanbark Road in South Hill after an argument broke out between a waitress and a customer. The waitress was giving out flyers of missing children to people in the bar. The male customer became upset and left the establishment without paying his tab. The waitress confronted the man outside and there was a scuffle. No one was arrested.

Home intruder. On Oct. 20, a man reported to South Hill police that an intruder broke into his house in the 850 block of Maple Circle while he was out to dinner and a babysitter was watching his children. The babysitter heard scraping sounds coming from an upstairs closet and found that a back patio door had been jimmied open. Police are investigating the incident.

Family dispute. On Oct. 26, a South Hill police officer went to the 120 block of Wichita Road where a woman and her 12-year-old daughter were arguing loudly and disturbing their neighbors. The officer found kitchen utensils scattered about the house and broken plates on the floor. Neither person had any injuries and the officer left the house after issuing the mother and daughter a warning.

Domestic dangers. On Oct. 31, South Hill police officers responded to the 120 block of Wichita Road after receiving a call about a domestic dispute between a husband and wife. The argument started when the wife became upset while reading a book about supernatural legends. While her young daughter looked on, the mother began tearing apart the closets in the house and overturning the beds, claiming she was looking for a demon. Her husband tried to restrain his wife and the woman tripped and fell, injuring her foot. Paramedics were called to the scene to treat the woman's injury.

From *The Girl Who Loved Halloween* (p. 36):

Teachers at South Hill Grammar noticed significant changes in Beverly as she entered the eighth-grade. Drawn to horror novels and scary movies, she was often brooding and sullen, rarely participating in class discussions or large-group activities.

"She wasn't getting enough sleep," recalls Tabitha Morgan, 44, a soft-spoken English teacher who had Beverly as a student. "Police had come to her house a few times to break up fights between her parents, and she had nightmares on a regular basis. Her relationship with her mother, in particular, was really falling apart."

As she talks, Tabitha walks past many examples of student work on the classroom walls, including drawings of lighthouses and dogs, poems about best friends and secret crushes, and stories of all genres. "Most kids don't mind, but Beverly never allowed me to showcase her work like this," the teacher says. "She could be very shy like that."

But for ten years, Tabitha has held on to one piece that Beverly wrote in the fall of 1973, a short story that the 13-year-old insisted that her teacher keep.

"I don't know why I still have it," she says. "It was supposed to be a fun little assignment—to write a spooky story for Halloween. I know Beverly was seeing a therapist by then, but something about her story really scared me."

Tabitha falls silent. She stands in front of the chalkboard, her voice now tense and guilt-ridden.

"I should have asked more questions," she says. "Beverly was a nervous girl, a haunted girl, consumed by death and tragedy. When I saw her picture on the news, I felt sick to my stomach."

"The Curse of the Woodsman," a story written by Beverly Dreger as part of Tabitha Morgan's eighth-grade English class, Oct. 1973:

Frank and Cherry, two teenagers out on their first date, were driving home from a scary drive-in movie called *The Legend of Boggy Creek*. They were on a lonely highway, and all around them were trees that looked like skeletons, raindrops that fell like knives, and a sky that was as black as gunpowder.

Lightning cracked like a whip above them. Thunder roared as loud as a mountain lion. Even though she was wearing Frank's band sweater, Cherry shivered in the cold.

"It's coming down hard," Frank said, turning the windshield wipers on full blast. The rain pounded the glass and the thunder made Cherry jump out of her skin.

"We could stop somewhere," Cherry suggested. "Wait until the storm passes. My parents don't want me home until eleven."

Frank nodded and began looking for a safe place to turn off the dark road. Frank felt nervous and excited. He had never parked before, but he really liked Cherry. She was nice and pretty, with soft blonde curls and skin that smelled like peaches, and she seemed genuinely interested when he talked about *Archie* comics and model airplanes. But the thing that Frank liked the most about Cherry was that she was never mean to anyone.

He spotted the turn-off sign that read "Black Oak Farms" and slowed down the car. Frank was feeling very happy. As he turned onto the exit, he took Cherry's hand and squeezed it gently.

"My grandfather used to raise horses out here," Frank said. "We can park by the stables. It's really peaceful and quiet."

Cherry looked concerned. "But isn't this the place where—"

POP!

The car began to skid across the road. Cherry held onto Frank with all her might as he tried to control the wheel. But the car was spinning wildly in the rain and suddenly they found themselves stuck in a ditch at the side of the road.

Terrified, Frank looked down at Cherry. She was still clinging to him, crying softly into his shirt. Rain hit the roof of the car like bullets.

"Are you okay?" Frank asked her.

Cherry nodded, looking up at him with wet blue eyes. Frank held her tight as thunder roared overhead.

"It sounded like we hit something," Cherry said.

"I'd better check it out. Stay here," Frank said.

Frank climbed out of the car. He tried to shield his face from the rain, but it was impossible. Once he climbed out of the ditch, he was already drenched. Then he saw it, curled up in the road like a rattlesnake.

A long strap of thick leather. The strap was filled with nails and shards of glass.

Someone had set a trap!

Cherry watched Frank through the backseat window of the car. With the storm raging all around, she could barely see him as he knelt down in the road to look at something.

Cherry smiled as she watched her date. Frank had always been friendly and polite, but Cherry now saw that he was also brave. She checked her reflection in the rearview mirror, making sure her hair was as perfect as it could be. She checked the spaces between her teeth. She wanted to look beautiful for Frank. But when she turned toward the window again, her pretty face froze in a look of terror.

Frank was gone.

Panicked, Cherry looked out the passenger window. Frank wasn't there. She looked through the windshield, trying to get a good view of the road ahead. All she could see through the rain were the empty horse stables in the distance.

Just then, she remembered the horror stories about Black Oak Farms. About the children who had died there. About the creepy man who hacked them to pieces with an ax.

"The Woodsman," Cherry whispered to herself. "Years ago, his own horse trampled him to death, and now his ghost haunts this land, killing anyone who comes near."

Cherry was getting scared. She couldn't see Frank anywhere. She noticed the keys in the ignition, but she didn't know how to drive yet. And the car was stuck in the muddy ditch anyway! Her heart started beating very fast.

Where was Frank? Did he run to get help without telling her?

Feeling dreadful, Cherry looked out toward the stables again. Lightning made zig-zags in the sky. The wind shook the car. And then she saw him coming through the rain.

A dark figure limping toward the car.

But it wasn't Frank.

It was a man she had never seen before. He was tall. He wore a floppy black cowboy hat. And in his hands he was carrying an ax with a long handle.

Cherry ducked beneath the dashboard, scrunching into a ball. She was terrified. She waited for what seemed like forever, watching the rain make crazy patterns on the car windows. Then she heard a loud thumping sound on the roof of the car.

Was it Frank? Did he need help? Cherry realized that she felt something much stronger than fear. It was her feelings for Frank. She liked him, maybe even loved him, and she didn't want to see him get hurt.

Slowly, she climbed onto the passenger seat and reached for the door handle.

Cherry was just about to open the door when blood started pouring down the windshield.

Then Frank's severed head rolled down the windshield and rested on its side on the hood of the car, his dead eyes staring back at Cherry through the bloody glass.

Cherry screamed. She reached out to lock the passenger door, but it was suddenly torn open and ripped off its hinges. A filthy hand grabbed Cherry and dragged her out of the car.

Cherry tried to crawl away from the big man standing in front of her, but she was confused and scared. Her fear made it impossible for her to move. The fall onto the pavement had scuffed her knees, and the rain pierced her skin like needles.

"Look at me," the man said.

Shaking like a leaf, Cherry opened her eyes and looked.

The Woodsman stood before her, his fingers tapping his ax. He lifted his hat so that Cherry could see his deformed face from where his horse had crushed the bones in his jaw.

"You should never have come out here," the Woodsman said. "I took your boyfriend's head for my collection. What part should I take from you?"

The old legend grinned a sick smile, the teeth and gums rotted with decay.

"You're...you're real?" Cherry whimpered.

The Woodsman did not answer with words. He answered with his ax. He answered twenty times, until Cherry's screams stopped, until blood bubbled out of her chest like lava, until there were pieces of her all over the road.

From "Beverly and *Halloween*: A Match Made in Hell" by Katherine Howard (originally published in *Underground Cinema*, Nov. 1983, p. 9-10):

The bogeyman hides under your bed. He crouches in the back of your closet. He lives in the abandoned house at the end of your street, and he hides in the attic among old toys and dust. He feeds off of your nightmares...

The *bogeyman* (a generic term derived from the Middle English *bugge*—a hobgoblin, scarecrow, or any folkloric creature that instills terror and fear) is a remorseless and aberrant figure conceived from the bedtime warnings of our parents and magnified by our darkest imagination. At the conclusion of John Carpenter's *Halloween*, after narrowly escaping a homicidal psychopath, a terrified brunette asks, "Was it the bogeyman?" Though the answer in the film provides a scant conclusion to a shoestring plot, we know that Beverly Dreger believed in this nightmarish conception with all her heart, a fear that began for her as a child (Raymond Sutcliffe cites "The Curse of the Woodsman" as Beverly's first attempt to invent her own version of the archetype) and culminated into a full-scale phobia by the time she attended Woodhurst State as a freshman in the fall of 1978.

In "Understanding and Overcoming Our Childhood Fears," Dr. Roosevelt Barnes classifies *bogyphobia* as a fear of ghouls, demons, ghosts, ogres, and of the Bogeyman itself, a nocturnal creature whose appearance and terrorizing methods vary among cultures throughout the world. In some folktales and fairy tales, "Bogey" takes the form of the Devil, especially in those stories in which the protagonist enters into a demonic pact or contract with Satan; in other tales, bogeymen are cannibals, shapeshifters, or mythological giants; they are often associated with fire, caves or underground dwellings, and dark places. In horror and psychological thriller films of today, they occasionally appear as child-mutilators, child-abductors, or child-killers...

In his article "What Happened to Beverly?" Stuart Norton argues that Beverly's exposure to violent horror movies at a young age (he cites 1960's *Psycho* and *Picture Mommy Dead* as examples) caused her irrational fear of the entity that Barnes describes. But Norton's thesis is limited in scope; it seems improbable that Beverly's paranoia would stem solely from watching exploitation and horror films on the VCR and late-night TV. While the killers in these movies most certainly had an adverse effect on her mental health, Beverly's condition stemmed from precursors that took place in real life, *not* on celluloid...

SOUTH HILL - Johnson County arson investigators are looking into two suspicious fires that broke out in the quiet community of South Hill on Thursday night.

Someone used matches to light two Halloween displays on fire, causing property damage and endangering the lives of homeowners and families nearby. Police believe the same person is responsible for setting the fires.

One of the victims, a man who has lived in the neighborhood for nearly ten years, was shocked to find his "graveyard" display burning in the middle of the night. "I was stunned at first," he said, "and then I realized how close it was. The house could've easily caught on fire."

The man said that his two dogs started barking sometime past midnight and that he woke up to the smell of smoke coming from the front yard. He could see the flames through his living room window.

"I ran to the side of the house and grabbed the garden hose. It took a minute or two to put out the fire," the man said.

Firefighters and police officers arrived minutes later, as they were already nearby responding to another call about a fire outside an apartment building on Morris Road.

"When I heard there was another fire in town, that's when I got suspicious," the victim said. "It felt like someone was playing a game."

The apartment fire erupted outside a residence that had been decorated with colored lights and paper streamers. The blaze was extinguished by the Johnson County Fire Department. The exterior of the building sustained smoke damage but no one was injured.

"This is a safe area," said building manager Shirley Potts. "Good families live here, and Halloween is supposed to be a fun holiday."

Police searched the wooded area near Morris Road for clues and found a book of matches from a nearby bar that they believe may be connected to the fires.

"Vandalism is very common on Halloween," said Donny White, division chief for the Johnson County Fire Department, "but two small fires like this, within close proximity to each other, is unusual. In my experience, this is either thrill-seeking, or someone's cry for help."

Investigators say that a person dressed in dark clothes was seen near Morris Road around the time of the fire, but that person has not been identified...

SOUTH HILL - A spokesperson for the Johnson County Police Department released new information today from its investigation of two fires that broke out in South Hill on Halloween.

According to the report, police are trying to locate the man who called 911 to report one of the fires. Investigators believe that the man may be able to lead them to their suspect.

911 dispatchers received the call at 11:34 p.m. on Halloween night. The male caller reported the fire that destroyed property at an apartment building on Morris Road. He also gave a description of a person he saw running away from the area.

Police hope the 911 caller can provide more details about what he saw. He identified himself as "Bill" and appeared to have a clear view of the fire and its surrounding area. Police have not been able to reach "Bill" since he made the call, and it is unknown if investigators have attempted to locate him at his place of residence.

With the hope that releasing this information will lead to their suspect, police have disclosed a transcript of the 911 call:

911 Operator: 911, where is your emergency?

Caller: There's fire at the apartments across the road. They could use some help over there.

911 Operator: What road, sir?

Caller: The corner of Morris and Ridgeway. The apartment building there. There's people all around. I hear sirens.

911 Operator: Emergency crews are on their way, sir. We've been getting a lot of calls tonight.

Caller: There's someone.

911 Operator: Excuse me, sir?

Caller: Someone's running away.

911 Operator: Running from the fire? Is the person injured?

Caller: She just threw something into the bushes.

911 Operator: Where is this person now, sir?

Caller: She's on the other side of the building. Heading toward the woods.

911 Operator: What was your name, sir?

Caller: My name's Bill.

911 Operator: Okay, Bill, I need you to stay on the line with me and tell me everything you see. You should see the trucks any minute now.

Caller: They're here.

911 Operator: Bill, where is this person now?
Caller: [inaudible]
911 Operator: Are you still there, Bill?
Caller: [inaudible]
911 Operator: Bill, stay with me, I'm going to get the Johnson police on the line.

It was at this point that the caller hung up, leaving investigators with more questions than answers about who might have ignited the blaze. Authorities described the suspect as a slender white female, possibly a juvenile, with dark hair and wearing black clothes…

SOUTH HILL - Police are still trying to determine a motive for an incident that occurred on Saturday night, when an argument with her teenage daughter caused Susan Dreger, 44, to become violent.

"The parents have been separated for months, but the mother showed up at the house and started raising hell, screaming something about sacrifice and devils," said the neighbor who called the police. "I knew the daughter was in serious trouble."

At around 10 p.m., Officer Anthony Donovan found Mrs. Dreger holding a kitchen knife while standing outside the house. When the woman refused to drop the weapon, the officer tackled her to the ground and handcuffed her.

"He's making me do this!" Mrs. Dreger was overheard shouting at police. "He's got me and he won't let go!"

A second officer put the woman in the backseat of a patrol car while Donovan entered the residence. He found the daughter, 14, hiding inside. The teen was uninjured and in stable condition. Police did not indicate the reasons for the argument with her mother.

While searching the house, Donovan discovered a circle drawn in black powder on the floor and occult-type items that police believe Mrs. Dreger brought to the residence.

"Our main concern was the daughter, and making sure she was unharmed," Donovan said. "She was subdued and did not give much indication of what may have started the fight. We are still trying to piece together everything that happened."

At the time of the incident, Jack Dreger, 41, was at a store five blocks away. Police believe that Mrs. Dreger staked out the residence until her husband left for the store. Then she entered the house and the argument with her daughter began.

When he returned to the residence, Mr. Dreger rushed to his daughter's aid while answering questions from the police.

"My wife has some serious issues with her mental health, and as the years have gone on, it's only gotten worse," Mr. Dreger said.

"I'll say this—I'll be damned if I let her near my child again," the father added.

Police determined that the knife came from the residence. They found three bottles of prescription medication and a book on ritual killing inside Mrs. Dreger's vehicle. She was arrested on charges of endangering a minor and resisting arrest.

From "Horror, Haddonfield, and Hallucinations" by Cameron Rhodes (originally published in *Exposure*, Jan. 1982, p. 13-14):

In December of 1974, Susan Dreger was convicted of one count of child endangerment after she threatened Beverly with a knife. She received a two-year suspended sentence that required her to attend parenting classes and family counseling. Jack Dreger filed for divorce later that month and maintained custody of his daughter.

"By then my only concern was Beverly," says Jack, a 49-year-old mechanic with knife-parted gray hair and tattooed arms. "Susan got dealt a raw deal in this life, but I wasn't going to allow her or anyone else to hurt my daughter anymore."

Jack tried hard to be a good father. He took Beverly to movies, ball games, and the planetarium; sometimes Beverly would spend the day at the auto shop, asking her dad questions about cars or chatting with customers. Jack encouraged her to write down her thoughts in a journal and to talk to him whenever she felt sad or angry.

"We always meant to take a road trip somewhere, but we never got around to it," Jack says. "There were places in the country I really wanted Beverly to see, places I wanted to take her to. Now I'm afraid it's too late."

For the next year, Jack and Susan fought constantly—mostly on the phone, sometimes in front of Beverly—as their lawyers hashed out the terms of the divorce settlement. They were close to finalizing their divorce just as their daughter was finishing up her sophomore year at South Hill High School...

"Everyone associates Beverly with slasher movies," says Victoria Menzies, a counselor at the school. "But there was more to her than that. She was a good friend, especially to some of the more troubled girls in her class. She liked watching the Chicago Bears with her dad. She acted in the plays and wrote movie reviews for the school paper. But the divorce was a crushing blow. As horrifying as her mother's behavior was, Beverly still cared about her. She believed they could be a normal family, even though they never were to begin with."

Around this time, Susan began renting a room in the home of Bob McNeely, a 45-year-old truck driver and frequent customer at the bar in South Hill where she served drinks. She began her parenting classes, maintained a consistent work schedule, and started receiving medical treatment at a psychiatric facility. Meanwhile, through phone calls and letters, she tried to stay in contact with her daughter.

On April 28th, 1975—just two weeks before Jack and Susan were scheduled to make a second appearance in front of a judge—McNeely came home to find several of Susan's "magickal" trinkets scattered on the floor.

"I thought maybe she was drunk and knocked something over," McNeely says. "But then I saw the trail of black powder leading to the bathroom, and I knew something was very wrong."

Moments later he found Susan's body, nude, on the floor in the bathroom. She had cut her wrists. Her landlord said he did not find a suicide note.

In an interview with newspaper reporters at the time, McNeely said, "She thought the judge might lock her up in the nuthouse. And even if not, she knew she was going to lose custody and never see her daughter again."

Two police officers went to the house in South Hill to deliver the tragic news to Jack. "When I opened the door and saw them standing there all hard-jawed, I knew Susan was dead," Jack says.

"After the cops left, I went into Beverly's room and told her. She had been watching *The Six Million Dollar Man*. We just sat there with Lee Majors on, and I held Beverly for a long time as she cried.

"Her death was a shock for us both because it seemed like Susan was slowly getting better. She was seeing a doctor at Crestwood, she was on medication. Bev thought there might come a time when they could have some kind of supervised visit," Jack explains.

Susan was buried in Franklin Grove after a brief funeral service. Jack packed her belongings into cardboard boxes with the intention of donating them to Good Will or to a local "new age" gift shop. And though her new therapist encouraged her to take some time away from school, Beverly stayed out for only three days.

"In hindsight, having Beverly return to school so quickly was a mistake," says Menzies. "She was a nervous wreck, not getting enough sleep, not focusing in class. But she wanted to come back as soon as possible. She was determined to go to college and do well."

Victoria Menzies flips through a school yearbook until she finds it: a picture of Beverly, smiling, brown hair layered to her shoulders, a green mood-stone pendant around her neck. The picture was taken at the start of her freshman year, almost two years before her mother's death.

"This is how I choose to remember Beverly," says Menzies. "She looks happy here. She had her whole life in front of her."

"Beverly Dreger: Teenage Sex Shocker" by Scooter Smith (originally published in *The National Buzz*, Jan. 1982, p. 5-6):

Lucy Billiet, Beverly Dreger's tight-lipped classmate from high school, has decided to come clean about her former gal pal's sex life in an upcoming exclusive article for The BUZZ.

Billiet will expose Beverly's biggest secrets, including her affair with a handsome therapist who was 39-years-old when he began sleeping with the troubled teen and self-described "horror nerd."

In an interview with veteran staff writer Franny Kurtz, Billiet will discuss Beverly's love of perverted horror movies like *Blood Bath* and *Orgy of the Dead*, and the scandalous affair that began between Beverly and her therapist when Beverly was a junior in high school.

Billiet, who is now 22 and works as a hairdresser in Chicago, will also divulge the shocking truth about Susan Dreger's suicide.

"By giving this interview, Lucy feels that she is washing her conscience clean," said Kurtz. "She's tired of feeling guilty and wants to end this chapter in her life."

Though Billiet makes an honest but meager living working in a downtown Chicago salon, she has refused monetary compensation for speaking with The BUZZ.

"That's not to say there isn't a book in her future," said a source connected with a major publishing house in New York. "A juicy tell-all could be a big hit, and I think she'd do it if the money was right."

Beverly was a 16-year-old virgin before she began sleeping with her therapist, according to a source close to Billiet.

"Beverly Dreger was pretty and shy, and the shrink was drawn to her innocence," the source explained. "But he also thrived off her dark side and the feeling that he was saving Beverly from her unstable background."

As a teen, Beverly was often moody and irritable. She dressed in black and listened to Satanic music groups like Alice Cooper and the Scorpions. Petty arguments with her father over simple house rules would explode into ugly shouting matches, which Billiet witnessed regularly.

"The shrink knew Beverly was a confused, underage kid, but he couldn't resist her," the source revealed. "And according to Lucy, Bev got off on all the personal attention."

The BUZZ will publish Billiet's interview in two installments that are sure to cause controversy and spark endless debate.

"Lucy Billiet will provide the answers we're all waiting for," said Kurtz. "Beverly can hide from the law all she wants, but that's not going to stop someone from telling truth about her and the entire Dreger family."

From "Horror, Haddonfield, and Hallucinations" (p. 14):

Around the time of her mother's suicide, Beverly was seeing Ted Worrall, a therapist who specializes in treating children and teens. Married with two young daughters, Worrall has never responded to the allegations made by the tabloid press that he had an affair with Beverly, telling the news media in 1981, "What occurs between me and my patients is a private matter. It's none of your business."

Helene Plummer, one of Beverly's classmates, says that the two of them bonded over their mutual experiences in therapy. "Both our doctors were unconventional. We did drawings, sculpture, nightmare analysis," Helene says. "Beverly and I would eat lunch together and swap shrink stories. She knew I came from a troubled home and was always understanding and supportive."

When asked if Beverly might have had a sexual relationship with Ted Worrall, Helene scoffs. "Get real. Her mother had just *killed* herself. Sure, we talked about boys and dating and stuff, but the last thing Beverly was thinking about was sex. She was focused on getting healthy and spending time with friends, and so was I.

"The media is spinning this out of control, making Beverly seem like a monster," Helene says. But on the table in front of her is a copy of the *Marion County Chronicle*, with the headline in bold-type: TRIPLE MURDER PROBE ON STUNNED CAMPUS.

"I still don't believe it," says Helene, crying now. "At graduation, she gave me the biggest hug. We promised each other that we were both going to make it."

"Nightmare Theory," an essay by Beverly Dreger (submitted as part of her Junior Research Project, 1977):

In the opening scene of *Nightmare* (1964), directed by Freddie Francis, a boarding school student wanders through a spooky house late at night. A ghostly voice calls out—"Janet? Where are you, Janet? I'm waiting for you"—beckoning the young girl to a door. The door creaks open, and inside a dark room Janet finds a deranged, laughing woman who tells Janet that they are both insane. Janet wakes up screaming in her bed.

A nightmare is an uncomfortable, distressing, and sometimes terrifying dream that occurs during rapid eye movement, or REM, sleep (Bridgeworth and Craig 1975). Nightmares are often associated with stress, anxiety or trauma; they will usually wake the sleeper, depending on the intensity of the dream or if the "noise" of the dream grows too loud.

"All sorts of things can cause nightmares," says Mercy Lassiter, who wrote the book *Dream and Nightmare Analysis*, "including lack of sleep, medications, and even a poor diet" (15). But Lassiter says that there can be more serious causes of nightmares, including childhood trauma. Children suffering from severe nightmares might have witnessed trauma or experienced it themselves. Yes, nightmares in children can be caused by an overactive imagination, but they can also be caused by family conflicts and even child abuse. "It was like having a demon inside my head," said one man about his nightmares. As a child, the man had been beaten regularly by his stepfather. "After waking up, I would lay in bed for hours, unable to move, unable to speak" (Baker 1975). Nightmares can also be defined by monsters and other scary sights that children see on TV and in the movies. Children who have nightmares all the time are more likely to believe that ghosts, goblins, and other supernatural creatures exist in the real world.

Psychologists have learned that women have more nightmares than men, though no one knows for sure why (Bridgeworth and Craig 1975). The most common nightmares for women involve being chased, kidnapped, murdered, or raped. *Dream and Nightmare Analysis* says that when women dream of being killed, they have recently ended an important relationship in their lives and are trying to cut themselves off from their emotions. The "killing" symbolizes the end of a part of their lives that they once loved and cherished (52). No one can say for sure if these interpretations are accurate, but we can all agree that dreams and nightmares are almost always weird and surreal. Why is this so?

The limbic system is an important part of the brain that deals with mood, emotions, and memory (Bridgeworth and Craig 1975). During dreams and nightmares, while the cortex area of our brain "sleeps," the limbic system ignites like a raging fire, making even the most bizarre nightmares seem real. When these nightmares grow violent or disturbing, people should pay attention to them. They might be the key to unlocking the secrets in our unconscious mind, or maybe even show the dangers or primitive desires that hide there. One woman kept dreaming that she missed her own wedding, which might have meant that she was unsure about marrying her boyfriend in real life. A man had a nightmare about finding bones scattered all over his house, which could represent his discovery of painful family secrets or betrayals (Lassiter 37). Nightmares can be the mind's way of warning people that they are heading down a destructive path.

By the end of the movie *Nightmare*, Janet's horrible dreams drive her insane. She attempts suicide, stabs an innocent woman to death, and gets locked up in a mental institution. In this surreal black and white chiller, Freddie Francis shows the unstoppable power of nightmares and the damage they can cause, both emotionally and physically. Understanding these bizarre visions might keep us from befalling the same tragic fate as poor Janet, one of the most lonely and terrified girls to ever appear on film.

"Sex and the Shrink" by Scooter Smith (originally published in *The National Buzz*, Feb. 1982, p. 5):

Ted Worrall, the middle-aged family therapist infamous for his shocking treatment methods and for sleeping with Beverly Dreger when she was a teenager, is now in for a shock of his own!

The BUZZ can confirm that Worrall engaged in several paid-for-sex encounters with an upscale prostitute in 1976—the same year that he was treating an adolescent Beverly Dreger for depression. The X-rated trysts took place in a no-tell motel miles away from the home in Salem that Worrall shares with his wife and three children.

The steamy allegations surfaced just after the brutal murders that have left Woodhurst State in bloody turmoil. Though Worrall has denied that the erotic escapades took place, the escort, a 31-year-old redhead named Clarice, insists that they are true.

"People have accused me of being a home-wrecker," Clarice said in an exclusive interview with The BUZZ. "But I'm tired of taking the rap for the choices that rich jerks make."

Clarice believed the therapist when he told her he was going to divorce his wife and end his infatuation with Beverly Dreger so that he and Clarice could be together.

"He talked about Beverly so much I started to hate her," Clarice told The BUZZ.

But insiders say that Clarice now feels guilty for despising a young woman whose situation was similar to her own. "From what I know, she was a kid with a lot of problems. I wouldn't be surprised if those people died because of all the crap he put in her head."

Worrall, now 45, and Clarice conducted their affair in between therapy sessions that the shrink held with patients at his office.

As The BUZZ revealed in a previous story, Worrall is notorious for his unusual approach to counseling children and teens.

"With Beverly, he would do something called rebirthing," said Clarice, referring to a controversial and dangerous form of therapy that requires the patient to be wrapped tightly in blankets and pillows in order to simulate the birthing process.

"She thought some creepozoid was stalking her, and the therapy was supposed to help her release those fears, to be born again and become a new person. I thought it was weird," Clarice said.

Clarice said having a romantic relationship with Worrall was difficult because he was constantly talking about Beverly.

"I've always been an upbeat person, and Teddy hated that," she said. "He wouldn't shut up about how dark and spooky she was. She loved scary movies, stories about murder, haunted houses, all that Halloween-type stuff. They fed off each other's misery. They were like vampires."

Clarice is quick to point out, however, that during all their sexy encounters, Worrall never admitted to taking young Beverly Dreger to bed. "He was paranoid enough about dating hookers," Clarice said. "Screwing a patient, never mind a teenage girl, would have probably given him a heart attack!"

Since the carnage at Woodhurst State, Worrall has remained mute about his connection with Beverly Dreger. But sources close to the bearded therapist have attempted to uphold the man's reputation in the media, denying that he paid prostitutes for sex and calling Clarice a golddigger looking to cash in on her story of hot sex and sleazy roadside motels. Yet the buxom redhead stands by her story.

"I have intimate knowledge," she told The BUZZ. "I can tell you what his manhood looks like, which kid is his favorite, what pills his wife takes, everything."

Clarice has recently returned to school and plans to leave the escorting world as soon as she graduates. "After the news broke about that poor kid, I realized that I wanted a different life for myself. I don't want to be around nutjobs like Teddy anymore."

ROSENDALE - Police are searching for a man in his mid-20s who frightened a high school girl while she was walking through a haunted house attraction in a Rosendale neighborhood.

The incident occurred on Halloween night inside a residence on Asbury Street. The girl, a junior in high school, was enjoying the attraction when she got separated from her friends.

The girl, 16, said that she found herself in a small bedroom that was decorated to look like a room in an insane asylum. Pillows were attached to the walls to make them look "padded," and there was a figure covered in a white sheet on top of a hospital gurney.

The figure sat up from the gurney, letting the sheet fall away, and cocked his head to face the terrified teenager.

The girl ran out of the house screaming. Once the crowd outside realized that the frantic teen was not part of the haunted attraction, someone called the police.

The man is described as white, 24 to 27 years old, broad-shouldered, with pale skin and thin, short hair, dark brown or black in color.

Rick Kolb, who owns the home and runs the haunted attraction every Halloween, says that there are no live actors in his haunted house, just a few plastic skeletons and rubber monsters. "I don't know what she saw," said Kolb, "but the stretcher only has a sheet with some ketchup on it. That's all."

When asked if someone could have gotten inside the house without him noticing, Kolb said it would have been impossible. "I'm at the door all night," he said. "And there were no signs of a break-in."

Police spent an hour searching the house and exterior property but found no sign of the mysterious intruder.

"We take every call we get seriously, and she was very specific in her description," said Johnson County police officer Jacob Meeks. "But we also understand that haunted houses can play tricks on the mind. She might have just been really spooked."

"We made sure that she had a ride home and that she was doing okay," the officer added.

Residents reported several instances of vandalism that night throughout the town, including an overturned headstone at the Old Rosendale Cemetery and some stolen items at a convenience store, but police do not think the incidents are connected.

Rick Kolb intends to keep his haunted house running for many Halloween seasons to come. "I've been doing this for over ten years, and I've never had any problems like this before," he said. "We run a safe, family-friendly haunt."

From *Shattered Mirror, Shattered Lives* (p. 46-47):

Susan Dreger slashed her wrists with a Mach-Extra II stainless steel razor blade. Her large-framed body was found nude, streaked with blood, on the bathroom floor of the house where she was renting a room. Signs of occult activity were everywhere, including several spooky drawings and a trail of bone powder leading to the body.

Adding to the grisly scene was the discovery of Susan's private notebook, which now serves as a bizarre testament to a life cut short by narcissistic paranoia and clinical depression.

Scotch-taped to the notebook's black cover was a newspaper article about the unsolved murder of Natalie Stubson, a 10-year-old girl found stabbed to death at the side of the road in 1964. But inside were even greater oddities: news clippings about murdered children, hand-drawn maps of residential neighborhoods, and creepy drawings of men with black faces and blood-red eyes. On some pages, Susan had scribbled notes to herself about the murders, about the children who died, and the violent ways in which they were killed.

"Her doctor encouraged her to write her feelings down," said Susan's landlord, Bob McNeely. "I'd see her writing or pasting in her notebook, sometimes until late at night, but I never asked to read it."

Police found the notebook tucked underneath copies of *Famous Unsolved Crimes* and *An Anthology of American Folklore*, books that undoubtedly fueled Susan's obsession with murders and superstition.

"Susan was fascinated by true crime, especially the murders of children and young women," McNeely said.

An 11-year-veteran of the SHPD, Detective Clayton Brewer was in charge of the investigation into her death. "We treat every death as a homicide, so the notebook was of some interest to us," he said. "But once it was determined that no foul play was involved, we had no use for it."

During the investigation, Brewer denied that Susan's notebook provided any insight into the state's long list of unsolved homicides involving children and teens.

"There is no evidence to suggest her writings would be valuable to any ongoing investigation," the stocky detective stated at the time. "The book is now in the possession of the decedent's immediate family, or somewhere in the city dump."

Brewer's first assumption was correct.

Once police had cleared the house, Jack Dreger gathered his wife's personal items—including the black notebook, her charms and protection incense, and an antique knife—and threw everything in a cardboard box. He took the box home and hid it away, high on a closet shelf behind a crate of broken tools.

"His first mistake was not throwing it all away," said McNeely. "It would've saved him a whole shit storm of trouble."

From "The Wrong Babysitter," by Katarina Topp (published in *Crime and Mystery Alert!*, May 1982, p. 12-15):

The brutal murder of Maggie Clark may provide clues into the fragmented world of Beverly Dreger and the Woodhurst Murders that occurred in October of 1981.

Margaret Nicole Clark was born on September 5, 1960 in Chicago, to Ronald and Deborah Clark. When Maggie was 11, her father died in a car accident. Deborah quit her job as a secretary and moved with her daughter to South Hill so that they could live closer to Deborah's parents.

In South Hill, Deborah worked at the post office while Maggie attended school. They lived in a small corner house on Wichita Road, next door to the Dreger family. Maggie, described by her teachers as a sweet and playful child, enjoyed drawing mazes and solving jigsaw puzzles. She and Beverly were in the same grade, and they became fast friends.

The two girls shared many interests, including spooky movies, television, and board games. Both of them liked to read *Nancy Drew* and *Encyclopedia Brown* mystery books. They had another friend, Lucy Billiet, and the three were often inseparable.

In 1974, while Beverly's family was falling apart, Maggie grew closer to her mother, who took her on day trips to amusement parks and antique shows. Possibly envious of this fruitful mother-daughter relationship, Beverly spent a lot of time at Maggie's house, enjoying dinners, *Monopoly* marathons, and late-night viewings of *Creature Features*. Sometimes Lucy Billiet would join them, and the three girls would stay up half the night watching TV and eating pizza.

Like Beverly, Maggie had trouble sleeping at night. She was on medication for rhythmic movement disorder, which caused her body to move involuntarily during sleep; as a result, she would sometimes bang her head against the wall or roll off her bed onto the floor. Her mother would have to wake her daughter up several times during the night so that she would not hurt herself. "She was used to waking up in the middle of the night and finding me there," Deborah Clark said with bitter irony in A.P. Bullock's *Shattered Mirror, Shattered Lives*.

It was at the Clark household where the tragic event would take place. The three girls graduated from high school in 1978. They spent the summer babysitting and making preparations to attend college in the fall. Maggie had been accepted to a state university in California; Beverly was excited to start her freshman year at Woodhurst State in Chicago; and Lucy had plans to attend cosmetology school.

"They wanted to have a fun and silly night like when they were kids," Deborah Clark has said. "They knew that their lives were about to change, and that they would probably go their separate ways. They were holding onto their childhood by a thread."

On the night of August 12th—the night before Beverly was to leave for Woodhurst—the three friends ordered a pizza from delivery and began acting out a radio play that Beverly had written as a school project earlier in the year.

"A little past 10, I heard them laughing and having a good time," said Deborah. "I took a sleeping pill because I knew her friends would watch out for Maggie if she needed help during the night."

Later, during the police investigation, a woman who lived on Wichita Road would remember seeing a tall, square-shouldered male with unkempt hair walking in the neighborhood at dusk. The man, who the woman thought was wearing a gray boilersuit, was not doing anything wrong and she did not call the police.

Sometime between midnight and one in the morning, all three girls fell asleep in front of the TV in Maggie's bedroom. Maggie slept on her bed, while Beverly and Lucy slept in sleeping bags on the floor. The television was on, showing a late-night movie called *See No Evil.*

At 1:15 a.m., Beverly awoke from a nightmare. She opened her overnight bag, looking for her sleep medication, but she couldn't find it. She began to have a mild anxiety attack. Longing for her own bed and needing her pills, Beverly decided to get dressed and return to her home next door. She left the Clark house without waking anyone.

Around two in the morning Lucy Billiet woke up. She had to go to the bathroom. As she sat up in her sleeping bag, her eyes adjusting to the dark, she realized there was someone standing in the doorway of Maggie's bedroom.

"Ms. Clark?" Lucy asked, assuming that the figure was Maggie's mother, there to wake her daughter during one of her sleep spasms. Giving no reply, the figure stepped into the room and went straight for Maggie's bed.

"It was a tall man dressed in black clothes," Lucy told reporters later. "He had no hesitation. He turned to Maggie's bed and started stabbing her. He was ferocious as he did it, full of rage, slamming the knife into her. And he smelled...like smoke. Like something burning.

"I couldn't save Maggie, so my only thought was to get help. His back was toward me, so I ran."

Lucy rushed straight to the Dreger house and pounded on the front door. Jack Dreger appeared on the porch in seconds, with Beverly behind him. He listened briefly to Lucy's tale of horror, then hurried to the Clark residence. The girls locked themselves inside the Dreger house and called the police, who arrived with wailing sirens in record time.

By then Jack was back on the street, holding a sobbing Deborah Clark against his chest, refusing to let her go, refusing to allow her back into the house after what he had seen in Maggie's bedroom.

"Maggie was the only one in the room when I got there," Jack told reporters. "I didn't have to check...it was clear she was dead."

Police found the 17-year-old's body, mutilated by several deep stab wounds to the chest. There was blood everywhere—on the bed, the walls and floor, even the ceiling. The young woman who was so excited to venture off to college had been slaughtered without reason or mercy.

South Hill Police scoured the town, searching for their suspect. Lucy Billiet's description of the killer and the subsequent composite sketch went out to as many TV and radio stations as possible. But with no fingerprints, no murder weapon, and no motive, police had little to go on. Investigators did discover an open window in Maggie's bedroom and footprints in the backyard of the residence, but they were unable to match them to anyone.

Margaret Nicole Clark was buried a week later in Rosendale. Over the next several months, the investigation into her murder stalled and her killer was never apprehended.

Lucy Billiet attended beauty school in another state. She moved away three weeks after the murder and never returned to South Hill.

Beverly Dreger postponed her departure to Woodhurst State in order to attend Maggie's funeral. She and her father left the day after the service, and Jack helped his daughter move into her first dorm room. Beverly began her freshman year at the school in the fall of 1978...

In "Beverly and *Halloween*: A Match Made in Hell," Katherine Howard argues that Beverly's belief in the bogeyman was the result of an anxiety disorder called *bogyphobia*. Others believe Beverly had a hyperactive imagination and wanted attention, while still others claim that an evil spirit *really did* appear in Maggie Clark's bedroom that night, perhaps from under her bed or from inside her closet!

I propose a more conceivable argument: someone very real was targeting Beverly, determined to take her life.

Beverly had a nightmare and fled the Clark residence before the killer could strike. Maggie's bedroom at the time of her murder was so dark that Lucy could barely describe the man who attacked her friend. Could it be that the murderer made a mistake and killed the wrong girl?

Deborah Clark was asked about this possibility in A.P. Bullock's *Shattered Mirror, Shattered Lives*. "What would it matter now?" she told the tabloid author. "All I know is that true evil exists in the world, and it walked into my house that night."

New information, in both the tabloids and mainstream press, is slowly being released about Beverly Dreger's background. We know that she felt "hunted for years by some evil, sinister force" (Sutcliffe 1983). Her mother, who committed suicide in 1975, was afraid that Beverly would die at the hands of some preternatural entity; she even kept a notebook full of descriptions and drawings of a sinister figure that abducted and killed children.

Just who was after Beverly Dreger, and why?

Four years have passed since the murder of Maggie Clark, and police are no closer to solving the case than they were on the night she died. Deborah Clark has given up hope that the case will be solved. "I don't think there will ever be justice for my baby," she has said, "and I really don't know how to live with that."

Lucy Billiet refuses to comment on that horrific night, especially after her awful experience with tabloid rag *The National Buzz*. "They wanted to interview me and I refused," Billiet told WLS-TV Chicago. "So they made up quotes I never said and attributed them to me. And they wrote a bunch of shit about Beverly that wasn't true. Even if the cops do catch her, there's no way she's getting a fair trial now.

"The media is the real monster in this case," Billiet added, "not Beverly."

Perhaps Beverly Dreger can provide the clues that investigators are looking for—only she's been missing for seven months, fleeing the scene of yet another gruesome murder and leaving police to question her involvement. My suggestion is that they look elsewhere. Someone was after Beverly—not the ghoul that the writings in Susan Dreger's notebook would suggest, but a man of flesh and blood. Someone who stalked the quiet neighborhood of South Hill, someone who followed her to Woodhurst, someone with a very big knife…

"The Haunted Closet," a radio play by Beverly Dreger (submitted as her final paper in Senior Composition, 1978):

"The Haunted Closet"

DRAMATIS PERSONAE:

ANNOUNCER
JOSEPH, family therapist
SUZANNE, Joseph's troubled wife
BETSY, Joseph and Suzanne's young daughter
DR. WOLFINGER, anthropology professor
AUNT MELINDA, Joseph's aunt
THE CREATURE
PRIEST

                    ANNOUNCER:
    Ladies and gentlemen. Please
    prepare yourselves for a sensory
    adventure unlike no other…

SOUND OF FOOTSTEPS.
A DOOR UNLOCKING.
A CREAKING DOOR.

                    ANNOUNCER:
    You have just entered…The Mansion
    of Horrors!

MUSIC: ORCHESTRAL IN BACKGROUND.

                    ANNOUNCER:
    Welcome, brave souls, to The
    Mansion of Horrors, an underground

radio series directed by the minions of Satan himself. If you dare, join me on today's descent into supernatural debauch and spine-tingling terror, into a fire lit underworld of demons and ghouls, witches and warlocks. You have opened a door into the unknown, a closet door to be exact, in the corner room of a centuries-old cottage house. Steel your spines, muster your courage, and step inside…

MUSIC: SYNTHESIZED STINGER.

ANNOUNCER:
"The Haunted Closet."

JOSEPH:
(NARRATES) When I was a boy, my friends and I delighted in telling ghost stories. We'd huddle in our sleeping bags late at night, pass a flashlight back and forth, and try to scare each other with tales of the Vanishing Hitchhiker, the Arkansas dog boy, and the bogeyman in the closet. But never did I believe, even in my youth, that there was any truth to these tales. How foolish I was. How naïve and foolish…

MUSIC: SOFT PIANO THAT CONTINUES UNDERNEATH.

JOSEPH:
(NARRATES) The first time it
happened, I thought my wife was
having a nightmare. Earlier that
day we had buried her mother in
the Church Street Cemetery, and
Suzanne was in deep mourning. She
woke up in the middle of the night
with this terrible scream.

SUZANNE:
(SCREAM)

JOSEPH:
What is it, my darling? Another
bad dream?

SUZANNE:
I'm not sure what it was!

JOSEPH:
Well, did you see something in
your mind, or was it here in this
room?

SUZANNE:
Oh—I don't know if I can tell the
difference anymore.

JOSEPH:
Tell me what you saw.

SUZANNE:
A figure. A man, maybe!

JOSEPH:
Where?

SUZANNE:
Inside our closet.

SOUND OF BEDSHEETS RUSTLING.

SUZANNE:
Joseph, where are you going?

JOSEPH:
To prove to you that there's
nothing to be afraid of.

SOUND OF JOSEPH'S FOOTSTEPS.

SUZANNE:
Don't – don't open it the rest of
the way.

JOSEPH:
That's exactly what I'm going to
do, my darling. It's the only way.

SUZANNE:
Oh, please—

SOUND OF CREAKING DOOR.

JOSEPH:
Now. You see? There's nothing in
the closet but our clothes. See
here? Here's the shirt you bought
for me from Hathaway. Here's the
dress I picked up for you in
Cairo. Here's my father's suit—

SUZANNE:
(INTERRUPTING) I see that now. I'm
sorry—you must think your wife
very foolish. Come back to bed.

SOUND OF CREAKING DOOR.

SUZANNE:
(PANICKED) Joseph, what are you
doing!

JOSEPH:
I'm opening the door. You need to
be able to see that there's
nothing inside it.

SUZANNE:
No—please. Close it. All the way.
You won't understand, as you are
so level-headed about such things.
But I need it closed. We might
even need to get a lock for it. Or
better yet—have it nailed shut!
Oh, I know how that must sound to
you. But please—close it firmly.

JOSEPH:
(HESITANT) Of course, my darling.

SOUND OF DOOR CLOSING. JOSEPH'S FOOTSTEPS AS HE WALKS BACK TO BED. RUSTLING SHEETS AS HE TUCKS HIMSELF IN.

A BEAT OF SILENCE.

JOSEPH:
Have you thought about seeing Dr. Pomeroy again?

SUZANNE:
I don't know. The poor man must think I'm mad.

JOSEPH:
Nobody thinks that, Suzanne. Certainly not Dr. Pomeroy.

SUZANNE:
Betsy does. Have you seen the way she looks at me? Like she's afraid! Very, very afraid! In what kind of world does a daughter want to see her own mother committed to an insane asylum?

JOSEPH:
(WITH SINCERITY) She wants nothing of the sort! Betsy loves you, my darling. We both love you. You've had a very trying day, putting

your dear mother to rest. You are
physically and emotionally
exhausted, which has caused your
mind to see things that aren't
really there.

                    SUZANNE:
It was a lovely service, wasn't
it?

                    JOSEPH:
Indeed it was. But now you must
take care of yourself. And you
should start by getting a good
night's sleep. Have you taken your
pills?

                    SUZANNE:
I got them down with a few
spoonfuls of applesauce. Dr.
Pomeroy recommended it.

                    JOSEPH:
That's my girl. Good night,
Suzanne.

                    SUZANNE:
Good night, Joseph.

A BEAT OF SILENCE.

                    SUZANNE:
Joseph?

JOSEPH:
(SLIGHTLY EXASPERATED) Yes,
darling?

SUZANNE:
I need to tell you something.

JOSEPH:
What is it?

SUZANNE:
You must promise not to laugh at
me.

JOSEPH:
I would never do such a thing.

SUZANNE:
The man I saw in the closet—

JOSEPH:
Suzanne, there is no man in the
closet—

SUZANNE:
Please! Just listen to me!

JOSEPH:
All right, all right. You'll wake
Betsy now.

SUZANNE:
I've seen him before. Years ago,
when I was a teenager, on the

night my mother had her first
stroke.

JOSEPH:
Are you sure you want to talk
about this now, Suzanne?

SUZANNE:
I had better get it all out now. I
may not have the courage to do so
in the morning.

JOSEPH:
Very well.

SUZANNE:
The year was 1946. I was sixteen-
years-old. There was a dance at
the community center in town, but
my mother refused to let me go. My
father was a carpenter and a
boozer, and my mother hated being
alone in the house while he was at
work or out drinking. She insisted
that I stay home with her.

JOSEPH:
But you snuck out with some
friends after your mother had gone
to sleep. You've told me this
story before, my darling.

SUZANNE:
Oh, but not all of it, Joseph! Not
all of it.

MUSIC: EERIE STRINGS IN BACKGROUND.

SUZANNE:
(NARRATES) As you know, I climbed
out my bedroom window and joined
my friends at the corner. By the
time we arrived at the community
center the dance was over, but we
met some nice boys in the park and
had a good time. Afterward, I
walked home alone with only the
moon to light my way. I remember
feeling like something was
terribly wrong, and by the time I
reached my street I was running
for the front door. The house was
pitch black. I hurried to my
parents' bedroom and turned on the
light. My mother was crumpled on
the floor, half of her face
paralyzed. I found out later that
she had suffered a stroke due to
the panic of finding me gone in
the middle of the night. As I ran
to her, the bedroom light popped
and fizzled, cloaking the tiny
room in darkness. And that was
when I saw him for the first time—
hovering over my mother like a
shriveled black ghost as the light

burned out before my eyes. When I
reached for the bedside lamp and
switched it on, I heard him call
my name…it was like a dead man
whispering in my ear! But then the
room was filled with light and I
was calling the police. My mother
and I were the only two people in
the room.

MUSIC: STRINGS FADING.

                    SUZANNE:
(NARRATES) I didn't tell anyone
what I had seen. Not the police.
Not my father. My mother returned
from the hospital a week later.
Though we never spoke of that
night, and I was never punished
for sneaking out, my relationship
with her was never the same after
that. I still feel guilty to this
day.

MUSIC: STRINGS FADE OUT.

                    SUZANNE:
Well, it's official now, Joseph.
Lock me up at the Chicago State
Hospital and throw away the key.

JOSEPH:
Don't be silly. I have a perfectly logical explanation for what you witnessed that night.

(BEAT)

You just said it yourself. You were feeling guilty for betraying your mother's trust. When you saw her helpless on the bedroom floor, that guilt manifested in the bizarre image you saw when the bulb went out. It was a trick of the light and your subconscious mind.

SUZANNE:
That's exactly what Dr. Pomeroy said. Only I don't believe it, Joseph. I don't believe it all.

JOSEPH:
And why is that?

SUZANNE:
Because that creature, that monster—whatever it is—has followed me my entire life. There are times when I think that he must be the devil himself!

SOUND OF SUZANNE CRYING.

JOSEPH:
Don't cry, Suzanne. Let me hold
you, my darling.

SUZANNE:
Is there someone else we can talk
to, Joseph? A colleague of yours,
or perhaps someone you've met on
your travels?

MUSIC: EERIE CELLO.

JOSEPH:
(NARRATES) I remembered an
acquaintance of mine from my
school days, long before I met
Suzanne. He was now a professor of
anthropology at the university in
the city, where he taught a
seminar on the role of ghosts and
spirits in folklore and religion.
His name was Dr. William
Wolfinger, and though we had not
spoken in many years, I hoped that
he could provide Suzanne the
answers she so desperately
needed...

SOUND OF DOOR CHIME AND OPENING DOOR.

SOUNDS OF PATRONS TALKING UNDERNEATH.

JOSEPH:
Cromwell's Coffee Shop. I haven't

been to this old haunt in years.

WOLFINGER:
(OFF) We made many fond memories
here, didn't we?

JOSEPH:
Oh! William, you startled me.

WOLFINGER:
I always did like to keep you on
your toes.

JOSEPH:
It's good to see you, old friend.
You're looking well.

WOLFINGER:
As are you. I have saved us a
booth in the back. Come.

SOUNDS OF PATRONS GROW LOUDER, THEN FADES.

WOLFINGER:
Here we are. I took the liberty of
ordering you the one drink that
kept our study sessions going long
into the night.

JOSEPH:
Oh, yes, black coffee. I don't
think either of us would have
survived without it. Thank you,
William.

                    WOLFINGER:
Of course.

(BEAT)

I have to admit, Joseph, I was
both intrigued and alarmed by your
phone call.

                    JOSEPH:
I apologize if I sounded panicked.

                    WOLFINGER:
Oh, don't get me wrong, old
friend; I am delighted to see you.
But why now, after all these
years?

                    JOSEPH:
(HESITATES) Well—are you still
teaching that class on the spirit
world? Ghosts, demons, that sort
of thing?

                    WOLFINGER:
I am. The class examines the ways
in which ghosts and spirits appear
in the folklore of societies
throughout the world. Speaking
frankly, it's the most popular
seminar at the college.

                    JOSEPH:
May I ask—have you ever seen a
ghost or a demon yourself?

                  WOLFINGER:
I'm not a ghost-hunter, Joseph.

                    JOSEPH:
You didn't answer my question.

                  WOLFINGER:
My friend, the tremor in your
voice betrays your true
intentions. I can tell that you
are deeply concerned about the
well-being of someone very close
to you.

                    JOSEPH:
You were always an expert at
deciphering my moods. It's you who
should have become a therapist—not
me.

(BEAT)

It's my wife, William. My poor,
dear wife.

                  WOLFINGER:
Tell me everything.

JOSEPH:
It all began when she was a
teenager. Her mother had fallen
victim to a stroke, and Suzanne
blamed herself…

MUSIC: EERIE CELLO TRANSITION.

JOSEPH:
…according to Suzanne, she has
seen the creature countless times
since that dreadful night back in
1946. One night, shortly after we
were married, she said it crawled
out from the closet and bit her
ankle.

(BEAT)

Doctor, she claims that the
creature *talks* to her.

WOLFINGER:
What does it say?

JOSEPH:
Excuse me?

WOLFINGER:
When the creature talks to your
wife, what does it say?

JOSEPH:
You're not saying you believe her!

WOLFINGER:
What I believe is irrelevant. What
matters is that your wife believes
that this monster is real.

JOSEPH:
I can't disagree with you there.

(BEAT)

The creature usually demands that
Suzanne play pranks on the family,
like steal my socks or hide
Betsy's books. But sometimes…
sometimes, Doctor, he tells her to
kill!

MUSIC: JOLTING STINGER.

WOLFINGER:
Hurry up and finish your coffee,
Joseph. I want to take you to my
office and show you something.

SOUNDS OF THE CITY RISE AND FADE.

FOOSTEPS IN THE HALLWAY. A DOOR UNLOCKING
AND OPENING.

WOLFINGER:
Have a seat anywhere and don't
mind the mess. I just need to find

some lecture notes from last
quarter.

SOUND OF WOLFINGER MOVING OFF, THE RUSTLING
OF PAPERS.

WOLFINGER:
Apparitions, poltergeists,
nonhuman entities…ah, here it is.

SOUND OF WOLFINGER RETURNING, SITTING DOWN.

WOLFINGER:
These notes are from a lecture
about the correlation between
mental illness, our fear of death,
and our longing to believe in
supernatural phenomena. Allow me
to read: "When faced with the
reality of death, especially the
death of a parent or child, some
people retreat into a fantasy
world of ghosts, spirits, and
demons rather than accept the fact
that their loved one is gone.
Others who claim to see
supernatural manifestations are in
fact suffering from a
psychological or medical
condition."

JOSEPH:
Are you saying Suzanne is mad?

WOLFINGER:
Not at all. When she walked into her parents' bedroom that night, Suzanne most likely believed her mother to be dead. Her inability to face that grim possibility, especially at the impressionable age of 16, caused her subconscious mind to conjure up the image of the creature.

JOSEPH:
So she transferred her feelings of guilt onto the monster. It was *his* fault, not hers.

WOLFINGER:
Precisely. Suzanne's mother had a lifetime of ailments, correct?

JOSEPH:
Sadly, yes.

WOLFINGER:
Then it's no surprise that Suzanne felt haunted by the creature for many years.

JOSEPH:
As her mother's physical health declined, Suzanne's *mental* health declined. That makes perfect sense, William! But why does the creature order her to kill?

WOLFINGER:
Joseph, I hate to tell you this—
but the only person the "creature"
wants Suzanne to kill is herself.

JOSEPH:
You mean...she's suicidal?

WOLFINGER:
I'm afraid so. Unless...

JOSEPH:
Unless what, Doctor?

MUSIC: JARRING VIOLIN THAT RISES AND FADES.

THE CREATURE:
(NARRATES) Unless the creature is
real? Is that what you were going
to say, my good doctor? Let me
assure you, I am as real as those
worthless degrees on your wall. As
the blood that curdles like sour
milk in your veins. As a creature
of the underworld, my skin burns
with the fires of hell. I enter
your earthly plane through portals
of time and space—closets,
tunnels, doorways. The wife is
mine; I will take her child too,
for innocent blood is pure. Don't
interfere, Wolfinger, and I may
just let you live.

MUSIC: VIOLIN FADES OUT.

JOSEPH:
William? William! Are you okay?

WOLFINGER:
(CONFUSED) Why…yes. Yes, I'm fine.
Just felt a bit queasy there for a
moment.

JOSEPH:
Perhaps we should get you
something to eat.

WOLFINGER:
No…really, I'm fine. I just need
to rest for a while. I'm not as
young as I used to be, Joseph.

(BEAT)

Go home. Tend to your wife and
daughter. I'll think of an
appropriate course of action and
ring you as soon as possible.

JOSEPH:
Thank you, old chum. I feel better
already.

MUSIC: EERIE CELLO TRANSITION RISES AND
FADES.

JOSEPH:

(NARRATES) I followed the doctor's advice and went home immediately. I took care of Suzanne as best I could over the next few days, attending to her every need. Drowsy from her medications, she would retire early to bed every night. Once Suzanne was asleep—with all the closet doors in the house firmly closed—my daughter and I would have our dinner and spend the rest of the evening reading adventure stories or playing board games. A mere ten-years-old, Betsy clung to me with a love unlike any I had ever known. She was a beautiful and tenderhearted child, and I doted on her without restraint.

SOUNDS OF A CRACKLING FIRE.

JOSEPH:

What game should we play next, Betsy?

BETSY:

(CHEERFUL) I don't know. You choose, Daddy!

JOSEPH:

We could try *Chutes and Ladders*, or maybe *Mouse Trap*?

BETSY:
I don't like those anymore. Let's
play the Halloween game!

JOSEPH:
The Halloween game? What do you
mean?

BETSY:
The "wee-gee" game. The board with
the plastic heart.

JOSEPH:
Oh, *that*. That's more of a game
for adults, honey—

THE CREATURE:
(DEMONIC LAUGHTER, OFF)

JOSEPH:
My gosh, what was that? It came
from upstairs!

BETSY:
Daddy, I'm scared!

JOSEPH:
Betsy, go to my study and lock the
door! Now!

SOUNDS OF RUNNING FOOTSTEPS, FOLLOWED BY
THREE FIRM KNOCKS.

JOSEPH:
(DESPERATE) Suzanne, are you in
there? Suzanne?

SOUND OF LOCKED DOOR RATTLING.

JOSEPH:
Suzanne, the door is locked! I'm
coming in!

SOUND OF SMASHING DOOR.

JOSEPH:
Suzanne? Where are you? (OFF) It's
so dark in here. I can't see a
thing. And what is that terrible
stench? I need to find the light
switch...

SOUND OF CLICKING LIGHT SWITCH.

JOSEPH:
Suzanne! Oh, Suzanne! No! No!

MUSIC: JOLTING STINGER THAT RISES AND FADES.

JOSEPH:
(NARRATES) Even as a veteran of
the war, never in my life had I
encountered a scene of such mind-
numbing horror. On the floor lay
my wife—my beautiful Suzanne—her
throat ripped open by what could
only have been a monster's claws.

From the open closet wafted a rotting, sickening smell, like burning flesh. It was all I could do not to pass out as I telephoned the police. Later, after making sure Betsy was safe and asleep in bed, I stayed up late into the night, walking the tiny cottage in a daze. Shortly before dawn, as I drifted to sleep on the couch, I heard evil laughter coming from the recesses of the home. I knew then what my wife had always known—the creature was real, and his hunger was insatiable...

MUSIC: EERIE CELLO TRANSITION.
SOUNDS OF BIRDS CHIRPING AND SOFT WIND.

PRIEST:
I commend you, dear Suzanne, to almighty God, and entrust you to Him whose creature you are. Having paid the debt of human nature in surrendering your soul, may you return to your Maker who formed you out of the dust of the earth...(FADES)

SOUNDS OF FOOTSTEPS ON GRASS.

WOLFINGER:
Joseph?

(BEAT)

Joseph, are you there, old friend?

JOSEPH:
Err—hello, William. I'm sorry.
Lost in my own thoughts, I
suppose. Has everyone gone?

WOLFINGER:
Yes. Betsy left for the cottage
with your aunt Melinda.

JOSEPH:
So many people came to say goodbye
to my Suzanne.

WOLFINGER:
Come with me. I'll take you home.

JOSEPH:
Home? I don't know if I can ever
go back home again.

WOLFINGER:
But you must, Joseph. Your
daughter is there waiting for you.
She needs you.

JOSEPH:
(HAUNTED) Suzanne was my entire
life, William. And she was torn
apart by that…that *thing*! Please—
please tell me you believe me!

WOLFINGER:
I do believe you. And that is why
we must act—*now*.

JOSEPH:
But what is there left to do?
Suzanne is gone.

WOLFINGER:
Joseph, listen to me carefully.
The killing of your wife was an
act of monstrous brutality—the
epitome of evil. This creature has
only one desire and, for whatever
reason, that desire is to destroy
everything you hold dear in your
life.

JOSEPH:
Are you saying—?

WOLFINGER:
Betsy might be in grave danger.

JOSEPH:
I was a fool to let her leave my
side. Get me to your car!

MUSIC: SUSPENSEFUL STINGER.
SOUND OF A CAR DRIVING IN BACKGROUND.

JOSEPH:
Tell me everything you're
thinking, William.

WOLFINGER:
My rational mind didn't want to
believe it—but it must be true!
You see, every culture in the
world has its own bogeyman. In
Bulgaria he is a long-haired
spirit who kidnaps misbehaving
children; in Hungary, a monster
with a sack for transporting his
victims to and from his lair; in
Italy, a tall man with a burned
face. His incarnations are as
varied as they are horrifying.

JOSEPH:
But what about here? In *this* city?

WOLFINGER:
Your wife was terrified of
closets. Did you ever think to ask
her why?

JOSEPH:
I assumed it had to do with her
childhood. Her father was a mean
drunk. When Suzanne was a child,
he would keep her locked in the
closet for hours.

WOLFINGER:
No, I don't think that's it. Oh,
how they prey on the weakness of
innocent blood!

JOSEPH:
William, I don't understand!

WOLFINGER:
For some monsters, closets can
function as a portal—a kind of
dimensional doorway. The bogeyman
that killed Suzanne uses closets
to traverse between its world and
ours.

JOSEPH:
I always thought that was the
stuff of legend.

WOLFINGER:
I only wish that were true.

JOSEPH:
William, there's something else.
When I found Suzanne's body, there
was an awful stench in the air…the
smell of burning flesh!

WOLFINGER:
Then we are dealing with a true
demon from hell. Tell me—is there
a closet in Betsy's bedroom?

JOSEPH:
Why, of course!

WOLFINGER:
Then I only hope we're not too
late.

SOUNDS OF CAR ZOOMING.

MUSIC: FRANTIC CELLO TRANSITION.

JOSEPH:
(NARRATES) My old friend drove
through town like his life
depended on it. As he sped toward
the cottage, he told me stories
that made my blood run cold—of
demons conjured up from old books
and sinister trinkets,
superstitions of the darkest kind,
and monsters that feast on the
blood of children. But it was hard
to concentrate...all I could think
of was Betsy and what a fool I was
for allowing my grief to take
precedent over her safety. By the
time we reached the cottage, I was
nearly mad with worry...

SOUNDS OF BRAKES SCREECHING.
FOOTSTEPS RUNNING ON GRAVEL, A DOOR OPENING
AND SLAMMING SHUT.

JOSEPH:
(CALLING OUT) Aunt Melinda! Betsy!
Are you home?

MELINDA:
(OFF) In the kitchen!

SOUNDS OF HURRIED FOOTSTEPS.

MELINDA:
Joseph! Dr. Wolfinger! You both
look white as ghosts.

JOSEPH:
Aunt Melinda, where is Betsy? Is
she all right?

MELINDA:
Why, she's perfectly fine. She
said she wanted to be alone for a
while. As soon as we got home she
took one of her board games from
the closet and went straight to
her room.

JOSEPH:
(RELIEVED) Oh, thank heavens.

WOLFINGER:
What kind of game was it, Melinda?

MELINDA:
Well, I'm not sure. She chose one
from the shelf and off she went.

THE CREATURE:
(DIABOLICAL LAUGHTER)

JOSEPH:
That voice! That evil laughter!
I'd recognize it anywhere!

WOLFINGER:
Take me to the child's room!

SOUNDS OF RUNNING FOOTSTEPS UP THE STAIRS.

JOSEPH:
(OFF) Betsy! Betsy!

SOUND OF DOOR OPENING.

JOSEPH:
Betsy, my darling, are you okay?

BETSY:
I'm fine, Daddy.

JOSEPH:
What is it...what is it that you're
doing there?

BETSY:
Playing the Halloween game.

JOSEPH:
Betsy, how many times have I told
you—the Ouija board is a game for
adults. Put it away this instant!

BETSY:
But it talks to me, Daddy. It

tells me things.

WOLFINGER:
Betsy, listen to your father! That game is *not* a toy. It is a doorway, a doorway to—

MELINDA:
(PIERCING SCREAM)

JOSEPH:
Aunt Melinda!

WOLFINGER:
Go to her! I'll stay here with the child!

SOUND OF RUNNING FOOTSTEPS.

WOLFINGER:
Betsy, let's put this game away and—

THE CREATURE:
(EVIL WHISPER) Make one move, Wolfinger, and I'll gut her before your very eyes. Leave now and I'll let you live.

WOLFINGER:
She is only a child! She doesn't deserve this. Fight me. Fight me instead!

THE CREATURE:
Do you really think you have the
willpower to take me on? A
pathetic old man like you?

WOLFINGER:
You attack children because they
are innocent and weak. Easy prey.
You are cowards—all of you!

THE CREATURE:
Try me, Wolfinger. Try us all!

JOSEPH:
(OUT OF BREATH) William, who are
you talking to?

WOLFINGER:
Never mind that. How is your aunt?

JOSEPH:
She's…she's dead.

(BEAT)

Betsy, come here, my dear. We must
leave this house at once.

BETSY:
Daddy, I'm afraid!

JOSEPH:
It's all right. I've got you now.
William, let's go.

WOLFINGER:
No. You go—as fast as you can.
Take Betsy with you and never come
back.

JOSEPH:
William, I'm not leaving you
behind!

WOLFINGER:
But you must.

(BEAT)

This is between us now.

JOSEPH:
If you insist. I'll send police
straight away. Goodbye, William.

WOLFINGER:
Goodbye, my friend.

SOUND OF HURRIED FOOTSTEPS DESCENDING, THEN
THE SLAMMING OF A DOOR.

WOLFINGER:
You let them leave. Is this what
you wanted the entire time? To
show me that all my work has been
in vain? To mock and to torment
me?

THE CREATURE:
We don't discriminate here, my
good doctor. We'll drain your
blood as easily as we would the
child's.

WOLFINGER:
And if I surrender to you without
a fight, will you leave the girl
be?

THE CREATURE:
Why would we do that?

WOLFINGER:
Because she deserves to live!
Because she is too young to know
the evil that exists in this
world!

THE CREATURE:
We make no promises, Wolfinger.

WOLFINGER:
Then come. Show me your face, and
I'll show you not to misjudge the
strength of the old.

SOUNDS OF FIZZLING LIGHTBULB...CRACKING WOOD...A
SCRAPING ACROSS THE FLOOR...

WOLFINGER:
Show yourself! Don't hide in the
dark like the heathen you are.

Prove it to me! Prove to me you
are real!

SOUND OF SNAPPING BONE...THE THUMP OF A BODY
AS IT HITS THE FLOOR...THE DRAGGING OF THE
BODY ACROSS THE FLOOR.

DRAGGING...DRAGGING...

SOUND OF A CLOSET DOOR CLOSING.
MUSIC: JARRING VIOLIN THAT RISES AND FADES.

ANNOUNCER:
And so concludes our horrific tale
for this evening. We hope you
enjoyed it. May you rest well
knowing that it was merely a
fictional story designed to chill
the blood in your veins...or at
least keep telling yourself that!
Join us next time for another trip
inside the Mansion of Horrors,
where creatures lurk around every
corner...and in every closet!

From *The Girl Who Loved Halloween* (p. 89):

For Beverly Dreger, Woodhurst State was supposed to be an escape from an adolescence scarred by conflict and tragedy. She loved the campus and its liberal-minded students. She enjoyed walking the sprawling green lawns and reading books in the enormous library. As her interest in film studies grew, the 17-year-old brunette thrived in a positive environment where she was encouraged to be herself and explore academics in new and creative ways.

"We worked hard, but had fun while doing it," says Lisa Brown, Beverly's roommate during their freshman and sophomore years. The pair took classes together, chatted over greasy meals in the cafeteria, and joined a film club that screened cult and "underground" movies in the college theater. According to Lisa, Beverly was like a lot of other students at Woodhurst: smart, introspective, and a little weird. "Sure, she was off-kilter at times. One of the first things we talked about was the murder of her friend back home, and how that had totally messed up her head," Lisa says. "But from what I could see, Beverly was dealing with it in her own way. She was a tough girl, and we got along great."

It was the fall of 1978, and Beverly Dreger seemed ready to put the past behind her...

"THE BLACK NOTEBOOK": VOLUME II

"I have a private theory, Sir, that there are no heroes and no monsters in this world. Only children should be allowed to use these words."

--Alfred de Vigny, Stello

From "The Beast Within: Psychoanalytical Responses to the Horror Film" by Martin O'Neill (UMT Dissertation Publishing: 1975), p. 3:

A psychology professor at San Francisco State University and the author of *False Memories and Repressed Trauma* (1974), David Felton has examined the emotional responses to some of today's most popular and accessible horror films, including *The Last House on the Left* (1972), *The Exorcist* (1973), and *The Texas Chain Saw Massacre* (1974). Through his research, Felton learned that some viewers were not only frightened or depressed by the material, but that those who felt a high degree of personal relevance to the graphic content had difficulty distinguishing between real and fictional events after extended viewings. "Most audiences are able to maintain an aesthetic distance from the violent situations found in horror movies," says the author. "However, when viewers are able to relate the content of these films to their own life experiences, the reaction can be tantamount to having a psychological collapse." According to Felton, this reaction is particularly common in victims of trauma, who recognize, amidst all the bloodshed and ghastly imagery, some aspect of their own lives…

"For the Love of Film" by Chris Shaw (published in *The Leader*, Sept. 1978, p. 2-3)

The first scary movie that Beverly Dreger saw in the theater was James Whale's *Frankenstein*, originally released in 1931. She was 11-years-old. Now a freshman at Woodhurst State, Dreger remembers the moment with a nostalgic twinkle in her eye.

"It was a revival screening that my father took me to," the new student says. "I was terrified of the monster, but I fell in love with him too."

Though currently undeclared, Dreger is considering majoring in Cinema Studies. This semester, she is taking two of the new film-related courses, and she plans on taking a winter class on writing film treatments.

Like many Woodhurst cinephiles, Dreger was delighted by the college's newfound interest in film studies. A few years ago, the school offered just three film courses, all within the English department. But since the establishment of the Cinema Studies Program (CSP) last spring, the number of film courses has tripled—and those are just the courses within the program.

"Due to high demand, we now offer film classes in departments throughout the college," says Lauren Reid, a professor of American Literature and current director of the CSP. "For the first time, Woodhurst students are learning how to watch and critique films, building a visual literacy that transcends the major."

Many of the courses offered within the CSP focus on specific film genres, including westerns, musicals, and comedies. But when asked to name her favorite genre, Reid responds with a wry smile. "Horror films can be scary and disturbing," she acknowledges, "but they are also cathartic. Movies like *The Blob* and *Night of the Living Dead* are about good triumphing over evil, about our refusal to back down in the face of a horrific and often violent adversary."

Faculty members who teach outside the CSP have been eager to get involved in the major. One of the program's most popular courses is the seminar on English filmmaker Alfred Hitchcock, best known for his films *Psycho* and *The Birds*. The course, taught by gender studies professor Rosemary Smith, requires students to write essays that analyze films through a historical and cultural lens.

"With *Psycho*, for example, we examine mental illness, gender reversal, the power struggle between men and women," Smith says. "By the end of the semester, students see films as puzzles that never end. There's always a missing piece just waiting to be discovered."

As a result of the popularity of the CSP, Woodhurst now hosts genre festivals in Wasserman Hall and monthly field trips to the local cinema. Fright Nights takes place in October, featuring classic horror fare like F.W. Murnau's *Nosferatu* and Robert Wise's *The Haunting*, and students attended a screening of John Carpenter's *Halloween* earlier this month.

"*Halloween* is one of the first horror movies that allows us to view events through the eyes of a killer," says Reid. "The theater was sold out with nearly all Woodhurst students!"

During the holiday season, the CSP has sponsored screenings of *Miracle on 34th Street* and *We're No Angels*, and a Marilyn Monroe festival is in the works for this spring.

Beverly Dreger sits in the courtyard outside Tupper Dorms and thumbs through the Woodhurst course catalog. She is considering adding 6 more units of film classes to her schedule, including a workshop on acting for the silver screen.

"Movies take us to places we've never been," she says with that familiar twinkle in her eye. "And I want to go there as much as I can."

FORT WORTH - Carpenter's film is bleak, nihilistic, cruel, and surprisingly dull for low-budget suspense...modeled after Norman Bates in Hitchcock's *Psycho*, the impotent killer wields his knife like a phallic symbol, and we are left to ponder why we choose to subject ourselves to such juvenile trash...

LOS ANGELES - John Carpenter's *Halloween* is a brilliant and seemingly effortless display of artful suspense, intense cat-and-mouse sequences, and brooding silence...a must-see for all horror fans.

SPOKANE - Heartless, gratuitous, and exploitative...I pity the young and talented actresses in this film, who struggle to rise above a threadbare plot and trivial script...nothing to see here except a few naked breasts and a masked killer with a chip on his shoulder...

SAN FRANCISCO - John Carpenter (*Assault on Precinct 13*) wants to scare the hell out of you. His latest flick, a jaw-dropping exercise in suspense and high tension, is horror the way it should be: visceral, grim, without a trace of humor...the murder set-pieces are devastating in their simplicity...*Halloween* is guaranteed to cause many sleepless nights...

From "Horror Film Shocks and Disgusts" by Eugene Stone (originally published in *The Leader*, Nov. 1978, p. 3):

As the closing credits of John Carpenter's *Halloween* appeared onscreen, I was disgusted and angry. Disgusted by the film's blatant misogyny and sadistic point-of-view, and angered that I had not spent my three bucks on tickets for a show at the Keys Playhouse instead.

Unlike classic cinema such as *Nosferatu* or *Creature from the Black Lagoon*, Carpenter's gloomy and nihilistic gorefest is the latest in a series of horror movies that wallows in sexual violence and the degradation of their female characters. After the opening scene, which depicts a young boy watching his teenage sister have sex before he stabs her to death, I considered walking out of the theater and demanding my money back. But Carpenter, the liberal hack behind 1976's laughable *Assault on Precinct 13*, was just getting warmed up...

The film delights in grime and sickness. Two nude teenage girls are stabbed and strangled to death; another teen abandons the child she is supposed to babysit in search of cheap sex, only to be choked and slashed across the throat. In other scenes, a dog is shown with its guts ripped out; a teenage boy high on drugs and booze gets stabbed through the heart; a bookish girl is stalked and tortured before having a mental breakdown at the end of the film. That all of the killings, religious desecrations, and animal sacrifices are committed by a lumbering sex fiend in a rubber mask makes the movie even more reprehensible. Does Carpenter watch the news? Do the names Gacy or Bundy mean anything to him? I'm sure the family members of the young victims of these real-life monsters would have a blast watching *Halloween*. I'm sure they would have a good chuckle...

When I left the theater, there was a line of excited moviegoers stretched around the block for the midnight showing of Carpenter's little cheerer-upper. I can only guess that these same people delight in woman-bashing, murder, and pornography. I see no other reason for this movie to attract so much unnecessary and undeserved attention.

From "Stone Gets It Wrong—Again" by Beverly Dreger (originally published in *The Leader*, Dec. 1978, p. 2):

For the most part, I enjoy Eugene Stone's movie reviews in *The Leader*. But I don't enjoy the factual and symbolic inaccuracies that pepper his critiques, including his silly and morally righteous rebuke of Carpenter's *Halloween*. Stone would have you believe that the film is the work of a lunatic, a Satan worshipper, or a pervert. *Halloween* does not feature any animal sacrifices, nor is any animal shown "with its guts ripped out." More importantly, the film does not end with the mental breakdown of its female protagonist. As the credits roll, Laurie Strode remains courageous and strong, a symbol of defiance against a dark force determined to kill her. Did Stone consider the undertones of female empowerment in the film? Did he even bother to watch the movie until the end? Perhaps he would prefer the dull and sheltered themes of *Oklahoma!*, currently staging at the Keys Playhouse...

Stone's invoking of real-life killers comes across as exploitative. More to the point, he fails to understand *Halloween*'s message. Gacy was a cook, contractor, and ex-husband; Bundy was a law student, campaign volunteer, and jilted lover. In other words, though they are cold-hearted killers, they are undeniably *human*. Michael Myers, on the other hand, is *nothing*—a faceless shape, void of soul, a barren vessel of terror and malice. And unlike Gacy and Bundy, who chose specific victim-types and worked in discernible patterns, Carpenter's bogeyman can come for you in any place at any time. He is your living nightmare, the monster your parents warned you about...

From *The Girl Who Loved Halloween* (p. 135-137):

A traumatic trigger functions like the rewind and play buttons on a videocassette recorder. The tape that rewinds is of the survivor's memory, returning them to the event of the trauma and playing it back with startling and deeply personal clarity. Triggers are activated by external stimuli that remind the survivor of the traumatic event. A woman who was attacked by a man with blond hair and acne scars might feel scared when she sees another man with similar features. A person who endured years of physical abuse as a child may react emotionally to seeing a parent spanking their son or daughter.

Already haunted by the death of childhood friend Maggie Clark, Beverly was deeply troubled by John Carpenter's *Halloween*, released in 1978. Though she saw the film many times and even defended it in her school paper, there is little question that the story of "bogeyman" Michael Myers functioned as a severe psychological trigger for the 18-year-old college freshman.

"Bev and I saw *Halloween* together three times, but I know she went and saw it by herself, too," says Lisa Brown, who noticed abrupt changes in her roommate in the weeks following the movie's release. "Her relationship with the film was very conflicted, as it reminded her of her mother's strange beliefs and Maggie's death. She even cried after we saw it the first time, realizing how close she came to being killed herself.

"But Beverly also wanted to be strong, like Laurie Strode in the movie," Lisa says. "Seeing *Halloween* that many times was like a test of endurance for her."

Lisa remembers waking up one night after she and Beverly had watched the film to find her roommate sitting upright in her own bed and pointing at the closet, her eyes wide and stricken with terror.

"He's in *there*," Beverly croaked. "He's *right in there*."

Beverly rarely remembered these incidents by morning, though one day, over breakfast with Lisa, she described the man she thought she saw. "He was tall, with dark hair, and his face looked like crinkled black paper," Lisa says. "Even though I never saw the guy, and I had no idea how he could realistically get inside our room, Beverly was so scared that I almost believed her. We went to campus security and reported it, just to make her feel better."

As *Halloween* cleaned up at the box office, Beverly continued to see the film, and her schoolwork suffered as a result. After visiting her father over the Thanksgiving holiday, she agreed to meet with one of the school counselors, who told her she needed to eat healthier foods and get more sleep. The counselor also encouraged Beverly to stop watching scary movies, advice that the stubborn girl refused to heed.

"It was like telling an alcoholic not to drink," Lisa Brown says. "It was a strange compulsion that Beverly couldn't control."

In those autumn months of her freshman year, Beverly spent most of her time at the movies, writing papers on the typewriter that she and Lisa shared, or watching films in the school library.

"She liked hunkering down in the stacks or the media rooms," says Lisa. "A security guard patrols the floors, and there's a few good places to settle in and hide out. She felt safe. Safe from the dude who killed Maggie, safe from her own fears and paranoia. No one could get to her down there."

It was on one of those nights when Beverly was holed up in the library that Lisa made a startling discovery in their dorm room.

"I had an essay to write for class," she says, "and I opened Bev's desk drawer to get some paper. A steak knife from the school cafeteria was right there in plain view. She hadn't tried to hide it or anything."

Lisa explains that she didn't think much of the knife at first, as kids swiped utensils and other items from the cafeteria all the time.

"But as I started writing, I couldn't concentrate," she says. "I'm not proud about this, but I got curious and started poking around."

As she searched their tiny dorm room, Lisa found knives hidden everywhere—in Beverly's dresser, under her mattress, taped beneath her chair, and in the pockets of her coat.

"People ask me all the time if I was scared of Beverly after that," says Lisa. "The answer is no, not at all. She was the first friend I made at Woodhurst and she was a sweet girl who had some fucked-up experiences. If anything, I felt sad. I wanted to help her understand that no one was out to hurt her."

"Beverly's Secret Library" by Scooter Smith (originally published in *The National Buzz*, Mar. 1982, p. 3):

The BUZZ can now disclose that girl-on-the-run Beverly Dreger was doing more than watching sleazy horror movies in the library of Woodhurst State, where the fugitive was once a student.

A source with close ties to the school has revealed the movies that Beverly watched in the library's media viewing rooms—but also the books that the slinky brunette allegedly checked out and the news articles she read for hours at a time.

"We all know about her obsession with *Halloween*, but now we have a sneak peek into a part of her life she desperately tried to hide," says the source.

The movies are the kind we've come to expect from the macabre Beverly—mostly horror flicks like *Dracula*, *Blood Feast*, and Satanic shocker *The Exorcist*.

But the books and newspapers reveal her fixation with unsolved murders and her delusional belief in a faceless killer that stalked both her dreams and her reality.

Books checked out to Beverly's account included *Helter Skelter*, the bloody saga of the Manson Murders; *In Cold Blood*, Capote's non-fiction story of the Clutter killings; and *Mary Ann Cotton: Her Story and Trial*, the tragic tale of an English woman who poisoned and killed her children.

The source added that Beverly spent a lot of time hunched over the newspaper racks and microfiche machine, searching Midwest-city papers for stories of mysterious crimes, unsolved murders, and home intruders.

"*Halloween* was the first ripple in the toxic waters of her mind," the source explained. "Now Beverly was determined to find proof that a real bogeyman killer was out there."

As law enforcement closes in on suspected murderer Beverly Dreger, keep your eyes glued to the pages of The BUZZ for all the latest news, including a full analysis of the crime scene at Woodhurst.

Three newspaper articles found among Beverly Dreger's possessions in 1981:

COLUMBUS - A Columbus University student walked into her dorm room early Sunday morning to find a man rummaging through her belongings, police reported in a campus-wide statement.

The student was returning from an on-campus "casino night" and entered her room shortly before 2:30 a.m., according to police.

The suspect was described as a white male with dark hair and a stocky build. He was wearing a long coat and dark pants. The student said he was wearing a Halloween-type mask and might have been wearing gloves. When the student screamed, the man fled the room and ran out of the residence hall.

Police did not release additional information about the incident, but the student did say that the man appeared to be going through her address book and photo albums.

"I didn't know who he was, or what he was looking for. But now I'm scared to sleep in my own room," the student said.

Police are investigating the possibility that the suspect was seen elsewhere later that morning. School officials are reminding students to keep their dorm rooms locked and to be cautious when walking on campus alone late at night.

MILWAUKEE - A nightmare befell two female college students as they slept inside their apartment in downtown Milwaukee.

Police say the two girls, freshmen at Haggerty University, were sleeping in separate bedrooms on Saturday around 3 a.m. Climbing through an open window, a strange man got inside the apartment and began ransacking the front room.

According to police, the man then walked into the first bedroom and peeled back the covers to look at one of the females. Moments later he crept into the other bedroom and shined a flashlight on the other girl.

"The young woman woke up and shouted at the man to get out of the residence," said Sgt. Bryant Morey of the Milwaukee Police Department. "In the hallway the suspect bumped into the other girl before fleeing the premises. Fortunately, she scratched at his face and came away with a piece of the mask he was wearing.

"The mask is the key we're looking for," Morey said, "especially if we can find out where the suspect might have purchased it."

The suspect is described as a white male between the ages of 23 and 30. He's about 6 feet tall with a stocky build and dark brown or black hair. He was wearing a black jacket, gloves, and big work boots.

Both girls said that the man had a coil of rope fixed to his belt, a detail that has police concerned.

"The rope indicates that the suspect had more than robbery on his mind," said Morey. "Had the girls not been more aware, we could be talking about a rape or kidnapping case right now."

Lakewood Apartments, where the incident took place, provides affordable housing for many Haggerty students.

"If you live in a crowded city, there's a chance you're going to get robbed or have your place broken into," said a junior who lives on the same floor as the two girls. "It goes with the territory."

Cynthia Leeper, a Haggerty senior and president of the school's Student Women's Association, feels differently. "It's 1978," she says. "They caught Bundy. They caught Berkowitz. But are women safe at school? Are they safe at home or the workplace? And who will speak up for them when they're dead?"

Morey says that the number of burglaries in residence halls has decreased over the past year and that college campuses are safe. "But in this case," he cautioned, "the suspect's M.O. has everyone in the department concerned and working overtime to catch him."

WAUKEGAN - A 19-year-old Greentown College student was found dead Monday morning in her dorm room, police said, and the body shows signs of a violent physical attack.

Shelly Caroti was pronounced dead in the dawn hours at one of the college's residence halls, according to the Westerview County Medical Examiner's office. Her body was found by her roommate, who had returned to the room that morning after spending the night elsewhere on campus.

Caroti's body was semi-nude and her throat was slashed. Police indicated that there were ritualistic undertones to the crime scene, including several lit candles and markings in blood on the wall.

In a statement issued to all students, the college stressed that stringent security measures are in place and the campus is safe. However, the *Waukegan Star* reported this morning that Caroti's death is one of many violent incidents involving young women that have occurred throughout the Midwest in recent months. Police would not confirm or deny that they are searching for a lone serial attacker. They did not disclose further details about the crime scene, but officials said that a homicide investigation is underway.

The *Star*, using student interviews and a police report as source material, said that Caroti, who grew up in Waukegan, was a well-liked student with aspirations of becoming a fashion model. The paper reported that her body was displayed in a ritualistic manner, but officials would not elaborate on her appearance.

A spokesperson for the Greentown College said that Caroti was a sophomore majoring in English. The school will hold a candlelight vigil on Wednesday night, while the Caroti family will hold a funeral service in Waukegan later in the week.

The spokesperson said that the college is "cooperating with law enforcement to ensure the safety of every student on campus."

From "Daily Crime Log" by Walter Canley (originally published in *The Leader*, Sept. - Dec. 1978):

TUPPER DORMS - On the evening of September 12, a physical fight between two freshmen female students took place inside Tupper Dorms. A student claimed that a girl who lived down the hall from her was insulting her, calling her a "witch," a "demon," and making fun of her black clothes and makeup.

The two students allegedly confronted each other in the hallway and began shouting at one another. The students then began hitting and slapping each other until the resident advisor broke up the fight. A campus security officer arrived and issued a warning to both girls. The warning was filed with both the housing and security office.

THEATER ARTS - On October 22, a student reported two lost bags on Sunday afternoon after accidentally leaving them unattended outside the Theater Arts building.

The student called campus police to report the lost bags, which she believes were stolen. The bags contained two masks and some clothes used in the school's current production of *Titus Adronicus*. The student said she placed the two bags outside the building before returning to one of the classrooms to retrieve a personal item. When she went outside again, the bags were gone.

The student gathered two other students and a faculty member who were in the building and the four of them searched for the bags. They also searched the backstage area of the campus theater, thinking someone might have brought the bags there. A campus police officer searched the area around both buildings but did not find anything.

The student said that the stolen items, especially the masks that were custom-made for the show, would be costly to replace...

STUDENT FARM - A campus security guard reported suspicious activity at the student research farm in the dawn hours of October 28.

The guard said he found a discarded shirt and pants near the mushroom house. The clothes were dirty and ragged. An officer from Woodhurst Police Department arrived at the farm to take the report.

The security guard told the officer that the farm is easy to access from Orchard Road and that there are limited security measures to keep trespassers out. The guard said there have been problems in the past with students playing pranks or having parties there.

The police officer searched the farm and found a stained black jacket near the packing shed. A faculty member from the Agriculture Department reported that a chicken was missing from the chicken coop and that there were drops of chicken blood on the ground...

OLIVER HALL - A student reported an act of vandalism in the laboratory washroom in Oliver Hall on Saturday.

Campus police officers arrived at the science wing and had the student take them to the washroom to show them the evidence.

Someone had scratched a woman's first name into the mirror above the washroom sink. Officers said that the vandal most likely used a pocketknife to commit the act. Most likely struck by a heavy object, the mirror was cracked down the middle. Officers did not reveal the woman's name scratched into the glass...

From *Shattered Mirror, Shattered Lives* (p. 98):

As winter turned to spring, Beverly fell into a strangely euphoric depression; she derived a bizarre kind of pleasure from her obsession with *Halloween* and the sex-starved killer who stalked its every scene. But much like the high from a drug, the pleasure was fleeting, leaving a dull, stabbing pain in the pit of her stomach. A smattering of violent news stories that she collected from the school library only added to her anxiety and fears. She kept it together for visits with her father in South Hill and for her thinning circle of friends, but the bleak, gritty realism of *Halloween* was slicing into her nerves with the precision of a surgeon's scalpel.

The movie, directed by John Carpenter and starring Jamie Lee Curtis and Donald Pleasance, tells the story of a mask-wearing, knife-wielding psychopath who butchers babysitters and horny boyfriends. An unflinching homage to teenage rebellion, sexual promiscuity, and sadistic violence, *Halloween* was an inexplicable box-office smash, a testament not to the merits of its sick artistry but to a country of marginalized youth searching for meaning in their lives.

For Beverly, the film was the stuff of revelation, a confirmation of her darkest fears but also a declaration of her independence and withdrawal from the world, a salutary "fuck you" to anyone who had ever cast disbelief on her claims that the bogeyman was real. At the Triplex movie theater in Woodhurst, she saw the film over ten times, feeding a twisted fixation that would fade and resurface over the next three years.

"I recognized her after her third visit," said Luther Doyle, 23, an usher at the theater. "Sometimes she came with a friend, but mostly she showed up by herself, usually to the late show, dressed in a *Night of the Living Dead* t-shirt. She'd order the same thing at concessions: a large buttered popcorn, a pack of Bottlecaps, and a Coke. She always sat in the back of the theater. She had a tough look, but she was very pretty. It was impossible not to notice her."

"Honestly, I always wanted to talk to her," Doyle said, "but she was kind of intimidating. I never had the guts."

Beverly would look either happy or distraught when she left the theater, the usher said. He recalls on one occasion her storming out before the slasher film was over, studded black purse thrown over her shoulder and a look of consternation in her flickering eyes.

"It was a mixed bag with her. I could never guess how she was going to respond," Doyle said.

In May of '79, as the school year was coming to an end, Beverly showed up at the Triplex with an older man on her arm. He was tall and lean, tattooed, dressed in blue jeans and boots.

"I didn't know it then, but it was her old man," Doyle said. "I've seen his picture in the paper since then.

"But it surprised me—they didn't see a horror movie. They saw *Love at First Bite* instead, which is a romantic comedy."

Though he had always supported her love of the macabre, Jack Dreger now implored Beverly to seek out more lighthearted sources of enjoyment. He knew his daughter was in pain, fighting demons both real and imaginary, but he had little clue how to help her.

"Jack couldn't forgive himself for what happened to Beverly as a child," said a family friend. "He felt guilty for putting his daughter in such an abusive situation for so long.

"So he did what good fathers do: he spent time with her, visited her at school, took her to silly movies, and tried to get her to see that she didn't have to life her life cowering in fear."

And for a while, the plan seemed to work. Now that *Halloween* was gone from mainstream theaters, Beverly told her friends that she was feeling better; her grades improved and she had fewer sleepless nights, rarely waking up from the blood-soaked nightmares that had haunted her for so long.

"Beverly was holding on to some bad memories, and the murder of that poor Waukegan girl really got under her skin, but her dad never gave up," the friend said. "Jack would have done anything for Beverly. He tried to give her everything she needed."

And Beverly was truly grateful. At the start of summer vacation, she allowed Jack to read one of her school assignments: an essay on one of the most sickening exploitation films to ever appear onscreen. The paper served as a twisted testimony to a daughter's love and the extreme lengths a father will go to in order to protect his only child...

"Portraits of Love in *The Last House on the Left*," an essay by Beverly Dreger (submitted to her Film Crit 101 class, 1979):

Wes Craven's graphic exploitation shocker, *The Last House on the Left* (1972), opens on a green lake dappled with sunlight and alive with feeding ducks. Birds chirp from the forest and tall trees stir in the wind. An elderly postman arrives at the home of J.H. Collingwood and his family. As he delivers the mail, he fancifully intones the name of the Collingwood daughter, Mari, who will turn 17 the next day. A close inspection of the postman's right hand reveals a sinister-looking black ring on his little finger, a strange choice for the older gentleman and a subtle indication of the mind-numbing horror that will befall the Collingwood family, shattering their pastoral surroundings and perverting their familial bond. Like the Manson Murders of 1969, *The Last House on the Left* signals the end of a generation marked by free love, radical music, and demonstrations of peace. In the metaphorical black forest of the film, rape and murder write the law.

At the start of the film, John Collingwood emerges as the heroic centerpiece, a concerned husband and father who exudes confidence, authority, and knowledge of the cruel world. He tells his wife, Estelle, that the news is filled with "murder and mayhem." He warns Mari, on her way to a rock concert with a friend, of the potential dangers they might face, and he criticizes her choice to not wear a bra on her night out. Here is a father who knows the evil that men do, a war veteran who is both stubborn and proud. But John also possesses a generous heart: before Mari leaves the house, he gives her a silver necklace adorned with a peace sign, an early birthday present that becomes central to the film's harrowing plot. When the natural order of their world is violated, when the love that Mari's necklace represents is shattered into a million bloody pieces, John Collingwood rises like a patriarchal giant, willing to avenge at any cost the blasphemy committed upon his daughter.

Before Mari and Phyllis drive to the city to see the concert, they take a walk in the woods. They talk about sex and drink champagne. Mari is excited that her breasts have filled out. Later, as Phyllis drives them into the city, the radio broadcasts chilling news: two convicted murderer-rapists, Krug Stillo and Fred "The Weasel" Podowsky, have escaped from prison, aided by a woman, Sadie, who kicked to death one of the dogs sent to capture the fleeing convicts.

The trio is joined by Krug's illegitimate son, Junior, whom Krug has hooked on heroin in order to control him. In these scenes, Craven excites his audience with images of young lust and carnality (embodied by Mari's budding breasts, glimpsed in an earlier shower sequence and discussed in the woods), then maligns that excitement by disclosing violent details of rape, murder, and the vicious killing of an animal.

This unsettling juxtaposition permeates all of *The Last House on the Left*. In the city, Mari and Phyllis buy ice cream before being abducted by Krug and his gang; while John and Estelle Collingwood set up decorations and bake a cake for Mari's 17th birthday party, Fred pulls a knife on Phyllis and Sadie fondles her breasts. Krug and Fred rape Phyllis while Mari is forced to watch; at the same time, John and Estelle toast cocktails to their "princess."

Later, as Estelle prepares their daughter's birthday cake, John tells her that he wants to take her in the other room and "attack" her. Craven's sexual innuendo is certainly not lost here, but it is John Collingwood's use of the word "attack" that is far more interesting. It is his second military reference in the film, an indication that he is willing to put his life on the line for those he loves, and a foreshadowing of the bloody battle to come. But in the calm before the storm, John tells Estelle not to worry when their daughter fails to come home by morning, believing that she is exhibiting normal teenage rebellion and will return soon. John vacillates here, refusing to face a horrific possibility not dissimilar to the unpredictable battlefronts of war. But when the police offer little assistance, the patriarch's worry and frustration begin to grow.

When Krug and his gang drag Mari and Phyllis to the woods, the film becomes increasingly vile and exploitative, turning urogphilia and bloodletting into a grotesque spectacle sport. In a brief off-screen sequence, Mari and Phyllis are forced to make love to each other. The only redeeming quality of this horrifying moment is the tenderness that Phyllis shows to Mari during their ordeal, comforting the girl and distracting the gang so that Mari might go free. While Krug returns to the car to get the killing knife, Phyllis makes a break for it. Fred and Sadie give chase, leaving Mari alone with the gullible Junior, the only member of the gang who feels guilt over what they have done. She renames him "Willow," a Celtic symbol for love and femininity, and secures her peace emblem around his neck. As Phyllis eludes Fred and Sadie, Mari tells Junior that she can get him his drug "fix" by going to her house nearby and raiding her father's medicine supply. Though Mr. Collingwood is absent in these scenes, Mari relies on the resources of her father to provide a path to her survival.

In the next scene, Phyllis stumbles into a wooded cemetery. She spots the highway through the trees and believes she has made her escape. But Krug, Fred, and Sadie appear and surround her. Fred stabs her several times, each thrust marked by electronic bursts from the film's jarring soundtrack. Half-naked, streaked with blood, Phyllis dies in agony. The film gives no indication that anyone, least of all her mother and father, will mourn for her.

Mari's plan to escape with Junior is thwarted when Krug and the others catch up to them. When Mari asks Krug if Phyllis got away, Fred drops Phyllis' dismembered hand on the ground. Mari screams in horror. Krug proceeds to rape her, his bloodied and razor-burned face pressed grotesquely against her cheek. As Mari stares dead-eyed into space, she realizes her death is near. The gang allows her to drift away from the group, floating like a ghost; she vomits into the grass and recites a prayer. Her words seem to find some trace of humanity within Krug and the others; they look pitiful and ashamed, their faces and hands sticky with innocent blood. Mari wades, zombie-like, into the lake, where Krug shoots her three times, killing her. The gunshots tear through the silence of the woods, alerting the Collingwood's dog. A universal symbol of companionship, and often referred to as "man's best friend," the dog links Mari's tragic death to her home nearby and to John Collingwood, the dog's primary caretaker.

As the killers wash the blood from their bodies and change into their Sunday best, the film cuts to the Collingwood house, where the gang finds refuge. When Estelle informs her husband of their guests, she finds John playing solitaire in one of the rooms. John Steinbeck employed this same motif in his 1937 classic, *Of Mice and Men*, in order to emphasize the role of chance in the universe. As Krug and the gang believe that chance has brought them good luck in the form of a new hideout, they are ignorant of what strong-willed, enraged parents will do when their hearts are broken beyond repair.

Though the naïveté of the Collingwoods serves to drive the film to its numbing climax, John remains keenly astute during the dinner scene. He notices a bite mark on Krug's hand and a small bandage on Sadie's forehead; he also observes Sadie's predilection for red wine. A nightmarish reality dawning on him, John sees that their guests are anything but normal. Later, Estelle spots Mari's silver peace emblem around Junior's neck and discovers bloody clothes in Krug's suitcase. Suspicion and terror mounting, John and Estelle run to the lake. They find Mari in the weeds, pale and cold. Estelle weeps over the broken body, while John remains more stoic, consoling his wife and refusing to cry for what cannot be undone. Like a grizzled veteran returning to the front lines, he will go back to his house to wage a war of blood.

In the next sequence, Fred has a nightmare in which he sees John and Estelle dressed in blue surgical scrubs. Estelle demands that Fred open his mouth. She hands her stone-faced husband a scalpel and a hammer. John places the scalpel over Fred's front teeth. When John brings the hammer down, Fred lurches awake. He gets dressed and wanders the house, finding Estelle in the living room. Meanwhile, in the basement, John prepares for battle by examining his stockpile of weapons, including a wrench and a rifle.

A plan of vicious revenge forming in her mind, Estelle seduces Fred, telling him that she "has always dreamed of a man who could take [her] easily." They go for a walk in the woods, the place of Mari's degradation and death. As his beautiful wife piles on the erotic charm, John puts his military expertise to use by booby-trapping the house. His attention to detail in this scene—constructing trip lines, setting up pratfalls, and swiping Krug's gun—reveals a father wholly dedicated to avenging his daughter and to upholding her honor and integrity.

Out in the woods, Estelle ties Fred's hands behind his back with his necktie; after mocking the diminutive size of his penis, she fellates him. During his orgasm, Estelle castrates Fred with her wrenching jaws, spitting out the remains in the dirt. It is a revolting, perverse moment, debasing Estelle to the level of beasts, not unlike the band of killers. But just as John steals Krug's gun to protect himself, Estelle rips away Fred's "weapon," protecting herself and any other woman who crosses the sick murderer's path.

At the house, John shoots Krug in the shoulder with the rifle as Sadie runs off. In the room where the grieving parents have gently placed Mari's body, John and Krug exchange blows. When Krug sees the deceased girl on the couch, he taunts the vengeful father: "Mari, Mari…she was a lot tougher than you, doc. She took a while to kill." To hear his daughter's name from the lips of her rapist-killer is too much for the wounded patriarch; it weakens his spirit and reveals the grieving heart beneath the gruff and reserved exterior. Krug prepares to strangle John when Junior suddenly appears and fires a gun at his father. When the bullet misses its target, Krug convinces his bastard son to turn the gun on himself. Junior does, dying before the icy-cold stare of the one man who was supposed to love him and never did.

The sound of a revving chainsaw distracts Krug from the bloody scene before him. John emerges from the basement with the powerful weapon, slicing through the door when Krug tries to lock him in. Two years after the release of *The Last House on the Left*, director Tobe Hooper shocked movie audiences everywhere with the sordid tale of a cross-dressing psychopath in *The Texas Chain Saw Massacre* (1974). But unlike the chainsaw-wielding Leatherface, who wears masks of human skin and eats his victims, John Collingwood is a relatable man whose grief we understand. With his mustard-colored turtleneck and sorrowful determination, he becomes the reluctant hero of a film that showcases the bond between a father and his daughter while exuding an unexpected sensitivity toward family relationships.

At the end of *The Last House on the Left*, John tears into Krug with the chainsaw, killing him just as police arrive at the scene. In the backyard, Estelle slits Sadie's throat before joining her husband in the house. Exhausted, the parents cling to each other. In the final shot of the film, the camera freezes on John's blood-streaked face, a searing portrait of a father's boundless love. The pictorial credits that follow show Mari Collingwood, angelic as ever, smiling in symbolic approval of all her father has done to defend his slain daughter's image.

From *The Girl Who Loved Halloween* (p. 164):

The summer after her freshman year at college, Beverly packed up her clothes and books and returned to her father's house in South Hill. She was happy to be at home, but she admitted to Jack that she couldn't get the brutal murder of Shelly Caroti out of her mind. In her imagination she saw the pretty girl nude, stabbed, and surrounded by burning votive candles...

That summer, she spent most of her time in her room, writing stories, watching movies on the VCR, and reading books about film, screenwriting, and acting. Occasionally, she would draw sketches of the man with the burned face she saw inside her dorm room closet, but she tore most of them up and flushed the pieces down the toilet.

Then, on a balmy night in July, trouble exploded at 127 Wichita Road.

While searching for a book that belonged to her mother, Beverly found a large box hidden away on a closet shelf. Inside were several of her mother's things, including magick weapons, prayer candles, and a tattered spiral notebook that smelled faintly of clove. Attached to its black cover was a newspaper clipping about a murdered child named Natalie Stubson.

"Bev called me that night freaking out," recalls roommate Lisa Brown. "She said she had found her mother's journal and that her dad had kept it from her. She said it was filled with all these awful things about dead kids and bodies found in ditches at the side of the road, and that all of the entries in the book were addressed to her.

"Her mother had made it for her. It was like a gift. A very weird, very fucked-up gift," Lisa says. "And what really tripped Beverly out was that she had done the exact same thing at school, collecting news articles in the library about murders and kidnappings and all that. It's probably the strangest mother-daughter bond you could ever think of, but it was a bond nonetheless."

With Lisa on the phone, Beverly recounted some of the articles pasted inside the notebook. As she shared the graphic details of one horrific crime after the other, her voice grew more despondent.

"I tried interjecting, to tell her that her dad must have hidden it for a reason, but she didn't want to listen," Lisa says.

Throughout the book, Susan Dreger had scribbled notes to her daughter, warning her of a burgeoning evil she called "the black thing in the dark, the taker of children."

"Just as I was getting her to calm down, her dad was shouting at her to hang up the phone," Lisa says. "I had never heard Jack yell like that—I think he was trying to get the book back—and then the line went dead. I called back three or four times, but no one picked up."

Over the next few days, Martha Porter, who lived three houses away from the Dregers, would overhear arguments from the residence while she was walking her dog at night.

"I could hear them up and down the street. Lots of yelling and slamming doors," Porter says.

Though disturbed by her discovery, Beverly argued to her father that the notebook might help her to understand her own fears. When Jack refused to let her have it, his daughter became irate.

"She wanted me to have it!" she shouted. "It belongs to me!"

But Jack was stubborn. The notebook was a filthy stain on their lives, he said, a gut-punch reminder of his wife's mental illness and abuse. He took the book from Beverly and threatened to destroy it.

"But you told me she was getting better!" Beverly reminded her father. "Maybe this can help me get better too!"

Martha Porter says she felt sorry for the Dreger family and even considered knocking on the door to see if she could help. "I could hear the girl pleading with him not to throw the book away," Porter says, "but in the end I thought I should just mind my own business."

In the days that followed, Beverly and her father rarely spoke to each other, except when they argued. "Jack wanted to tell her about the book and let Beverly make her own decision on what to do with it—just not right then. He knew the possessions in the box were the only remaining things connecting Beverly to her mother," Lisa Brown explains. "But Beverly had come so far by then, and he didn't want to set her back. He wanted to wait until she got even stronger.

"But Bev didn't see it that way. She thought she had a right to it. It got to the point where Jack had to carry the stupid thing around with him, just so Beverly wouldn't try to take it."

One afternoon, while her father was at work, Beverly called Lisa and told her she wanted to get out of the house.

"I thought she meant go to the movies or something," Lisa says. "But she wanted *out*-out. She asked me if I knew a place where college kids could go for the summer, like a hostel or an art commune. I told her about this place called Wasawillow Ranch. My cousin had visited there and really dug it."

Beverly spent the rest of the afternoon in the South Hill library, where she read articles about the ranch in *Reader's Digest* and *People* magazines. She learned about the people who lived there, the farmers and the hippies, the writers and musicians. That night, in a moment of calm, she presented the idea to Jack.

"He thought Beverly was just running away from her problems, but she had really latched onto the idea of going," Lisa explains. "She convinced him that it wasn't about the notebook or their fight; it was about taking a break, about getting away from a past that was clearly causing major problems between the two of them."

That same night, Beverly gave her father copies of the articles to read and showed him the location of the ranch on a map.

"She had the address and the bus route all written out for him," Lisa says. "She said she would write once a week and call from a pay phone in town. Jack eventually said yes, but they made an agreement to put the mother's possessions away and figure out what to do with them when Beverly got back."

Three days later, Beverly's bags were packed. Jack gave her food for the bus ride and the cash in his wallet. He tucked a letter inside one of the bags that told his daughter how much he loved her.

"Jack was worried," Lisa says. "He didn't understand what was pushing Beverly to do this, but he had done some soul-searching himself when he was her age and camped out all over the country. He understood her need to find her place in the world. And to that aim, Wasawillow was the perfect opportunity."

"The Mysteries of Wasawillow" by Prudence Gravelle (originally published in *Appalachian Voices*, Feb. 1982, p. 2-5):

Sipping licorice root tea on the patio of her parents' house, Prudence Gravelle says that Wasawillow Ranch is an artistic retreat that focuses on spiritual health and egalitarian principles, and not a religious cult that some make it out to be.

"I wanted out of the mainstream world," she says. "I wanted to go back to Mother Earth, to eat food I grew myself, and build my own personal space. Wasawillow promised me all that and it delivered."

Prudence, 23, is speaking for the first time about the two years she spent at the 25-acre ranch nestled in the foothills of Willow Creek Forest in eastern Kentucky. Though the organization has never been in any legal trouble, some have linked the Wasawillow Ranch to cult-like practices, including indoctrination and shunning.

"Wasawillow stands for a rejection of capitalism, an expression of artistic spirit, and a belief in communal living for the greater good," says Prudence. "I no longer live there, but I have a duty to correct the mistruths that have been printed in the media."

Prudence openly admits that she has another reason for coming forward: she was there when Beverly Dreger joined the group. Dreger is suspected of killing three college students in October of 1981, and has been missing since the murders occurred.

"She came to the ranch in the summer of '79," Prudence recalls. "Her first night in camp, I held a purificatory ritual in her honor and she slept in my cabin. By the next morning, she was one of us."

Prudence stresses that Beverly enjoyed her stay at the ranch, denying that the psychological impact of living in an unfamiliar and isolated community could have played a role in the murders.

"There's no way the young woman we came to know killed those poor girls," she says. "Beverly was struggling with some family issues, but that applied to just about everyone who visited or stayed there.

"At the ranch, we lived differently than most people," Prudence adds. "We believed in communal possessions and housing. We didn't eat or wear animal products. We had certain rules and structures to follow. But that didn't make us a cult."

Prudence was never one for a traditional life. Her father was a folk singer, while her mother sold oddities—gas masks, wooden dolls, medical supplies, vintage toys—that she found at garage sales and city dumps. The family lived in Pinewood, a suburb of Kentucky, where Prudence dropped out of high school at age 17. A friend told her about a nearby "farming community" that included log cabins, vegetable orchards, a stable for animals, and areas for sculpture, painting, and performance art.

"My parents encouraged me to go. To them, it was alternative education at its best," says Prudence, who has earned her GED since leaving Wasawillow. "I gathered up my poetry books and my dad's old six-string, and I hitchhiked to the ranch in less than a day."

When she first arrived in the spring of 1978, Prudence knew she had found paradise. "The air smelled like fresh laundry. Hippies were everywhere, young men with long beards and women with kinky hair and big chests. There were a few families with children. Everyone was good-looking and kind. They lived either in tents or cabins that they built themselves. They didn't have electricity, but they cooked their own food over fire pits and played live music every night."

But Prudence quickly discovered that life at the ranch was not always what she expected. "On my second morning in camp, I was given a list of rules that dictated everything from my work schedule to when I could eat. I admit, I was taken aback at first," she says. "But I soon understood that these rules were no different than the laws back home; in fact, they were better than laws, because we *followed* them. They spoke to the hyper-organization of the ranch and how aligned everyone was with the same beliefs and goals."

Prudence learned that group members were required to attend spiritual services at the Wasawillow church—an outbuilding in the center of camp. But she says that church services at the ranch focused more on moral and ethical living rather than strict religious devotion.

"Joel allowed us to explore our own spirituality and decide for ourselves the role of God in our lives. He was there to guide us if we needed it, teach us if we requested it, but we were mostly free to make own choices."

Prudence smiles warmly at her first mention of Joel Flannery, a man in his early 40s who started the group from his log-cabin home in Kentucky in 1971. Flannery, Prudence says, was a motivational and charismatic visionary who had important ideas about the future of Wasawillow. "He wanted to build a school and marketplace, an entire self-sustained town. He taught us how to live off the grid, to survive in a society of our own making," she says.

"Yes, Joel had strict rules about labor and food rations, but his main objective was to sustain the camp and treat each man, woman, and child equally."

Prudence admits that communal living at Wasawillow was not always easy. "Some people defied the rules, or tried to obey the rules but found them too restrictive," she says. "We had a safe, honest, and consistent punishment system in place when infractions occurred. No one was ever beaten with switches, or starved to death, or any of the other crazy things you've read." Prudence insists that the core values of the ranch always centered on hope and productive change. "Some of us talked about living there indefinitely, while others had plans to return to society and open up an art gallery, music club, or theater. The vibe was always supportive and inspiring."

Around this time, over 250 miles away, Beverly Dreger was finishing up a turbulent freshman year at Woodhurst State. Though she earned good grades and made a few friends at school, the 19-year-old was depressed and lonely, haunted by the memory of her mother's suicide and struggling to overcome various psychological afflictions.

"She told me about her mother, the notebook, her feelings about *Halloween*, all of it. We became very close," says Prudence. "Beverly thought the movie was speaking to her in code, telling her she wasn't crazy, and that the bogeyman really existed. And while that brought her some comfort, it also scared her to death.

"To help Beverly transcend and grow as a person, we ditched her black clothes for basic cotton blouses and dresses. We taught her how to use meditation as a tool to let go of the past and to shape her future.

"One night, during one of Joel's midnight concerts, I gave her an evil eye bracelet to wear, which would bring her protection and positive energy. I think she started feeling a lot better after that."

Prudence says her positive relationship with Beverly kept both of their intellectual minds healthy and active. "She enjoyed talking about movies, books, art, music," she says. "I was an actress in high school, and she became very interested in that, in the ways to play different characters and bring their stories to life."

Prudence and Beverly were among the many young artists and free-thinkers dedicated to the principles of Wasawillow. 23-year-old Shawn Cote was in charge of organizing the ranch's holistic activities, including yoga, sculpture, and painting classes. Like Beverly, he came from a troubled home. He also had an older brother who fought in the Vietnam War.

"Shawn said his brother had been hexed by Vietnamese monks, and Beverly took strange comfort in that," Prudence explains. "She felt like she wasn't the only one tormented by something invisible." As the weeks went on, Beverly and Shawn grew close. "It was sweet to watch them fall for each other. And Beverly looked beautiful when she was around Shawn—nothing like in those awful, washed-out pictures that came later in the paper."

Throughout the summer, the trio worked hard building cabins, growing their own food, and learning from Joel Flannery how to self-sustain. For fun, they smoked pot, played guitar, and acted out old scripts that Prudence had brought from home. "Getting stoned helped us all open up," Prudence says. "I told Bev about my depression when I was a teenager, and she told me about her mother and the infamous notebook. Beverly said it was like looking at a car accident; she knew there was something terrible inside, but she couldn't look away. We spent a lot of time together, talking it out, helping each other to heal."

On the late-August morning that Beverly left the ranch, Shawn sprinkled her bags with blackberry flowers and lilies. The entire camp gathered to say goodbye. "She was much thinner, but the hard work had given her strength and muscle," Prudence says. "She was wearing an embroidered blouse and the bracelet I had given her. She told me she was excited to go home, see her father, and return to school. She even said that she wanted to become an actress! I kissed her on the cheek—I remember that very clearly—and said, 'Just don't forget to be you.' Shawn drove her to the bus stop and I never saw her again."

As Prudence watched the pretty college student drive away, an overwhelming feeling of melancholy came over her. She knew it was time for her to leave Wasawillow too. "I hadn't finished high school at the time, and I missed my friends and parents back home," Prudence says. "I loved my life at the ranch, but I was exhausted all the time. At the end of September, I was ready to leave."

Prudence has never returned to Wasawillow, but she insists that it's not because she harbors any feelings of ill will toward the ranch or its founder. "Cults target people dissatisfied with life—and that was definitely me at age 17—but they also manipulate your dreams, your fears, and then use them against you," she says. "For me, Wasawillow did the opposite. I left the ranch feeling ready to start my new life."

Just as Prudence was finishing up her GED in 1981, news of the brutal slayings at Woodhurst State exploded across television screens nationwide. When she saw Beverly's picture there in fuzzy black and white, Prudence felt ill.

"People are saying all kinds of crazy things about her, that she's a cold-blooded killer, that she's left the country, that she went to the woods and shot herself and police haven't found her body yet. From what I've read in the papers, the police don't really understand Bev, the way her mind works. They're not even *trying* to understand her, and that's their biggest problem.

"Like I said before, the girl I knew was not capable of violence, let alone that kind of savagery," Prudence says. "Unless everything we shared, all our dreams and late-night talks, our nature walks through the forest, the love between her and Shawn…unless all of that was one big lie, then I believe Beverly Dreger is innocent."

From "Horror, Haddonfield, and Hallucinations" (p. 14-15):

Released in 1979, *Day of the Woman* (later renamed *I Spit On Your Grave*) played for three nights at the Dixie 4-Screen Drive-In outside Chicago. Oozing with low-budget slime, the grimy shock-fest tells the story of one woman's rape and her subsequent revenge on the greaseball rednecks who attacked her...

Lisa Brown recalls seeing the flick with Beverly as they prepared to start their sophomore year at Woodhurst. "We went as a joke," she says. "We smoked out, got loaded on vodka Slurpees, and drove over to Bartlett to watch it.

"I didn't bring up all the crazy stuff that happened before she left for the ranch," Lisa adds. "We were having too much fun and I didn't want to spoil it."

After the movie, on the quiet drive back to campus, Beverly would not stop talking about what they had seen—the rape sequences, the graphic nudity, the castration and the disembowelments and the drownings. "She knew it was garbage, but she thought it was still an important film about female empowerment and survival." That night, Beverly wore a blouse with bell-shaped sleeves and a strange-looking bracelet that Lisa had never seen before. "She called it her protection amulet," Lisa says. "She was always worried that it was going to break or fall off."

Lisa and Beverly stayed up late listening to Bruce Springsteen's *Darkness on the Edge of Town*. They smoked pot and decorated their dorm room. They talked about the boys they liked and Beverly told Lisa about Shawn Cote. They shared their plans for the year. Inspired by her summer internship at a law office, Lisa had decided to major in Political Science and become a lawyer. Beverly said that she wanted to be an actress, that her dream was to make a horror film, to get lost inside her role, to emerge from the creative process an entirely new person...

From "Girl on Fire" by Juliette Gossamer (originally published in *The Review*, Dec. 1983, p. 13):

In the summer of 1979, 20-year-old Nathan Moon wrote a script for a low-budget "rape and revenge" flick called *Carol Refuses to Die*. He wanted to make a movie that was crazy, like *The Texas Chain Saw Massacre*, but also scary as hell, like *The Exorcist*. A movie that used real people instead of professional actors. A movie where you couldn't quite trust the guy making it. "I want my audience to feel unclean," he told his college paper that fall. "Like, they can't go out to a club after watching my movie. They have to go home first and take a shower."

Today, on a rainy afternoon inside a Chicago diner, Moon leafs through an old copy of the script. Now 23, he stares at the pages as if searching for some hidden meaning in the words. "This is the original copy," he says. "One of the few things that survived from the shoot, other than our corporeal bodies."

Moon wears a carrot-hued sweater, ripped jeans, and a St. Jude medallion around his neck. His looks tired, his complexion wan under scruffy patches of beard. He tells me he has two other screenplays in the can, including one about a haunted funeral parlor, that he's been struggling to get made. But he admits that, after his first experience shooting a feature film, he no longer has the same enthusiasm about the medium that he used to. "People say to me all the time, 'Dude, you were making a drive-in movie, get over it.' But we were artists," Moon insists. "We believed in what we were doing."

Moon was an undergraduate student at Woodhurst, a state school located in a western suburb of Chicago. There, in the fall of 1979, he began gathering the resources he would need to turn *Carol Refuses to Die* into an actual movie.

"It was derivative trash," says Janet Holt, a 22-year-old drama major who Moon recruited to be his cinematographer. "But it was our first film and we were committed to the process. Nathan revised the script, I scouted locations and rented the equipment, and Robbie was in charge of casting."

Like Moon, Robbie Bruckner was a sophomore at Woodhurst, a soft-spoken student actively involved in community theater. "Casting the role of Carol Hartley was left up to me," he says. "Nathan wanted someone real, someone off the street. I was handling props for a local production of *The Bad Seed*, and Beverly Dreger came to see it one night. I met her in the lobby after the show. She was wearing a purple skirt over blue jeans. Not a touch of makeup on. She looked gorgeous, and she was perfect for the part."

Moon agrees that Dreger had the right look for his bohemian protagonist, a young woman who gets beaten and violated within the first ten pages of the script. "I figured she'd hate it and that we'd have to find someone else," Moon says. "But she dug it. She read the script and actually had notes for me the next day. She dove into the whole experience head-first, and that's what made us cast her." Holt also recalls Dreger's enthusiasm for the amateur project. "She was a movie nerd, just like all of us in the crew," she says. "You could tell being in the film meant a lot to her."

At the time, Moon had no idea that Dreger's input would reveal the most disturbing experience of her life. "In the original script, after Carol kills Bluto and Tomato Face, she drives into Death Valley and blows her head off," he says. "Beverly hated the scene and asked me if she could rewrite it. I wanted her in my movie, so I said yes."

In Dreger's version, Carol slits her wrists and bleeds to death on the bathroom floor of a motel room. "We were at the pub, drinking, and I asked her why she changed it. We ordered another pitcher, and that was when she told me.

"Her mother killed herself, and Beverly found her body," Moon says.

Over the next few hours, Dreger described for Moon the horror of that terrible day: the dirty house, the bathroom smeared in blood, her mother dead on the tiled floor. She told Moon that she ran like hell after discovering the body—out of the house, down the stairs, into the busy street. She took the bus back to the house where she lived with her father and didn't tell anybody what she saw.

"I don't know why she wanted it in the script or why she told me about it. We hardly knew each other, really. Maybe she was drunk or high on something, or she just got carried away with the excitement of being in the movie.

"Here's what I do know—that kid was in a lot of pain, and I was a novice, snot-nosed director who didn't know how to take care of his actors," the young filmmaker concedes.

But Moon is quick to add that he will never forgive Dreger for what took place during the filming of *Carol Refuses to Die.*

"It was my American dream, and Beverly's demons tore it apart. And now, whenever I smell gasoline, I feel like killing somebody."

"Students Unite to Make Feature Film" by Russell Burger (originally published in *The Leader*, Nov. 1979, p. 4-5):

Carol Hartley's life has become a living hell. Her pretty face has been disfigured by seeping wounds and bruises the color of eggplant. Her clothes are torn and clotted with gore. But she laughs as she takes a skinny greaser by the neck and slices into his bobbing Adam's apple with a switchblade. Blood begins to flow and spurt, coating her hands and arms in red goo. Her laughter becomes the scream of a deranged banshee as she raises the blade and drives it into one of the punk's terrified eyes…

This is just one of the balls-to-the-wall scenes from sophomore Nathan Moon's screenplay *Carol Refuses to Die*, a sickening slice of exploitation gore-pie that the 20-year-old director plans to shoot this winter.

The Leader sat down with Moon and fellow sophomore Beverly Dreger, who will take on the blood-soaked role of Carol Hartley, to find out what delicious torments and ghastly treats they have in store for their first collaboration together.

LEADER: What drew you both to the exploitation genre and to this story in particular?

BEVERLY DREGER: I read Nathan's script and saw genuine humanity in Carol's battle to stay alive. Sure, the movie's filled with some of the most gross-out scenes you could ever imagine, but the character arc really spoke to me. You have a heroine who overcomes the most vile assault possible, not only on her body but on her mind, and she rises like a phoenix from the ashes to take her revenge. I could relate to that feeling of wanting to take back control of your life.

NATHAN MOON: I watch a lot of movies and I'm constantly being exposed to different genres, from the sick, bottom-of-the-barrel exploitation flicks like *I Spit On Your Grave* to classics like *Citizen Kane* and *The Godfather*. Watching the good films as well as the bad ones helps me to have a clearer vision of the kinds of movies I want to make. I want people to be moved by *Carol Refuses to Die*, I really do, but I also want them to feel unclean after watching it, like they have to go home and take a shower afterward. The thing is, even when you hate an exploitation movie, you can't get it out of your mind either. The images stay with you whether you want them to or not.

LEADER: *Carol Refuses to Die* is a "rape and revenge" film not unlike Zarchi's *I Spit On Your Grave*. Since this is the first feature film for both of you, how concerned are you with the script's graphic sexual content and violence?

DREGER: I don't want to sound like a nihilist or someone who doesn't take tragedy and death seriously, because I do. But the reality is that people, young women especially, are being raped and killed every day all over the world. Have you heard of Kitty Genovese? She was raped and murdered and people *saw it happening*. Her killer was caught and went to jail, but there are many more victims out there who die at the hands of these monsters and no one knows a thing about them. As hard as it is to swallow, *Carol Refuses to Die* presents life as it really is.

MOON: I'm not a violent person by nature, but I like watching scary movies in which terrible things happen to good people. I don't want to see anyone get hurt in real life, but when I watch a horror movie I expect to be thrilled, horrified, and shocked. I want to be kept on edge, never knowing what's hiding around the corner. Sex, blood, and violence can do that to you!

LEADER: Beverly, as a first-time actress, how are you preparing for the role of Carol Hartley? Are you studying other actors or looking to other films for inspiration?

DREGER: I've watched a few biker flicks here in the library, and I adore *Easy Rider* and all the Roger Corman stuff, but mostly I've been talking to Nate about the character. I learned to meditate over the summer, so I've been doing that to get more in touch with myself and relax more. I've never been in front of the camera like this, so I'm very nervous! Also, Nate has given me the freedom to create my own backstory for Carol, so I've been working on that in between my classes and homework.

LEADER: Can you tell us about the special effects in the film and how you intend to pull them off on such a limited budget?

MOON: Some of my favorite films, especially *Rosemary's Baby* and *The Texas Chain Saw Massacre*, actually have very limited gags. But the camera work, the lighting, the editing—if handled correctly, your audience imagines things that aren't really there. The devil baby in *Rosemary*, the hook scene in *Chain Saw*—these sequences are masterful for what the camera *doesn't* show us. But I will also admit, while I hope *Carol* has some style and finesse to it, we're stocking up on karo syrup and red food coloring to satisfy all the gorehounds out there.

DREGER: The effects are going to be insane. There's death by corkscrew, death by acid-spiked drink, tampons soaked in cyanide...I don't want to give too much away!

LEADER: Nathan, we know this is a sensitive subject, but have you done any research into the psychological or emotional mindset of rape victims in order to present your heroine in a realistic light?

MOON: To be honest, I didn't do any research when writing the script. I just thought about how I'd feel if I were raped and brutalized, subjugated to the point where I felt like an animal. The scenes and the dialogue sprang out of my reaction to that scenario.

LEADER: How has it been working together so far? Is it hard to have fun when working with such graphic material?

MOON: We've done several read-throughs of the script with students from Lauren Reid's screenwriting class and from the theater program. There's a lot of gallows humor in *Carol*, so we're having a blast with that. It's definitely the most collaborative project I've ever worked on. Beverly's input on the script has been great—very gutsy and bold. The only problem we ran into was during location scouting at the cemetery in Bellwood—some creepy dude dressed in black kept watching and staring at us the whole time!

LEADER: Beverly, you mentioned giving Carol your own backstory. In what ways did you add to the character and how do you think this process will help you portray her onscreen?

DREGER: I took Carol all the way back to her childhood home in Chicago Heights, a rough place to grow up, imagining her as a child of divorce and being raised in a home where the line between love and hate was very thin. She was a sweet kid but angry a lot of the time. Her mother committed suicide when Carol was a kid; her father was a good man who did the best he could. Giving Carol this story has helped me *become* the character, which I know sounds really affected, but it's true! Hopefully this preparation will translate well on camera.

LEADER: How do your families feel about you making a movie with such violent and explicit content? Do they support what you do?

MOON: We're not pornographers! We're just a bunch of goofy kids trying to make a name for ourselves in a cutthroat business. My dad kicked in a good amount of dough for us to get started, and my mom works in a nightclub on the south side with live music and weird art installations on the weekend. They support what I do.

DREGER: My dad loves horror movies and monsters, especially the Universal ones, but I haven't decided yet if I'm going to tell him about this.

LEADER: How has the Woodhurst faculty and student body responded to the project?

MOON: With the CSP increasing in popularity over the past year, Woodhurst could not be a more creative and supportive place for aspiring filmmakers, or artists in general. We had so many people turn up for auditions, there's clearly a strong interest in movies and anything that promises to shake up the status quo in some way.

DREGER: Everyone has been great. A few of my friends got cast as extras in the movie, so that will be fun. Lauren Reid is an awesome teacher and has been an advocate of the project from the very start.

Keep your eyes riveted to the pages of *The Leader* as we bring you further exciting details from *Carol Refuses to Die* as they roll in. With the recent success of gruesome flicks like the *Dawn of the Dead*, *Phantasm*, and the sci-fi shocker *Alien*, horror fans from all over the country are demanding more guts, more gore, and more glory! Let's hope the talented Nathan Moon and his cast can deliver...

BELLWOOD - Police officers went to the cemetery on Harper Road on Saturday morning after being notified that desecrations had occurred on the premises.

When officers arrived at the scene, they found three tipped-over headstones. The base of a mausoleum at the rear of the cemetery was covered in broken glass and debris from ruined flower arrangements.

"It's inexcusable. There is nothing more sinful than dishonoring the dead," said Margaret Dalley, who arrived at the cemetery to visit her father's grave only to find police searching the grounds for clues. She remained shaken for the rest of the day.

Coral "Tiffy" Henry, who works for the Marion County Museum Association, said that the cemetery attracts vandals because there is no security system to keep them out. "All they have to do is jump the fence and the place is theirs," Henry said.

A group of college kids was seen taking pictures of the cemetery around the suspected time of the incident, but police have cleared the students of any wrongdoing.

Guy Nelson, a truck driver who has lived in Bellwood all his life, has an ominous feeling about the wreckage.

"This is more than the average prank or destruction of property. The person who did this is very sick and very angry," Nelson said.

Police have made no arrests in connection with the vandalism. The investigation is ongoing.

From "Horror, Haddonfield, and Hallucinations" (p. 15):

Gone were the skin-tight black dresses and horror-flick tees, the Gothic jewelry and military boots; Beverly now favored braided headbands and flowing skirts, leather belts and macramé bracelets. A sophomore in college, she cruised through her course load of general education and film classes, earning good grades and recognition from her professors.

"She had a tendency to be melodramatic in her writing, drawing parallels that I didn't think always worked, but her efforts stood out," says Rosemary Smith, who had Beverly as a student in the fall of '79. "There was an energy to her work, a passion for film studies and art in general."

Beverly declared her major that term, writing to her father that nothing meant more to her than "the language of movies, the baptism of watching film." However, the stark brutality of *Carol Refuses to Die* was a constant reminder of her mother's suicide. In that same letter to Jack, she admitted for the first time that she had discovered her mother's body: "I know I wasn't supposed to see her, but I dropped by to say hi. I thought we could have lunch or something. I'm sorry I lied to you, Dad. I was too scared to say anything."

While working on the film, Beverly never broached the subject of Susan's notebook with her father, but it must have weighed heavily on her mind when she rewrote the script so that the heroine cuts her wrists and bleeds to death. If only briefly, she wanted to *become* her mother, to feel her anguish—a catharsis of blood and B-movie fantasy that had dire consequences for the entire project.

Despite Beverly's new look and demeanor, Smith knew that the 19-year-old was masking her pain.

"Beverly seemed preoccupied with not only the horror genre, but also far more serious issues, including violence against women and suicide. That term, she gave me a paper to proofread that had me concerned," says the professor. "But she never came back for it, and I never could figure out what class it was for." Smith brought the paper to the attention of the school's health services, but she never heard back from them...

From "Untitled Fall Paper" written by Beverly Dreger, 1979:

...rawboned Georgina Spelvin moves bug-like across the screen, the existential prisoner of 1973's *The Devil in Miss Jones*, Gerard Damiano's X-rated spiritual masterpiece. The prologue finds Justine Jones, the character played by Spelvin, in deranged sexual psychosis, pleading a strange man to make love to her, a jarring display of nymphomania that foreshadows the devil tarot card of the opening credits. Damiano then takes us moodily into the past, into Justine's threadbare city apartment, where she climbs naked into a bathtub. Plummeting piano chords signal her doom as Justine drags a razor blade across her wrists. A gory prologue to the sexual odyssey about to unfold, her veins spout blood into the water, dripping from her lifeless body, mingling with the bushel of sopping pubic hair. Her head slumps to one side, her face as pale as winter, a gruesome image that sends a message to the person unlucky enough to find her: *you never understood my pain...*

In 1976's *The Omen*, a gruesome suicide clears the way for the young anti-Christ and his rise to familial and political power. The child, Damien Thorn, has a life of wealth and ease; his father is the ambassador to Italy and his mother showers him with affection. But on the boy's sixth birthday—six being the number of sin, the devil, evil spirits, and sorcery—his nanny commits the most gleeful suicide ever captured on celluloid ("Look at me, Damien! It's all for you!"), hanging herself before a crowd of awestruck children. The nanny was powerless in the face of monstrosity, manipulated by Satanic forces beyond her control. The loopy smile that she wears at the moment of her death is the smile of freedom, an escape from an ugly world in which nameless evil reigns and the innocent suffer...

From 1973's *The Exorcist*, Damien Karras is the picture of guilt; tormented by the death of his elderly mother, troubled by his dwindling Catholic faith, and terrorized by a biblical evil inside a Georgetown house, the priest commits suicide in the film's climax. During his confrontations with the demon-possessed child, Karras witnesses Regan speaking in foreign languages that she has never learned, committing grotesque acts of self-mutilation, and moving objects with telekinetic power—things that the brooding priest can't rationalize, despite how hard he tries. With the aid of Father Merrin, Karras realizes that to defeat the demon he must choose blind faith over reason and logic. Always the brawny athlete—the film shows him running and boxing—Karras accepts the ultimate physical challenge when he confronts Pazuzu and commands the evil spirit to enter his body so that the child may live. In a savage demonstration of his restored faith, Karras, while battling the demon within, throws himself down the treacherous city steps outside Regan's window. His suicide ends the cycle of evil, returning the angelic child to health and preventing others from falling victim to the devil's black magic.

Of course, it didn't take long for the Prince of Darkness to show his horns again. After all, *The Exorcist II: The Heretic* was released with embarrassing fanfare in 1977...

"Nathan Moon's Grindhouse Opera" by Fiona Bridge (originally published in *CityArts Magazine*, Winter Edition, 1979, p. 2-4):

Visiting the on-location shoot of the student film *Carol Refuses to Die*, Woodhurst State sophomore Nathan Moon's tale of female vigilantism currently being filmed at a farmhouse near Bell Forest, is a humbling experience. The small cast and crew remain remarkably quiet as Beverly Dreger, the first-time actress playing the titular role, prepares for the movie's most violent and graphic sequence: a rape scene that will leave her and her co-star, Solomon Hall, covered in dirt and fake blood. It's a disturbing scene made all the more chilling by the funereal tone on set. As Moon directs, everyone seems hyper-aware and respectful of the potentially volatile material.

The first shot of the day is a rough-and-tumble fight sequence between Carol and tattooed hoodlum Bluto, played with menacing relish by the lanky and handsome Hall. Moon vows to keep his actors safe as they trudge their way through a grueling shooting schedule for a film that the 20-year-old director hopes to have in the can by late January.

As Moon runs through the scene with his actors, CityArts meets Robbie Bruckner, a 19-year-old sophomore who cast the film. Behind the farmhouse, standing next to a table piled high with textbooks and empty fast-food containers, Bruckner says that the cast and crew have essentially been living on the set. "We do our homework here, we eat here; Nate and Sol even slept here last night. We have put so much work into this, we want to get everything right.

"No one's denying that we're making a trashy movie," he admits with a smile. "But we have respect for the story we're trying to tell and for what the actors are doing, especially Bev and Sol. They're going to have to go to some pretty dark places in order to pull off their scenes together. We're all a little edgy on set because of the violence. It's all simulated, of course, but Nathan wants it to look as real as possible. Beverly, Sol, Lenny—they're all troopers, putting up with this script."

As if on cue, Lenny Coleman, who plays Bluto's vicious sidekick Tomato Face, comes limping around the corner of the farmhouse. Fortunately, the 22-year-old senior isn't really hurt; he's just staying in character while on set. "Tomato Face is like Igor or Quasimodo, but even more screwed up," he explains. "Because of his limp, he's been bullied all his life. When he sees Carol at the rest stop, dressed in her Grateful Dead tank top and short shorts, he thinks she's teasing him. He can't take it anymore and shows her to Bluto. From there…well, you'll just have to see the movie!"

A lunch break on set gives CityArts the chance to sit down with cinematographer Janet Holt and ask about her stylistic approach to the flick. "I'm a huge fan of documentary film, dark stuff like *Asylum*, *Faces of Death*, *Manson*," says Holt. "That's the look we're going for. I call it 'gutter realism.' You're going to wallow in filth for 80 minutes and have an awesome time doing it. But as Nate says, it's not all about grime and sludge. I respect Carol—or, I should say, I respect the way Beverly has chosen to portray Carol. She's a beautiful, independent, and smart woman who gets into serious trouble with a bunch of degenerate creeps. She has to use her wits and physical strength to survive, and it's my hope to capture this in a cool and poetic way."

Holt hustles back to the set, granting CityArts the opportunity to meet Mitch Arsenault, a Woodhurst junior who does makeup and prosthetics for the college's theater productions. More subdued than the rest of the crew, Arsenault appears hesitant to discuss working on the project. "I've done Poe onstage, and *Titus Adronicus*, but nothing this demented," he says. "Sometimes I question what we're doing, the morality of it."

After Arsenault shows me some of the prosthetics for the film, including a severed eyeball and tongue, he continues. "Nate's script calls for gallons of blood, a corkscrew in the stomach, decapitation by bone saw, a corpse that's been eaten away by acid. It's pretty gross, and speaking frankly, we don't have the budget for half the stuff he wants done."

As the visit comes to an end, CityArts regrets not being able to chat with stars Beverly Dreger and Solomon Hall, who left for campus to get some rest before returning for the night shoot. Director Nathan Moon was able to spare a few minutes to explain.

"We're not making a nice movie," he admits. "And when you're not making a nice movie, things go wrong on set. They've had a long day, they're exhausted and hungry and a little pissed off, but they'll be back tonight, ready to go."

Moon appears confident in his ability to deliver an impressive first film. "We've drained our bank accounts, begged our parents for money, sold clothes, books, records, whatever we need to do to make this movie, we've done it. And I really hope people get a chance to see it, even if it's just at festivals or colleges. It's demented, operatic, and bloody as hell!"

"Beverly Dreger's Personal Horror" by Lara Hanley (originally published in *The National Buzz*, May 1982, p. 5-6):

Before her schizo-meltdown at Woodhurst State in October of last year, Beverly Dreger was set to star in a sleazy "horror-porn" film that involved numerous simulated grotesqueries, including rape, devil worship, and bestiality. But an exclusive source tells The BUZZ that the movie, titled *Carol Refuses to Die*, was more real than Beverly could have ever imagined!

The film, which was never finished due to a suspicious accident, featured one scene in which the heroine, played by Beverly, is brutally attacked by a tattooed punk named Bluto. During the shoot, the actor playing Bluto got too rough with Beverly and caused the actress to storm off the set, says the insider.

"He basically assaulted her on camera, and the wimpy director did nothing to stop it," reveals a source close to the film.

"He knocked her to the ground and held her down against her will. Bev did what she had to do; she fought back. She wasn't going to let these sick wackos do whatever the hell they wanted. She thought they were making a fun movie and it nearly turned into a snuff film!"

Beverly, now 21, has been missing since the murdered bodies of three Woodhurst State students were found on the morning after Halloween of last year. *Carol Refuses to Die* was the first film for the actress-turned-murder-suspect.

At the time, police began investigating the possibility that at least one crime had occurred during the filming of the movie, but some people say the incident involved more than just a few punches and shoves. Campus scuttlebutt had it that Beverly and the male actor engaged in a violent and unscripted fight while the director let the cameras roll.

"Rumors began circulating at the school," says the source, "and then someone told a teacher about it, and the teacher contacted the authorities.

"As police checked it out, Beverly retreated back into her bubble of gloom and darkness, spending most of her time holed up in the library or her dorm room. The only person who ever saw her was her roommate."

Nathan Moon, the hotheaded director of the unfinished horror film, was outraged by the allegations. In a furious editorial published in the Woodhurst State newspaper, he wrote: "Nothing illegal took place on my set and everything was scripted in advance. Don't believe any of the rumors going around. They're being spread by sick people who are determined to destroy me!"

The BUZZ's insider believes that Beverly's experiences on the set of Moon's sick flick caused a shocking chain reaction that has left three innocent people dead and a city in torment.

"Beverly was physically and psychologically abused that day on set," said the source, "and she was going to make people pay."

From *My Roommate, My Friend: The Untold Story of Beverly Dreger* by Lisa Brown (unpublished manuscript):

Beverly ran into our dorm room to find me folding laundry. She threw her arms around me, crying out my name. She was practically screaming. When she pulled away, I saw scratches and red marks on her cheeks and nose. She had a bruise on the left side of her face.

"Oh! Beverly, hey…"

Her eyes were wet, ringed with vampire-brown circles. She was wearing her costume from the movie: a Grateful Dead t-shirt ripped down the middle and streaked with stage blood.

She was shaking. One of the buttons on her shorts was undone. "Tell me what happened," I said, but she wouldn't talk. She took off her clothes. There were pockets of broken skin on her stomach. She had dirt caked onto her thighs.

"Let's get you in the shower," I said. I checked the bathroom in the hall to make sure it was empty. She went into the last shower stall. I held her towel and waited for her to clean up.

While she was drying off, she said, "Sol hit me," and I asked her to repeat what she had said. She said, "He cracked me across the face with a stick, he held me down, and they got it on film." I told her I was confused—that I didn't know if she was talking about a scene from the movie or if this really happened—or both.

We went back to our room. Bev put on a sweatshirt and clean underwear. We sat on the floor, our backs against the lower bunk, and I cleaned the cuts on her face with witch hazel.

She took a shuddering breath and told me everything. The long hours on set. The camera breaking down. The whispers between Nate and Solomon. The shitty script that kept getting shittier every time Nate rewrote it.

Then, while they were "fighting," Beverly said that Sol broke off a piece of wood from the horse trough and threatened her with it. She said, "It wasn't in the script. I didn't know what the hell he was doing. I thought he was going to rape me. I could taste dirt in my mouth and Sol was on top of me, hitting me with the stick. I started fighting back, clawing for his eyes, when Janet finally shut the camera off.

"And his face, Lisa…his face *changed* while he was hitting me."

"What do you mean, it changed?" I asked.

"It became black and shriveled," Beverly said. "Like it had been burned to a crisp. Like the man. Like the man inside our closet!"

We sat there for several minutes not saying anything, and then I told Beverly, "We need to call the fucking cops." She said no; she said she wasn't totally sure what had happened, despite what she had just described. I said, "It's obvious someone hurt you," and she shook her head, saying, "It's a crappy horror movie. We all look like this."

I insisted that we call the police, or at the very least go to health services. Beverly refused, claiming they were all useless. She popped some aspirin. She found some pot in a beaded purse that someone gave her at that hippie camp. We smoked two bowls before Beverly said, "I need to get out of here." She looked a little panicky. "I need some greasy cafeteria food," she said.

"Did he really hit you, and you guys hadn't rehearsed this at all? Because if he did then we really need to go to the cops." She looked at me with the kookiest expression on her face and said, "Lisa, you're so crazy!" Then she laughed like nothing bad at all had happened. She was acting manic and was starting to really scare me.

She threw on her black jeans and Chucks and her big coat with the furry hood. Then she took a bundle of papers from her desk. It was Nate's script, the pages crinkled and stained with nicotine.

"Piece of shit makes no sense," I said. "It's called *Carol Refuses to Die*, but she kills herself at the end. I don't think Nathan is smart enough to be ironic."

We laughed, and our laughter felt good. Cathartic.

Then, using the lighter, Beverly set the script on fire.

"Jesus! Beverly!"

The pages burned and crackled in her hand. We screamed and ran circles around the room with our "torch" like the spiteful villagers in *Frankenstein*. Then Bev dumped the blazing pages in the trash and we stomped out the flames.

"Am I going crazy?" she asked.

"Beverly, *no*," I said. "Those guys are assholes. Solomon Hall is borderline retarded, and Nathan is a coke-snorting loser. You should never have gotten mixed up with them."

"But what about the burned man? I saw him!"

Beverly started to cry then, and I held her. I told her I loved her. She said she needed to be alone, that she was going to grab some food at the dining hall and that she would be right back. "Okay, but let's watch a video tonight," I said. "*Blazing Saddles*, maybe, or *The Bad News Bears*. Whatever you want."

Beverly kissed me on the cheek and left.

And that was it. She never came back to the room. Two weeks later, someone from housing showed up and hauled away her clothes and books...

From *Carol Refuses to Die* by Nathan Moon (revised final script, Jan. 1980):

72 EXT. ABANDONED FARMHOUSE – DAY

An old farmhouse in the middle of a field. Burning high above it, a liquid sun, dripping with heat. Farm equipment everywhere: chipped shovels, rusty backhoes, bale spears sticking up out of a horse trough filled with mud.

73 EXT. FARMHOUSE ROAD – SAME DAY

Carol, her Grateful Dead shirt slick with blood and grime, squints her eyes against the blazing sun. She's got scratches and cuts all over her face.

Carol's POV – the farmhouse, surrounded by a halo of molten sunlight.

Carol limps toward it.

74 EXT. ABANDONED FARMHOUSE – SAME DAY

Carol reaches the horse trough and stops, exhausted. She eyes the farmhouse. Cracked windows, twisted nails in the door, a deformed porch swing hanging from one hinge.

CLOSE ON one of the bale spears jammed into the muddy horse trough. Carol wraps a

bloodied hand around the spear and yanks it
free.

                    MALE VOICE (O.S.)
          You gonna need more than that to
          whip me, you hippie bitch.

Carol whirls around and comes face to face
with Bluto, his busted lip curled into a
freakish snarl. His neck and shirt sticky
with blood.

Carol's voice is a throaty gargle, choked
with phlegm.

                    CAROL
          What more do you want from me?

                    BLUTO
          I want what the other fellers got.
          And yer gonna give it to me.

Carol tightens her grip on the spear.
Glances at the farmhouse, wondering if
there's someone there that can help...

                    BLUTO (CONT.)
          Take off yer clothes.

                    CAROL
          No. No more!

                    BLUTO
          Scream all you want. Ain't nobody

gonna hear ya way out here. I said take off yer clothes. Or you want me to cut 'em off?

Carol's face is a mask of rage...

                    CAROL
You come near me and I'll stab you! I'll stab you in your fuckin' balls!

Bluto laughs, a demon in human form. He removes a buck knife from his belt.

                    BLUTO
You know how cops figger out the time a body died? They stick a ther-mom-ter up its butt. I ain't got a ther-mom-ter...

Bluto grins at his big knife. The blade flashes in the sun.

                    BLUTO (CONT.)
...but I got this.

Bluto glides the knife along his neck and shirt, getting it slick with blood.

                    BLUTO (CONT.)
Here I come, *mont cherry*.

Bluto charges at Carol, jutting the knife forward.

But Carol doesn't run. Instead she bursts forward, a screaming wild animal of revenge.

Carol's rage startles Bluto. He grazes her cheekbone with the knife, but she stabs his belly with the spear.

Bluto falls to the ground, writhing in pain. Blood pumps from his wound.

                    BLUTO (CONT.)
          You whoring bitch! You stabbed me!

Carol stands over him with the bale spear.

                    CAROL
          I'm gonna stick this up your ass
          til it splits your tongue on the
          other side.

                    BLUTO
          (screaming) Try it! Just you try
          it, bitch! We'll come for you, me
          and the boys! You ain't never gonna
          be safe! Never!

CLOSE on Carol, her face streaked with tears and grime, but her jaw set, her eyes steely cold.

                    CAROL
          I was minding my own business. I
          never did a damn thing to you. You

and your hillbilly friends took
everything from me.

                    BLUTO
And I'll do it again! I'll take
you home with me! Chain you up in
my yard and make you my dog!
Bring you to my altar in the woods
and show Satan your soul!

                    CAROL
Scream all you want, you redneck
piece of rapist shit. Ain't nobody
gonna hear ya out here.

Carol lunges at Bluto with the spear, but it
clashes with the buck knife.

She drops the spear, and Bluto kicks her
feet out from under her.

One hand clutching his stomach, he rises to
his feet, knife in hand.

Carol scrambling away on her butt as Bluto
lurches forward, collapsing on top of her.

The knife inches away from her eyes, Carol
pushing it away with all her might. Bluto's
face is a twisted mask of pure evil.

> BLUTO
> This is how us redneck greasers
> like it. Up close and personal.
> Yeehah!

They grapple in the dirt, kicking up plumes
of dust.

> BLUTO (CONT.)
> Gonna take one of yer eyes fer my
> collection!

Bluto is too strong. Carol faltering beneath
his power. He's about to cut out one of her
eyes when she kisses him forcibly, driving
her tongue deep into his tobacco-stained
mouth.

Stunned at first, but then grotesquely
aroused, Bluto begins kissing her back with
a black veiny tongue that looks diseased,
cancerous.

CLOSE on Carol, as she puts every ounce of
strength into clamping her mouth against
Bluto's...

And then we hear a sewer-like GURGLING from
the back of Bluto's throat and
realize...Carol's got his tongue in her
jaws, BITING and CHEWING and WRENCHING it
right out of his throat.

Bluto rolls off Carol, blood spewing like a
geyser from his hole of a mouth.
Carol gets to her knees. She spits Bluto's
tongue into the dirt. Wipes her mouth with
the back of her hand and watches Bluto choke
on his own blood.

                    CAROL
          That's for my collection, you
          inbred fuck.

Carol stands shakily, her body wracked by
abuse. She picks up Bluto's buck knife and
tucks it into her shorts.

Above her, the ochre sun is a tempest of
fire in the sky. We hear it burning,
rippling with heat, as Carol heads for the
farmhouse, determined to survive...

WOODHURST - The remains of a fire were discovered inside a storage room at Woodhurst State on Sunday morning. Located in the theater arts building, the room housed personal items belonging to students, including costumes, lights, props, and footage from various films and projects, witnesses said.

The building was cordoned off as firefighters investigated the scene in the early morning hours. It was soon determined that the fire would be treated as arson, according to Marion County Police.

Campus security believes that someone broke into the building sometime past midnight in the remote part of campus where drama classes are held. The suspect targeted the storage room, setting fire to several items inside and then dousing the charred fragments with water.

Though no one was injured and no other rooms were damaged inside the building, the financial and emotional losses are significant.

Senior Janet Holt, who had been shooting a movie with friends, was dismayed to discover that their work had been destroyed in the blaze. "This is heartbreaking," said Holt. "We have invested countless hours and money into our film, and now it's all gone."

Nathan Moon, a sophomore involved in the same project, was outraged by the incident, saying, "I'll be demanding a thorough police investigation. My father's a lawyer, so I can promise you one thing— we'll get justice for this."

The cause of the fire is under investigation, and school officials are urging students to come forward with any information.

Police refused to comment on the signifcance of the evidence found in the wreckage, but they are hoping it will lead to the identity of their suspect...

From *The Girl Who Loved Halloween* (p. 201):

The timing of the campus fire and Beverly's sudden departure from Woodhurst did not go unnoticed by Lisa Brown—or by the arson detectives who canvassed the school looking for clues.

"They came by the room, asking questions," Lisa says, "but Bev and her stuff were long gone by then. They showed me a bracelet and some gloves they had found near the fire, and asked if they belonged to Beverly. But I told them I had never seen them before.

"Two weeks went by, I got a new roommate, and people stopped asking questions," Lisa says.

Lisa was aware of Beverly's fascination with fire, but she doesn't believe that she started the blaze that destroyed Nathan Moon's film. "I get that it's a huge coincidence," she says. "But Beverly was in such a bad place then. I can't imagine her creeping around campus in the middle of the night with a gasoline can and a book of matches.

"Besides, if the footage contained what Beverly said it did, why would she want to destroy it? It was the only evidence she had against Nate and Sol. God knows Janet Holt wasn't about to risk her precious neck by saying anything."

Lisa looks distraught as she remembers the night when Beverly told her about what happened on the set of *Carol Refuses to Die*. She describes the cuts and bruises on Beverly's skin, the terror in her sad eyes. Her voice teeters on the edge of anger and grief. "Have you read the script? It was vile, twisted shit. It was a chance for those creeps to act out their perverted fantasies on an unsuspecting girl. I wouldn't be surprised if Nate and Sol set the fire themselves so that they wouldn't get busted…

"For a while I had the dorm room to myself. I would lay awake at night, wondering where Beverly might have gone. I thought maybe to that ranch place, maybe to find Shawn. So when I heard what really happened, my heart just broke all over again."

JOHNSON - A panicked father was forced to call 911 when his 19-year-old daughter suffered a mental breakdown inside their home in South Hill last night.

The man told the 911 operator that his daughter woke up from a restless sleep, screaming that there was an intruder in her room.

She had been diagnosed with nightmare disorder at an early age and often experienced sleep hallucinations, said the father.

He told police that earlier in the evening he and his daughter had gone through some possessions that had belonged to her mother, who had died a few years earlier. This included a personal journal that discussed the mother's turbulent history of psychosis, including afflictions that the daughter believes she has now inherited.

"When my daughter has a nightmare, she is totally at the mercy of her unconscious mind," the father said. "When she wakes up, she'll believe that what happened in the nightmare is happening in real life. There was no one in her room, but she really thought there was."

The daughter, who recently took a leave of absence from college, had plans of becoming an actress, but she was deeply troubled by the gruesome and violent images she saw in horror magazines and scary movies.

Before the daughter went to sleep that night, she and her father had sat down to go through the deceased mother's possessions.

"She was having a rough time, and she wanted to learn more about her mother who passed away," said Officer Glenn Marino, who was the first responder at the scene. "But some of the items were of an unusual or disturbing nature. I walked in on a very stressful domestic scene."

After she woke up, the young woman began shouting that there was an intruder in her room, her father told police. She leaped from her bed and began swinging her fists in the air, sometimes hitting the wall. After injuring his wrist while trying to hold her down, the father called 911, afraid his daughter might hurt herself. Police were forced to restrain her once they entered the room.

"I made a terrible mistake," the father said. "But I thought, if we looked through the box together, I could help her understand that her mother was very sick and that we did all we could to help her."

Paramedics treated the man for his injury, while police took his daughter to a nearby hospital for a psychiatric evaluation.

"I hated to see her go off like that, but I didn't know what to do. I don't want my daughter to think I don't love her," the father said.

"We tried to help her relax and understand we were not there to hurt her. Eventually, she agreed that medical treatment was her best option. She packed a bag with some clothes and personal items and left with us calmly," said Officer Marino.

"It is always hard to see a family hurting like this," the officer added. "But a hospital will get this young woman the help she needs."

"THE BLACK NOTEBOOK": VOLUME III

"There is nothing that gives more assurance than a mask."

--Colette

Excerpt from session #1 interview with Beverly Dreger, conducted by Dr. Bruce M. Walker (Crestwood Behavioral Health Center, Franklin Grove, Mar. 1979):

WALKER: Hello. Are you Beverly? May I come in?

WALKER: My name is Doctor Walker. I'm going to sit down here, across from you, if that's okay. I trust everyone has been treating you well. Are you comfortable?

WALKER: You arrived late last night. Past midnight, wasn't it? Were you able to get some rest?

WALKER: It's okay to be quiet, considering all you've been through. We don't have to talk about anything serious today. I really came by just to meet you and see how you're doing.

WALKER: What have you got there? That is an interesting-looking ring. Does it open? Can you keep things inside it?

WALKER: Beverly, I'm going to have to take that ring for now. I hope you understand. Would you mind handing it to me?

WALKER: Beverly, please. I need to take it.

WALKER: Thank you. Now, I read about what happened last night. It sounds like you had a very frightening dream.

DREGER: What about my stuff?

WALKER: Your stuff?

DREGER: The things they took from me when I got here.

WALKER: Hospital policy requires us to remove any personal items when you're first admitted—that's why I had to take your ring. But I understand how frustrating that must be. Did the nurse take some belongings that you really care about?

WALKER: Having our possessions taken away from us would make anyone angry. I can understand that.

DREGER: Those are private things, *my* private things. I don't want the whole world reading what's in there.

WALKER: I can see that you're upset. I would react the same way.

WALKER: Beverly, I will work on getting you your things back. How about today, we talk about—if I could ask you about your background, your medical history, find out how you're feeling—and then when I leave I'll ask the nurse about returning your personal items to you.

DREGER: Fine.

WALKER: Great. Let me start with a few basic questions...

From Dr. Walker's notes, regarding session # 1:

Today I had my first meeting with Beverly Dreger, who arrived at Crestwood last night after suffering a psychiatric breakdown at the home where she lives with her father. The police report indicated that the 19-year-old college student experienced a lucid nightmare and a hypnopompic hallucination of a strange-looking man in her bedroom.

At admittance the following items were removed from Beverly's person: a duffel bag, three matchbooks, two horror-movie magazines, and a black spiral-bound notebook.

When I entered the room, Beverly kept her face turned away, but I could still make out her physical features. She is an attractive young woman but has a rough look about her. Her brown hair was unbrushed. Her clothing—a black *Night of the Living Dead* shirt and ripped jeans—was clean. On her right hand she wore a black ring in the shape of a coffin, which I had to confiscate for the time being (note: all jewelry should have been taken at admit.).

Beverly's skin is pale and free of blemishes; she is a slender girl, with prominent cheekbones and a stern jaw. Eyes are brown and clear and show normal pupillary constriction. She sat in a chair across from me and made consistent eye contact during our session.

Through some gentle but persistent questioning, and my verbal agreement to return her personal items as soon as possible (she was especially concerned about the notebook), I was able to get Beverly to begin talking about the circumstances that brought her to Crestwood.

Beverly admitted to feelings of melancholy and paranoia, which stem largely from her troubled childhood and her mother's suicide in 1976. Beverly discovered her mother's body, but she kept this a secret from everyone she knew for several years. The violent trauma of that scene (her mother cut her wrists) has contributed greatly to Beverly's psychosomatic distress and nightmare disorders. When asked about the content of her nightmares, the patient returned to the topic of the notebook. I agreed to return the book during our next session, with the stipulation that Beverly talk about its contents with me...

Our first session ended with Beverly discussing her more recent past, including the year and half she spent studying film at college. Beverly is currently on a medical leave of absence from school, but she is determined to return in the spring, perhaps with a lighter course load. She dismissed my suggestion that her fixation on horror movies like *Halloween* has contributed to her fears, but she admitted to focusing too heavily on the gloomy and macabre.

In accordance with the DSM-IV, Beverly appears to be suffering from parasomnias (night terror disorder and REM behavior disorder) that have contributed to her manic and depressive state. The DSM-IV criteria indicates that these types of parasomnias are not the result of substance abuse or some other medical condition, which is in keeping with my initial diagnosis of the patient. I am anxious to meet with Beverly again to learn more about her experiences and feelings, and to come up with a treatment plan that will enable her to continue her studies in the spring.

Excerpt from session #2 interview with Beverly Dreger, conducted by Dr. Bruce M. Walker:

WALKER: I'm happy to see they returned your notebook and other belongings. I hope you understand about the matches. At some point I'd like to talk to you about them. I noticed you had three packs but no cigarettes.

DREGER: I don't smoke.

WALKER: That's good. It's a terrible habit. But why the matches?

DREGER: I'm not a pyro, if that's what you're asking.

WALKER: Oh, no, I didn't mean that. I just found it odd and wanted to ask you about it. I saw in your medical file—you were burned as an infant?

WALKER: Okay. We can talk about that later. How are you feeling today? Did you have breakfast?

WALKER: They do their best with the food around here, but it's not like getting a home-cooked meal, is it?

DREGER: They ruined my notebook.

WALKER: I see that the spiral binding has been removed. I'm sorry about that. But I assure you that all the pages are intact.

WALKER: Now, Beverly, the last time we met, we agreed to discuss the contents of your notebook. Do you think we can do that?

DREGER: Did you read it?

WALKER: As your doctor, I skimmed through it, just to get an idea of what might be in there, but I didn't want to invade your privacy. I see that it's a notebook that originally belonged to your mother. I saw her name on the inside cover. Is that right?

DREGER: Yeah.

WALKER: How do you feel about the notebook?

DREGER: I hate it.

WALKER: I didn't expect that answer. By the way you're holding it, it would seem it's of great value to you. Can you tell me why?

WALKER: Beverly?

DREGER: It was her record.

WALKER: Her record of what?

DREGER: I thought you read it.

WALKER: Well, I skimmed it, and I saw a few things, but I'm not sure I understood everything that I saw. I was hoping you could explain it to me.

WALKER: Do you think you could do that, like we agreed?

DREGER: It's about murders, okay?

WALKER: Okay. Like real-life murders, or murders that you see on TV or in the movies?

DREGER: Real life. My mother hated the movies.

WALKER: She was more interested in true crime, wasn't she?

DREGER: She thought there was a reason these murders were never solved.

WALKER: And what was that?

WALKER: We don't have to talk about that yet. I understand that this must be a sensitive issue for you.

DREGER: You *don't* understand.

WALKER: Well, I want to understand, but I need your help. Can I ask you—these murders in the book—they were the murders of children?

DREGER: Mostly teenage girls. A few younger than that.

WALKER: And your mother kept a record of these murders— news reports, clippings, that sort of thing?

DREGER: Yeah.

WALKER: Now, this nightmare you had, did it have something to do with the notebook?

DREGER: I don't remember.

WALKER: You had an extreme reaction to your dream. Your father injured himself when trying to restrain you.

DREGER: I didn't mean to hurt him!

WALKER: Of course not. We never intend to hurt the people we love.

DREGER: Is he all right?

WALKER: From what I was told, he's fine. He's worried about you.

WALKER: Beverly, how do you feel now that you have the notebook? You said earlier that you hated it, and yet you seem drawn to it at the same time.

DREGER: My dad hid it from me for a long time. He's not going to be too happy when he sees that I took it from the house.

WALKER: Why do you think he hid it from you?

DREGER: He loves me. He was only trying to protect me. But…

WALKER: But what?

DREGER: She addressed the book to me. She wanted me to have it.

WALKER: That sounds like a strong possibility. I would like to get a better understanding of why your mother kept this notebook. Do you know when she started to keep it?

DREGER: My dad said sometime after the party.

WALKER: What party was that?

DREGER: The Halloween party. Years ago. I don't remember it. I was three, maybe, or four years old.

WALKER: Did something happen at this party?

DREGER: I guess. They were playing with a Ouija board. People said my mom conjured up an evil spirit.

WALKER: Do you know how a Ouija board works?

DREGER: Sure. It works by the power of suggestion. You put your fingers on the pointer and your mind tells it where to go.

WALKER: So you don't think your mother actually conjured an evil spirit that night?

DREGER: I don't know. Do you think that's possible?

WALKER: My honest answer is that I think our imagination, or even our dreams and nightmares, can get the best of us sometimes. It can make us see things that aren't really there, or believe in things that don't really exist—things like monsters or demons.

DREGER: But that's the excuse everyone gives.

WALKER: That's true. I hope it didn't sound like I was reading from some textbook. Do you really think it's just an excuse?

DREGER: I'm not sure. I mean, what if you're wrong? What if it's not just our imaginations and the monsters are actually *real*? My mother thought they were. And lots of people in movies and books believe in them too.

WALKER: You're certainly right about that. But you do understand that your mother was seriously ill.

DREGER: Yeah, I do. And the people in movies and books aren't real. I get all that. But it doesn't change the fact that nightmares can really suck sometimes.

WALKER: I don't disagree with you there. I'm guessing your mother had terrible nightmares too. Her descriptions of the evil spirit were probably fueled by some very frightening dreams. For example, in her book she calls the monster "the black thing in the dark, the stalker in the corn."

DREGER: You have a good memory.

WALKER: Well, your mother's language is very descriptive. It was hard not to notice that passage. Do you like to write too?

DREGER: Sometimes.

WALKER: What do you like to write?

DREGER: Short stories. Some poetry. I tried writing a screenplay, but it didn't turn out so good. I took some film classes this semester and got to write about movies and stuff.

WALKER: Horror movies?

DREGER: Mostly, yes.

WALKER: Is that your favorite genre?

DREGER: Yeah. I grew up watching scary movies. My dad took me to see them all the time.

WALKER: I'd like to explore that with you, perhaps during our next session. I'm wondering if there's a connection between the problems you've been having and these scary movies that you like so much.

WALKER: Beverly, what is it? You look concerned.

DREGER: It's just that you never answered my question.

WALKER: I'm sorry. What question was that?

DREGER: What if the monsters are real?

WALKER: Well, it might surprise you to know that I *do* think they're real. But what I hope to show you is that they're inside you.

They're like thieves trying to rob a house. The thieves have gotten inside your subconscious—your house—and we need to find a way to get them out and make sure they don't come back.

WALKER: You don't look convinced.

DREGER: I…I have a hard time trusting what people say.

WALKER: That's a very natural reaction. Being in a hospital like this, surrounded by people you don't know, I would have my doubts too.

WALKER: But let's turn that negative into a positive. You came here voluntarily. You must have thought it could do some good.

DREGER: I want it to.

WALKER: That's good. That's really good, Beverly, to have that drive within you to get better. I hope you don't mind me bringing this up, but I noticed in our records that your mother stayed at Crestwood a few times. Was that part of your incentive to come?

DREGER: I don't know if I really thought that far ahead. But it makes sense.

WALKER: How so?

DREGER: My dad said that she was improving. She was getting help from one of the doctors here. If she could get better, then maybe I can too.

WALKER: You definitely can, and you will.

DREGER: Of course, then she went and offed herself, so maybe this is absolutely the worst place I can be.

WALKER: Well, let's make this a good place for you, a safe place. A place where you can be yourself and really get to the bottom of what's troubling you. I have this idea. Why don't we go through the notebook together and talk about what's real in there and what's not? You have my word that you can stop any time and ask me to take a hike, or we can switch topics and talk about something else.

DREGER: All right. I think I can do that.

WALKER: Fantastic. Let's turn to the first page and see what your mother wrote…

From Dr. Walker's notes, regarding session # 2:

Beverly was in fairly good spirits during the most of our session, making eye contact and speaking clearly. She had bathed and brushed her hair and eaten some food, and she looked more rested than in our previous meeting. The return of her mother's notebook seems to have brought her a strange kind of comfort...

From what I have gathered from the notebook's contents, Susan Dreger believed that these unsolved murders were the work of a true and bonafide *bogeyman*, a supernatural monster, and not the work of a human being. The incident with the Ouija board when Beverly was a child seems connected to her mother's delusion. My concern is that Beverly suffers from this same delusion, resulting in her self-imposed isolation and depression.

While Beverly was generally aware of how a Ouija board works, she hesitated when I asked if she believed that her mother could use the game to conjure an evil spirit. Eager to learn more, I located a newspaper article from 1964 that describes the incident at the party. Police were called to the Dreger residence after Susan used the Ouija board and became violent. She believed she had summoned an entity that she called the bogeyman, which appeared at the party as a cloud of green smoke. According to the entries in the book, this entity began stalking Susan, taunting her and threatening to kill her. Believing she would never be able to live a normal life, Susan committed suicide...

While I do not believe Beverly has suicidal ideations, I hope to explore the impact that her mother's persecutory delusions have had on Beverly and her belief in "monsters." I also hope to discuss her father's need to protect Beverly from what he sees as a danger and a threat, and Beverly's natural desire to know and understand her mother, even after her death...

Excerpt from session # 3 interview with Beverly Dreger, conducted by Dr. Bruce M. Walker:

WALKER: Hello, Beverly. I haven't spoken to you for a few days. How are you feeling this afternoon?
DREGER: I'm fine. I just wasn't in the mood for talking much.
WALKER: That's quite all right. What have you been up to?
DREGER: Reading. Catching up on sleep. Oh, and I met a woman at breakfast who thinks she's a vampire. And the girl across the hall eats dirt and glass.
WALKER: It's called pica.
DREGER: Excuse me?

WALKER: Pica. It's a pathological condition that compels the patient to ingest non-nutritive substances.

DREGER: Oh. Did you know that my neighbor thinks that her pastor is the devil?

WALKER: That's Alexis. And yes, I know. She's my patient.

DREGER: She was screaming so loudly last night. The nurses had to come and give her something to make her quiet.

WALKER: That must have been a frightening experience, to hear her scream like that.

DREGER: Is she going to be okay?

WALKER: I'm sure she will. Does that concern you—whether or not she will be okay?

DREGER: Yes.

WALKER: Why?

DREGER: Because girls shouldn't hurt like that.

WALKER: That's true. But the reality is, sometimes they do.

DREGER: Well, someone should watch out for them and care for them.

WALKER: I absolutely agree. And that's why they're here. To receive the proper treatment and to get better.

DREGER: I hope so.

WALKER: What about in these scary movies you like? Aren't young women hurt in them? In fact, isn't that pretty standard for films like that?

DREGER: But the strong ones survive. That's the whole point.

WALKER: I understand. Well, I'm certainly no expert. I think the last scary movie I saw was *Rosemary's Baby*, and that one terrified me.

DREGER: That's one of my favorites.

WALKER: You didn't get scared near the end? When the lady was holding the knife and saw her baby for the first time?

DREGER: That's the best part!

WALKER: Well, you are a far braver person than I.

DREGER: You know, it's interesting you brought up that movie.

WALKER: Why's that?

DREGER: Because, as weird and as twisted as it sounds, it's about a mother's love. At the end of the movie, Rosemary is rocking her baby to sleep. And he's the *anti-Christ*!

WALKER: Wow, I never thought of it in that way. You sure know your scary movies. Listen, Beverly…can we talk about the notebook some more today?

WALKER: Beverly?

DREGER: I found something inside it.

WALKER: That certainly sounds intriguing. What did you find?

WALKER: I can see that you would rather not talk about that. That's okay, though you have indeed piqued my interest. Is there something else on your mind today that you would like to discuss?

DREGER: I'd like to go home.

WALKER: Do you think you're ready to go home?

DREGER: It's been over a week. I want to see my dad. And I want to go back to school.

WALKER: I don't blame you. Your father loves you and it sounds like you go to an awesome school. But how do you feel? See, that's where I come in. I need to know how you're doing, what you're thinking, and to talk to you about that.

DREGER: I feel better. Much better.

WALKER: Well, that's good news. Do your feelings have something to do with what you found in the notebook? You've been spending a lot of time reading it.

WALKER: I'm sorry. I didn't mean to be pushy. Let's get back to the idea of you going home. You're here voluntarily, so the first step is to write a letter to our medical director, indicating that you wish to leave the hospital. I can help you with the letter, if you'd like, after today's session. We can even write it on our hospital's fancy stationery.

DREGER: That would be great. Thank you.

WALKER: But I need to feel confident that you are healthy and strong and not a danger to yourself.

DREGER: All right.

WALKER: Let me ask you this—and, please, correct me if I'm wrong. In a roundabout way, the writings in your mother's notebook seem to have brought the two of you closer together. Do you feel a stronger bond with your mother, even now that she's passed?

DREGER: Especially now.

WALKER: Even though, when you were a little girl, there were several incidents where she tried to hurt you?

DREGER: No. In her mind, she was trying to *protect* me.

WALKER: That's an interesting way to look at it. Protect you from whom?

DREGER: From the man she believed would one day kill me.

WALKER: The bogeyman. The "black thing in the dark."

DREGER: He has many names.

WALKER: And what does the bogeyman—what does he do exactly?

DREGER: You must have seen movies or heard stories about him.

WALKER: Well, sure, but you already know that scary movies make me squeamish! Besides, I'm far more interested in what you have to say.

DREGER: He hunts you down. He kills off everyone in his path, all your friends, until you're the only one left.

WALKER: Do *you* believe the bogeyman was trying to kill you, like in the movie *Halloween?*

DREGER: It doesn't matter what I believe. What matters is that Mom thought she was trying to keep me safe.

WALKER: But she *did* try to hurt you.

DREGER: Lots of times. More times than the police even know about.

WALKER: So how does taking your life keep you safe?

WALKER: Beverly, I'm sorry. I didn't mean to upset you.

DREGER: I'm sorry for crying.

WALKER: There's no need to apologize. I understand. Take some tissues.

WALKER: Beverly, I'd like to return to what you said a moment ago. You said what you believe doesn't matter. I'm here to tell you that it does. What you believe matters very much—for lots of reasons.

DREGER: Yeah? Like what?

WALKER: Well, first, I'm your doctor, and I care about you. And second, I'll be asked to provide a written evaluation of your mental state as part of your letter to the medical director, so I want to make sure we are openly communicating.

DREGER: Okay. I'm here. I'm talking.

WALKER: Good. Let me ask you a hypothetical question then, and I'm merely asking for your opinion here. Had your mother taken your life, God forbid—how would your death have kept you safe? How is dying better than living?

WALKER: It seems like such a simple question, but it's actually quite complex, isn't it?

DREGER: I haven't thought about it until now. Until reading all this.

WALKER: We've got time. Take a moment.

DREGER: By ending my life, my mother would have denied the world's monsters the pleasure of torturing me. And for her, that was a kind of love.

WALKER: But she never went through with it. She took her own life instead.

DREGER: I've thought a lot about that.

WALKER: Have you come to any conclusions?

DREGER: I think she took her own life so that maybe the bogeyman would spare mine.

WALKER: Is that what you believe? That your mother bartered for your life with her own? She made a deal with the devil, so to speak?

DREGER: I don't know. It sounds crazy, doesn't it?

WALKER: Well, I don't think your mother was crazy, but the scene of her death was quite unusual. It does seem like she was acting out some kind of ritual.

DREGER: I didn't...I didn't spend too much time looking. After I saw her, I just ran.

WALKER: Well, you needn't feel bad about that. I would have done the same thing. I think just about everyone would. And I want you to know—I'm so sorry that this happened, to you and your mother.

DREGER: All I know now is that she didn't hate me.

WALKER: Of course not. She may not have been well, but I'm sure she loved you very much.

WALKER: Beverly, I see you smiling today and it is a wonderful sight. You have a nice smile. I hope you don't mind me asking again—what did you find in the back of the notebook?

WALKER: I'm sorry. Another time, then.

DREGER: How long after the hospital receives my letter do I get to go home?

WALKER: Most likely three days. Certainly no more than five.

DREGER: And you can help me write it? Convince them that I'm well enough to go?

WALKER: I won't sidestep the troubles you've been facing, but I can certainly help you with the letter, yes.

DREGER: I found her suicide note.

WALKER: Well, that is quite a discovery.

DREGER: She spread it out across several pages so that only I could find it.

WALKER: Did you read the note?

DREGER: Well, yeah. She wrote it to me.

WALKER: How did the note make you feel?

DREGER: No longer...*marked.*

WALKER: That's an interesting choice of words. What do you mean?

WALKER: Take your time. There's no need to answer right away.

DREGER: Ever since I was a kid, pain and death have always followed me around. It started with the fire when I was a baby...and just never stopped.

WALKER: And now you feel...?

DREGER: I feel confident. I finally feel in charge of my own life.

WALKER: You feel stronger now than when you first arrived here at Crestwood?

DREGER: Yes. Absolutely.

WALKER: Beverly, a suicide note can often generate feelings of blame and guilt in the reader. You're still grieving over your mother's death, and as your doctor I would like—

DREGER: I know how to kill him now.

WALKER: Kill whom?

DREGER: The bogeyman.

WALKER: You mean the one in your mind? The man in your dreams and nightmares?

DREGER: Yes, of course! He doesn't actually exist, like you and me. He's not out there, like, *walking around.*

WALKER: Well, that's a relief!

DREGER: I know the difference between reality and illusion, Dr. Walker.

WALKER: Tell me about that.

DREGER: I know that the monsters on the movie screen aren't going to come to life and start attacking people in the audience. I know that Michael Myers from *Halloween* is a fictional character who can't really hurt me.

WALKER: That's good. So what do you see as your primary problem? What do we need to fix?

DREGER: If I can take control of my dreams and not have such a bad reaction to them, I think I'll be fine.

WALKER: Now, let's go back a moment—in one of our first sessions you asked me if I thought monsters were real.

DREGER: That was over a week ago. I was still feeling the effects of my nightmare…sort of like how you can still see the glow of fireworks after they've gone from the sky? I see now what a silly question that was.

WALKER: I don't think it was a silly question at all, but let me ask you what I think is a *difficult* question. Suppose you did kill this bogeyman—the one in your mind. Doesn't he have the ability to return to life? To rise and kill again? Isn't that part of his mythology?

DREGER: That's only in the movies. In real life, he's much easier to destroy.

WALKER: And why is that?

DREGER: Because he's a fake. A phony. He only lives in my head.

WALKER: I like that kind of language. You're showing the bogeyman just how unimportant and meaningless he is. He's the manifestation of all your childhood fears and experiences.

DREGER: And all the horror movies I've ever watched or scary books I've read.

WALKER: But he's not real. You're not giving him any power.

DREGER: That's right.

WALKER: So how do we stop him from appearing?

DREGER: Only watch Disney movies?

WALKER: Well, I'll take *Bambi* over *Rosemary's Baby* any day of the week!

DREGER: You have a good sense of humor, Dr. Walker.

WALKER: And you've been very forthcoming.

DREGER: It feels good talking about it. It makes me feel normal.

WALKER: You *are* normal. Trust me.

DREGER: Thanks, Doc.

WALKER: Now, all of that said, I do want to caution you about your mother's book. If it promotes the idea that supernatural monsters are real, and that there are actual rituals that show you how to kill these monsters…well, I think there's potentially great harm in believing in all that.

DREGER: Of course. I do too.

WALKER: It's one thing to enjoy being scared by movies like *The Exorcist* and *Halloween*. It's another thing to believe the characters in these movies exist in our world.

DREGER: I understand. I know that they don't.

WALKER: Beverly, here's what I would like to do. I want to talk about some steps you can take after you leave Crestwood to make sure you don't have another episode like the one before you arrived. This will include some medications that I'll go over with you thoroughly. I also have the phone number of a therapist-friend of mine who works in Glen Heights, which is right near your school. I think you should give him a call when you return to Woodhurst. How does all of this sound?

DREGER: It sounds good, Dr. Walker. Thanks again.

WALKER: And after all that, we'll get a ballpoint pen, and that spiffy stationery I talked about, and compose the greatest letter that the Crestwood Behavioral Health Center has ever seen.

DREGER: Dr. Walker?

WALKER: Yes?

DREGER: You've never seen *The Exorcist*, have you?

WALKER: Of course not. I was trying to establish a little street cred. Did it work?

DREGER: Yes, it actually did!

WALKER: I'm glad I could make you laugh. Let's make a deal— you can keep teasing me if you hear me out on some ideas I have for your treatment.

DREGER: Sounds like a good deal.

WALKER: Okay. Well, for starters, I would like you to start exercising regularly, which will increase the quality of your sleep…

"Beverly Dreger's Mother in Suicide Shocker" by Lara Hanley (originally published in *The National Buzz*, June 1982, p. 12-13):

Susan Dreger, mother of alleged "Woodhurst Butcher" Beverly Dreger, committed suicide when her daughter was just 16, slashing her wrists inside her home. The BUZZ has learned that the deceased woman, an occultist who believed in evil spirits, left behind a chilling suicide note addressed to her only daughter.

This is just one of many shocking revelations that The BUZZ has uncovered in its exclusive investigation into a story that began on October 31ˢᵗ in 1981, when three college students were found brutally slain on the college campus where Beverly was a student.

Even more bizarre is that the suicide note, which featured odd drawings and passages, was hidden in a place intended for Beverly to find, a source close to the suspected killer reveals.

"The mother kept a journal of all these unsolved child murders," the source told The BUZZ in an exclusive interview. "And inside this journal, scattered about in weird bits and pieces, was the suicide note left for Beverly.

"The mother was a sick woman who believed that the murders were committed by a supernatural creature, which is why she thought the police could never solve them," the source explained. "You can't catch a killer that exists only in your imagination."

Beverly discovered her mother's suicide note during her stay at a psychiatric facility when she was 19.

"Beverly was in rough shape when she showed up for treatment. She had dropped out of school after supposedly being attacked by a classmate. Then she had a crazy nightmare and practically broke her father's wrist," the source told The BUZZ.

After her mental collapse, Beverly was voluntarily committed to a mental health facility and spent two weeks reading and studying her mother's private journal. Within those creepy pages, she discovered writings from her mother that she never knew existed.

The suicide note revealed to Beverly that there was a bizarre method to her mother's madness.

"In Susan's mind, she could either kill her daughter and spare her the pain of a tormented life, or she could offer up her own life as a sacrifice to the monster in her head," the source said. "After years of mental distress, she finally chose the latter.

"Susan died trying to satiate the monster. And from beyond the grave, she encouraged Beverly to fight her demons rather than submit to them," the source said. "She died so that Beverly could live."

As part of this special story, The BUZZ contacted Lon Burns, the author of *The Dictionary of Demons* and a specialist in the occult who described Susan's suicide as "an appeasement ritual."

"Throughout history, people have tried to placate angry entities through sacrifices and offerings. These rituals often involve the use of special powders, blessed salt, strange drawings, and other signs of the occult.

"But when appeasement fails," Burns added, "those under great distress will attempt to bargain with the demon in order to be spared, which can become a very risky venture.

"The troubling fact is this," the author continued. "There is only a small window of time—a sliver, actually—between the appeasement ritual taking effect and the demon returning to torment its victims.

"It's the nature of evil in our world," Burns concluded. "It never goes away, no matter what we do."

The BUZZ has obtained a snippet of the suicide note that Susan Dreger left behind as a forewarning and bizarre token of love for the daughter she never really knew.

She wrote: "I was born to feed his hunger. And you were born to destroy it. Be brave. Get strong. Find the blessed knife and show him he can no longer hide in the darkest hour. Drag him into the light and watch the black thing burn."

From *The Girl Who Loved Halloween* (p. 195):

A summer of counseling, daily exercise, and meditation brought a
nervous smile to Beverly's face. Her relationship with her father was
strained, but Jack was pleased to see his daughter's health improving.
They spent most of their time reading and going for walks in South
Hill. One afternoon they went to see Chevy Chase in *Caddyshack*, and
they had a great time. That same night, they went through Susan's
things, choosing the items they wanted to keep in remembrance and
discarding the rest.

Beverly returned to Woodhurst State in the fall of 1980 as a
second-semester sophomore, determined to reclaim her personal and
academic life. Jack agreed to pay most of the rent on an off-campus
apartment. Beverly got a part-time job at a head shop in town, selling
new-age herbs and bongs, in order to pay for the rest.

At school, she enrolled in mostly film classes, including two with
Lauren Reid, director of the school's Cinema Studies Program.

"She was excited to leave the past behind and get a fresh start,"
Lauren says while sitting inside Juke's, a bar near campus—the same
bar where Beverly and Lisa Brown used to drink beer and play songs
on the jukebox. "One of Bev's first assignments in my screenwriting
class was a short script about an arsonist who falls in love with the
man whose house she burned down. It was dark, quirky and weirdly
romantic—I thought it was great. I didn't ask too many questions,
but I got the impression Beverly was trying to make amends for
herself. She was writing from the heart."

Now 20, Beverly enjoyed the solitude of living off-campus, but
she wasn't entirely alone. Her father wrote her letters and visited
when he could. Lisa Brown dropped by each week, and the two
would go out for pizza, pinball, and beer. She also received monthly
visits from Shawn Cote, who by that time had abandoned
Wasawillow Ranch and was attending a junior college in Indiana.

"She still had that free spirit that I fell in love with at the ranch,
but without as much baggage," he says. "She was enjoying her
studies, writing, drawing. We stayed in most of the time, watching
movies, reading, playing board games. She was in a groove, learning
how to be at peace with the world."

Beverly also attended an outpatient treatment program in Glen
Heights, a short bus ride from campus. "She got a lot of help there,"

Shawn says. "They had counseling, Jazzercise, and writing therapy. Beverly really dug it."

When he could get time off work, Jack Dreger accompanied his daughter to family therapy sessions at the treatment center in Glen Heights. Their relationship improved. They laughed more, reminisced more. They could talk about Susan without shouting at each other. In a letter to his daughter in September of 1980, Jack wrote, "I believe in you...I believe you can succeed at anything you put your mind to. But if darkness falls, I'll always be here to protect you, no matter what."

Though each day she left campus immediately after her classes ended, Beverly worked hard in school. Lauren Reid saw reflections of Beverly's renewed confidence in the short scripts and film treatments that her student turned in each week.

"She was still focused on horror, but she was doing things in her storytelling that modern horror movies weren't doing," Lauren says. "Her characters were falling in and out of love. They were learning to face the consequences of their choices. They grappled with God and spiritualism and the false promises of earlier decades. All while being chased by a homicidal maniac or a bioengineered zombie. Bev was a unique talent, and her work was a lot of fun to read."

Lauren leaves her table and goes to the Dracula pinball machine in the back of the bar. She drops in a quarter and begins to play.

"You're not the first person to ask if I feel responsible," she says as fiery skulls and coffins light up the machine. "For the record, I was trying to help Beverly, not destroy her."

Lauren is referring to the potluck dinner she held at her home in November of 1980—an opportunity for her and her students to bond over vegetarian food and some fun videos. Beverly and Shawn went together, bringing along a garden salad and a pitcher of ginger iced tea.

"Beverly wore this lovely white ankle-length dress and turquoise earrings," Lauren recalls. "She looked radiant. The kids were sweet to her, and her boyfriend was totally smitten."

Everyone was having a great time at the potluck until, during dessert, someone popped *Halloween* into the VCR. As the professor and her students gathered around the television to watch, Beverly disappeared into the back of the house.

"I found her in the bathroom," Lauren says. "She was really embarrassed—she was crying, and she told me she had problems with that movie. I asked her if she wanted to talk about it. She said she admired the heroine's strength, but that the film's bogeyman reminded her that right then, in the real world, women and young girls were being killed all the time."

It was later that night, after *Halloween* had been replaced with *The Kentucky Fried Movie* and the potluck was over, that Lauren suggested to Beverly that she write an analytical thesis on Carpenter's slasher film. She could write the paper for one of Lauren's film classes that would begin in the spring.

"I'm not a psychiatrist, but I knew Beverly was up against some serious issues," Lauren says. "Pardon the expression, but I thought the paper could be an exorcism of sorts. She was skeptical at first, but as the night went on, she seemed to take to the idea. She left the party feeling good, holding her boyfriend's hand."

At the end of the spring semester, Beverly turned in her paper, 20 pages devoted to *Halloween*, handing it to her teacher with a shy smile. Attached to the first page was a note: "Thank you for believing in me."

That same day, Lauren sat down in her office to read the essay.

"I was pleased with the paper, but it made me sad too. You can find fragments of Beverly's psychosis scattered throughout the entire text. And the way the essay ends, her interpretation of the final shot of the film…it's the complete opposite of how she originally reviewed the movie during her freshman year. What I'm saying is, I don't think Beverly ever really believed she was going to get better."

Lauren allows the last ball in her pinball game to pass through the flippers. She returns to her corner table and orders another beer.

"After the murders, I was terrified. It was like Manson all over again. Those girls were good students, nice kids. Everyone was in a total state of shock.

"But from what I know, the police actually found little evidence that connected Beverly to the killings," Lauren says. "And most of the time, knowing this makes me very happy."

She pauses. Her eyes are wet, ringed with tears she refuses to let go. She takes a long pull from her beer.

"But sometimes late at night, when I hear a strange sound from inside my closet, or a noise under the bed, I start to wonder: what if Beverly was right? What the hell are we supposed to do then?"

"Beware the Bogeyman: A Dissection of John Carpenter's *Halloween*," an essay by Beverly Dreger (submitted as her final paper in Story Analysis, spring semester, 1981):

The opening credit sequence of John Carpenter's *Halloween* (1978) transposes the pumpkin as a symbol of plentiful harvest into a force of destructive and masculinized power. As the glowing jack-o'-lantern fades into view, the hypnotic theme song intensifies, piano and synthesizer working in a chilling tandem that prepares us for the slaughter to come. By the end of the sequence, the flickering pumpkin dominates the left side of the screen. Its orange glow fades, replaced by two white-on-black titles: "Haddonfield, Illinois" and "Halloween Night, 1963," backed by an off-key children's rhyme of "black cats and goblins on Halloween night." The eerie metal rattle of a child's party toy cues the first scene.

Nighttime in suburban Haddonfield. A figure darts from behind a tree, moving toward a two-story home several yards away. Bound by the constraints of the seedy first-person camera, we are forced into a perverse world of nocturnal stalking, while crickets and the hooting of an owl signal our growing terror.

The figure reaches the steps, pausing at the sight of a young couple (Sandy Johnson and David Kyle) kissing in the foyer, the view blurred by white curtains on the front door. The yellow light, the first-person point-of-view, and the phallic lamp turn youthful passion into erotic performance, a peep-show for the voyeur in the sticky theater seat. The psychosexual horror has begun.

The couple steps out of view. The shape slips around the house to track them. A moment later the couple appears through a window, necking and fondling each other. In this era of *Deep Throat* (1972), *The Devil in Miss Jones* (1973), and *Debbie Does Dallas* (1978), the moment is semi-pornographic and incestuous, for we soon learn that the girl is Michael's sister, Judith. According to Diana Foster (1977) in "The Phallus-cy of Sex in Shock Cinema," sexuality in horror movies "may be diluted as producers clamor for the legitimacy of an R-rating over an X, but the sex scenes are still overtly suggestive of hardcore pornography, sadism, and, in extreme cases, rape and incest" (p. 12).

As the young Michael (Will Sandin) watches, the couple heads upstairs. The boyfriend holds a plastic clown mask, reminiscent of the crude rape-wear in Kubrick's *A Clockwork Orange* (1971); with his other hand he reaches for his Judith's rear end. Like Norman Bates in Hitchcock's *Psycho* (1960), who spies on Marion Crane through a peephole in his office, Michael is spurred on by erotic imagery. In "Psychosexuality and Monsters," Kim Churcher (1977) contends that "sexual behavior in the horror film—including kissing, fondling, voyeurism, exhibitionism, and intercourse—almost always precedes a misogynistic, bloodspill-as-orgasm killing" (p. 44).

As Michael returns to the front of the house and checks the upstairs window, we get our first aural "stinger" in the film: a sudden burst of music designed to highlight a significant event (and to get us jumping out of our seats). Here, the synthesized stinger resounds as the upstairs bedroom light turns off, implying an imminent sexual act, and providing the child outside the cover of darkness he needs to move undetected.

Michael walks to the back of the house and enters through an open kitchen door. The night is dark, blue-tinted, filled with shadows. In the foreground, a small table, shelves, and a stand mixer on the counter; in the background, a dining table with two tall, unlit candles, a Gothic setting not dissimilar to domestic scenes in *The Addams Family* (1964-1966) or *The Munsters* (1964-1966). A kitchen light comes on. The child goes to the sink. He opens a drawer and removes a large kitchen knife (the weapon of choice in *Psycho* and *Rosemary's Baby*, 1968, among others). We catch a blurred glimpse of Michael's clown costume, complete with satin sleeves and frilled cuffs (not three months after *Halloween*'s release, a real "killer-clown" terrified the country when John Wayne Gacy, who entertained at children's birthday parties as "Pogo the Clown," was arrested after confessing to the murder of over 20 teenage boys).

Knife in hand, Michael enters the living room. Near the stairs, he watches the boyfriend leave the house. For now, the impenetrable male is spared from the phallic kitchen knife. Michael moves up the stairs and into the darkness of the second floor. On the floor in front of him is the boyfriend's plastic clown mask, which Michael picks up in one of the film's more surreal shots: as he reaches for the disguise, his arm appears eerily elongated and disembodied, a spooky touch accentuated by the haunting synth-piano soundtrack.

The child puts on the mask—just like little Alice in *Alice, Sweet Alice* (1976). The POV becomes limited to the darkened eyeholes that remind us of the Lone Ranger's mask (but without its accompanying moral code) from the 1950 television series; moreover, Halloween masks have echoes of ancient Druid customs and sacrificial rites, embuing those who wear them with demonic, shapeshifting, or supernatural power (Markett, 1954, p. 72).

Michael enters the forbidden parlor of his sister's bedroom, the effect not unlike looking through a coin-operated booth in a sex shop. Another stinger resounds at the sight of her sitting half-naked at her vanity and brushing her hair. Michael glimpses the symbolic bed, the sheets tousled, before approaching his sister. As she cries his name, she instinctively covers her breasts. The knife plunges into her nine times, justifying Foster's claim that women in horror films experience "a vicious and sexualized punishment that unites sex and death" (p. 13). In a display of primal, masturbatory male exhibitionism, Michael watches the rise and fall of his knife as Judith collapses to the floor, her right leg closing off the tempting entry point between her thighs. His sister's sexual life ended, her soul dispatched to God, Michael becomes the heavy breather of *Black Christmas* (1974), or even Darth Vader in *Star Wars* (1977). In a single take that has now lasted more than four minutes, he descends the stairs and exits the house.

Outside, an adult couple has just pulled up in a car. Dressed in a suit and tie, the man—Michael's father—removes his son's mask, and for the first time we see the child's cherubic face, half in shadow. He looks confused, drugged, standing in his feminine clown costume and holding the killing knife. Michael's mother, wearing a long coat, puts her hands in her pockets, a strangely casual response to the sight of her dazed son. As the camera pulls up and away, we see a gnarled tree in the front yard of the Myers house, its open-mouthed knot reminding us of the secret place where Boo Radley hid his treasures in *To Kill a Mockingbird* (1962). But there is no wise Atticus Finch in *Halloween*; parents are useless and nearly mute in Carpenter's universe, unable to prevent their children from being strangled or stabbed to death by a deranged psychopath. Their incompetence gives birth to the bogeyman himself.

The next title card reads "Smith's Grove, Illinois," and then "October 30th, 1978," set against the sound of driving rain and roaring thunder—a common motif in horror films, including *The Old Dark House* (1932), *Psycho*, and *Suspiria* (1977). Lightning cracks, wind whips, and rain falls as a car curves around a desolate highway. Cut to

Dr. Samuel Loomis (Donald Pleasance) sitting in the passenger seat, a solemn and brooding presence. Driving the car, Marion Chambers (Nancy Stephens) is a heady mix of Little Red Riding Hood and the "sexy nurse" archetype that began with exploitation films like *The Student Nurses* (1970) and *Candy Stripe Nurses* (1974).

As they near the entrance to Smith's Grove Sanitarium, where they are to pick up 21-year-old Michael Myers and transfer him to another county, Loomis does not refer to Michael as a human being; instead, he calls him a monster, an "it," not unlike Chaney's werewolf or Lugosi's vampire. Our psychological reaction to this sequence is a confusing brew of dread, anxiety, and titillation. We fear the bogeyman as much as we long to meet him. Darren Belfry (1973) calls this personality trait "sensation seeking," a direct relation between the "monster on the screen and our own arousal" (p. 5).

With a nod to George Romero's wandering zombies in *Night of the Living Dead* (1968), Loomis and Marion spot some mental patients stumbling near the sanitarium's entrance. Our fear of the mentally ill, touched on in *The Exorcist* (1973), explored in *One Flew Over the Cuckoo's Nest* (1975) and made shockingly real in Geraldo Rivera's exposé of the Willowbrook State School in 1972, manifests in this scene as Michael leaps onto the hood of the car. Marion careens the vehicle into a ditch as Michael lunges for her through the open window. Michael smashes the passenger window with his open palm. Churcher notes, "Like Frankenstein's monster, the horror-film killer often possesses superhuman strength that makes him an indomitable and terrifying adversary" (p. 62). Frankenstein's monster is not a far cry from Michael Myers: both are called "monsters" and "devils," and both are condemned by the doctors who hunt them.

The nurse flees the car and tumbles into a wet patch of lawn, allowing Michael to get behind the wheel and drive away. The scene shows Michael at his most energetic, alive with muscular power. However, while evil may look attractive and seductive, as in Milton's *Paradise Lost* (1667) or Stoker's *Dracula* (1897), Michael's spirited performance outside the sanitarium is a disguise, as thin as his flimsy hospital gown, for his ego-dystonic compulsion to kill teenage boys and girls. The next title card, "Haddonfield," underscored by drifting October leaves, signals the bogeyman's cruel homecoming.

Halloween morning in small-town suburbia. The camera pans along a white, two-story house surrounded by bushes and trees. Like the Gothic mansion in Poe's "The Fall of the House of Usher" (1839), the windows of the Strode residence resemble a skull, a death's head leering at rain-soaked streets.

With an armful of schoolbooks, Laurie Strode exits the house. Dressed in plain clothes and dull colors, she is a natural beauty, with shoulder-length honey-brown hair and unblemished skin. Carpenter marks this virgin territory with the fashion of innocence and purity, including Laurie's lengthy flowery skirt, white stockings, and penny loafers. In fact, *Halloween*'s protagonist shows almost no skin at all, a striking contrast to the embattled heroines of such films as *Don't Look Now* (1973), *Carrie* (1976), and *I Spit On Your Grave* (1978).

As Laurie heads to school, her realtor father asks her to drop off a key at the abandoned Myers house. Though Tommy Doyle (Brian Andrews) protests, "that's the spook house," Laurie has no qualms about approaching the crumbling haunt and slipping the key under the mat. As she does, the camera perspective changes to Michael's POV as he watches Laurie from behind the door, ever the sexually repressed voyeur. He then emerges, silently, to see Laurie strolling down the street and singing a lover's tune that mirrors Michael's perverse desire. Michael's ability to not make noise or to draw the attention of anyone in the neighborhood suggests the merging of his maniac-killer persona with a supernatural ability. As Richard Daniel (1980) has explored, "the latest trend in horror films is to present a duality of the psychopath as both man and preternatural entity" (p. 39). The fast cuts between Laurie and Michael outside the Myers house suggest an impending battle, an antediluvian fight between angel and devil, so relevant in films like *Rosemary's Baby, The Exorcist, Beyond the Door* (1974), *To the Devil a Daughter* (1976), and *The Omen* (1976).

The song that Laurie sings while walking down the street—"I wish I had you all alone, just the two of us"—is fictitious, though its lyrics reflect the subject matter of many of the love songs of the 1970s, including Roberta Flack's "The First Time I Ever Saw Your Face" (1972), Donna Summer's "Love to Love You, Baby" (1975), and Heart's "Crazy on You" (1976), all of which could serve as depraved declarations of Michael's sick obsession with teenage girls (later in the film, Annie Brackett will also sing a fictitious song of young love and lovemaking, for which she will be suitably punished). As Laurie sings these words, she becomes psychologically vulnerable, revealing intrinsic sexual desires that she cannot bear to vocalize in normal speech. Meanwhile, her siren's song serves as an auditory trigger for Michael, whipping up his homicidal frenzy and leading him to action, much like Ophelia's fragmented melody propels Laertes in *Hamlet* (1603).

Cut to Laurie in high school English class, legs firmly crossed, introspective and lovely. As the teacher talks, the droning intonation like the "mwa-mwa" voice in *You're in Love, Charlie Brown* (1967), Laurie spots Michael Myers standing across the street. In this scene, Carpenter establishes a dichotomy within the spectra of Laurie's own fate. On one side, she is drawn to all the beauty and discovery that the world has to offer, represented by the globes and encyclopedias surrounding her in the classroom. On the other side, she is being lured into Michael's taboo world of perversion, violence, and death; she is a weird sister in Stoker's *Dracula*, a bride for the monster in Shelley's *Frankenstein* (1818), Satan's concubine in *The Exorcist*.

Meanwhile, Michael loiters outside the school in the film's first of many pedophiliac moments, watching Laurie through the window, escape vehicle at the ready. Standing with legs apart and arms rigid, Michael remains in control, manipulating Laurie's movements throughout Haddonfield and invading her subconscious. In "Visual Stimulants in Horror," Jean Beck (1978) argues that Michael's "death stare" from outside the classroom window accentuates "Laurie's subjugation and feminine passivity, her submission to the monster's hypnotic will" (p. 17).

Tommy Doyle, shuffling out of school with a huge pumpkin in his arms, believes in the innocence of Halloween. He wants to make popcorn and carve jack-o'-lanterns and watch *The Thing from Another World* (1951). That night, while Laurie symbolically prepares for motherhood by babysitting Tommy, the boy will display his trust in Laurie's ability to keep him safe. But at school, with no one there to protect him, Tommy is tormented by the older boys; the holiday of candy and make-believe becomes one of terror and persecution. "The bogeyman is coming," the boys taunt Tommy. "He's gonna get you." In a bullying sequence that echoes *Massacre at Central High* (1976) and *Carrie*, the older boys push Tommy to the ground; he falls on top of his pumpkin, exposing its pulp, a tongue-in-cheek foreshadowing of the viscera that the bogeyman will cull from his victims.

Outside the school, in the film's second pedophiliac scene, Tommy is stalked by a panting Michael. The killer is separated from the child by two cages: the chain-link fence outside the school, which Michael fetishsizes by running his fingers across it, and the partition in the backseat of the hospital car. As an escaped mental patient, trapped within the prison of his polluted mind, Michael is constantly barred from his desires by windows, locked doors, fences, and closets.

In *Universal Monsters and Magic*, Anthony Pogue (1980) connects the appeal of horror cinema to the nature of revelation: "The narrative in many horror films is propelled by the audience's inherent desire to explore, discover, hypothesize and resolve" (p. 62). In the next scene of *Halloween*, Carpenter engages his audience in this pursuit as Loomis tracks Michael 73 miles outside of Haddonfield. At the side of the road, he finds Michael's discarded hospital gown, an abandoned garage truck, and the "Rabbit in Red Lounge" matchbook, evidence that points to Michael's newfound identity and destination. Carpenter lets the audience discover the corpse of the poor mechanic, naked and bloody in the brush.

The language in *Halloween*, especially of the adolescent girls, focuses on sex, often sadomasochistic sex, recalling young Michael's use of the knife in his sister's bedroom and her breasts splattered with blood. Foster argues that "horror films are grossly unrestrained in their overlapping of sex and violence," a relevant comment in light of the conversation between Laurie and her friends as they walk home from school (p. 13). Wild-child Lynda smokes a phallic cigarette and Annie says that her boyfriend "dragged" her into the "boys' locker room," the place of so much testosterone and chauvinistic glee. As Michael passes in his car, threatening the girls with his death stare, Lynda says, "I think he's cute." Meanwhile, Annie's cry of "speed kills" functions as another auditory stimulus for Michael: he responds intuitively to the word "kill" by slamming on the car brakes. As he drives off and the girls pass under oak branches that resemble an enormous tentacled hand, Carpenter suggests that they are never far from reach of the dominant male grasp.

Moments later, after Lynda goes into her house, Laurie spots Michael several yards ahead, standing behind a large bush. But when the girls reach the corner, he has vanished, engaging in psychosexual foreplay that confuses and troubles Laurie. Annie tells Laurie that the stalker "wants to take [her] out tonight," and that she is "seeing men behind bushes," a juvenile play on words that implies Laurie's repressed sexual desire. She soon confesses to Annie that she has a crush on Ben Tramer and wants to take him to the school dance. As Laurie matures sexually, embracing her womanhood, she moves closer to her confrontation with "boyfriend" Michael Myers.

Unlike Judith Myers' bedroom, a den of eroticized vanity and death, Laurie Strode's bedroom is painted in virginal creamy white; a heart-shaped pillow sits in the corner and a Raggedy Ann doll rests on the dresser (in Carpenter's macabre landscape, Raggedy Ann lingers like a specter of death; in 1915, Johnny Gruelle created the doll for his young daughter, who died after receiving a smallpox vaccination).

Above Laurie's dresser is a reproduction of Belgian painter James Ensor's *Self-Portrait with Flowered Hat* (1883). Ensor was known for surreal and grotesque paintings that featured carnivals, skeletons, masks, and puppets. 1883's *Scandalized Masks* shows a couple wearing nightmarish, long-nosed carnival masks, while 1890's *The Assassination* depicts a ghastly scene: masked figures pin a man down and eviscerate him, drawing a stream of blood from his neck into a bowl on the floor. *Christ's Entry into Brussels in 1889* features a blue-faced ghoul, an old witch, a fat man in a clown mask, and a grinning skeleton in a green and black top hat. On the left side of the canvas, squeezed between a flute player and a woman with rouged cheeks and puckered lips, looms a white-masked figure with a puff of orange hair. This last figure resembles Michael Myers, and the ghostly manner in which he hides among the surging crowd correlates to the killer's furtive movement throughout Haddonfield. Carpenter places Ensor's image in Laurie Strode's bedroom—tacked above her, gazing down upon her submissive frame—to echo the monstrosity of the painter's work and to contaminate Laurie's place of solace.

Inside her bedroom, Laurie goes to close the open window; the billowing curtains parallel the billowing bedsheets on the clothesline in the yard next door as Laurie finds Michael staring at her from below. He stands erect among the bedsheets, enveloped by them in a way the impotent killer could never experience with a lover. Laurie does not look away from the window before Michael vanishes, further proof of his supernatural ability, which Richard Daniel argues is "representative of the horror film psychopath's indestructible form" (p. 41). Troubled, Laurie collapses on her bed. Though a telephone is visible in the room, she does not call her parents, rejecting them as a source of comfort or protection. In "Fear of Family in Psychological Thrillers and Horror Films," Nicole Porcelli (1980) explains that, "Parents in horror films are rarely present, leaving their children to face terror and brutality on their own. In those horror films in which the family unit has disintegrated completely, the children are prone to violent attacks that not even the sanctuary of home can prevent" (p. 31). Without any parental guidance, in an empty house that appears open to threats of any kind, Laurie is entirely alone. Like the alienated Carol Ledoux in *Repulsion* (1965), she begins to question her own sanity.

In a brief sequence, the film returns to Samuel Loomis and his unrelenting pursuit of Michael. A groundskeeper (Arthur Malet) leads the doctor through a cemetery in search of Judith Myers' grave. When they find the gravesite, Loomis discovers that Michael has stolen his sister's tombstone, a feat that would require immeasurable strength and the supernatural ability to go unnoticed on a popular holiday in the middle of the afternoon. Michael's desecration of sacred ground and his act of vandalism reveal premeditation on the part of the killer, as he will later use the stolen tombstone to create a ghastly tableau of sacrificial horror.

One of the Four Horsemen of the Apocalypse and a symbol of the Black Plague that ravaged 14th-century Europe, the Grim Reaper appears with dark humor in *Halloween*'s next scene. As Laurie and Annie smoke a joint in Annie's car (that "good girl" Laurie partakes in the drug is surprising, but reflective of the shifting, more liberal cultural landscape of the late 1970s), Blue Oyster Cult's "(Don't Fear) the Reaper" (1976) plays on the stereo. The song inverts the scythe-wielding Reaper into a figure of warmth and acceptance, escorting a young woman (the "baby" in the lyrics) into the afterlife. Michael Myers would gladly do the same for Laurie Strode, their "romance" as tragic and doomed as young Michael's relationship with his sister.

The subtleties of *Halloween* point toward the ugly and sadistic world beyond the cinema screen. In 1975, Utah police discovered the following items in Theodore "Ted" Bundy's VW Beetle: a ski mask, an ice pick, handcuffs, and rope. These were just some of the tools that Bundy (now on death row in a Florida state prison) used to abduct and kill young women in a murder spree that began in 1974. "Bundy was clearly possessed by Satan," Dwight Jones (1978), psychologist and author of *Please Let Me Go: Murder in America*, has said. "That is the only way you describe such evil" (p. 172).

Bundy's presence haunts the scene outside Nichols Hardware in downtown Haddonfield. Annie's father, Sheriff Lee Brackett (Charles Cyphers), tells the girls that someone has broken into the store and stolen a Halloween mask, rope, and "a couple of knives," actions that mirror Bundy's addiction to breaking and entering, shoplifting, and petty theft. As the sheriff speaks with the girls, a wide shot of the interior of Annie's car reveals blood-red upholstery (Bundy used cars as a lure and place of capture for his female victims, and investigators found traces of blood in his VW Beetle). In the next scene, as Loomis waits to confer with Brackett, Michael Myers drives right past the hardware store, playing a "cat and mouse" game that echoes Bundy's ability to evade police during his spate of murders in the Pacific Northwest. As Jones reminds us, "Most killers of this type don't get caught. We don't even know who or where they are" (p. 175).

As they drive off, Annie and Laurie continue smoking dope, but Laurie is worried about Sheriff Brackett. "I'm sure he could smell it," she says. The double entendre of her words reveals a fear of female sexuality (as seen in *Cat People*, 1942; *Repulsion*, *Psycho*, *Play Misty for Me*, 1971; *The Exorcist*, *Emmanuelle's Revenge*, 1975; *Carrie*, *I Spit on Your Grave*), perpetuates the myth of the vaginal douche, and marks the womb as "a madwoman's grotesquerie of flesh and blood" (Foster, p. 18). Annie encourages Laurie to ask a boy named "Dick" to the school dance, but Laurie again admits to having a crush on Ben Tramer. Annie uses a desexualized word, "cute," to describe Ben, and for the second time in the film it prompts Michael's emergence in the scene. Like a dog to blood, he scents out his prey: a doe-eyed virgin uncomfortable and unfamiliar with her body.

As Laurie and Annie begin their babysitting jobs for the night, Loomis and Sheriff Brackett pull up to the deserted Myers house in a patrol car. The house looms like an abattoir, not as large as the family estate in *The Texas Chain Saw Massacre*, but just as threatening. "Every kid in Haddonfield thinks this place is haunted," says Brackett. "They may be right," Loomis responds.

The "haunted" Myers residence is predated by several "haunted house" and "old dark house" genre films, including *The Cat and the Canary* (1927), *The Gorilla* (1939), *The Uninvited* (1944), *13 Ghosts* (1960), *The Haunting* (1963) and, more recently, *The Amityville Horror* (1979). The latter film, directed by Stuart Rosenberg, shares some similarities with *Halloween*: both feature intersibling abuse and murder, a babysitter tormented by an evil presence, and an on-the-market house that serves as an embodiment of evil. As they enter the foyer, Loomis and Brackett find the Myers house in a state of Gothic decay that mirrors the crumbling Victorian estate in Charlotte Perkins Gilman's 1892 short story "The Yellow Wallpaper" (also see Marie Ashton's short film of the same name, produced by *Women Make Movies* in 1977), or the haunted ancestral mansion in Poe's "The Fall of the House of Usher" (also see Roger Corman's 1960 film version, titled *House of Usher*).

Near the stairwell on the first floor of the Myers house, the two men discover an (unshown) eviscerated dog. Loomis states that Michael "got hungry." The eating of the dog has echoes of Samhain, a pagan celebration of "summer's end" during which ancient Druids sacrificed animals (see also the exploitation films *Mondo Cane*, or *A Dog's Life*, 1962; and *Faces of Death*, 1978). It is one of many taboos that Michael violates—a rejection of the symbiotic relationship American families have had with dogs for thousands of years—leading Loomis to tell Brackett that Michael "isn't a man." Later in the film, Michael will kill another dog so effortlessly that we wonder if he has committed this monstrosity since he was a child.

Loomis walks to the second floor in a slow-moving motion shot that resembles Milton Arbogast's walk up the stairs in *Psycho*. The doctor and the sheriff enter Judith's room, now barren and dark. As Loomis begins to describe Michael's boyhood voyeurism, a broken downspout shatters the window in the film's first "jump scare."

Jump scares have appeared in horror films for almost as long as the genre has existed. Notable examples include the lurching bus in *Cat People*; the discovery of Kathleen's underwater grave in 1963's *Dementia 13*; the resurrection-cum-baptism of Jason Voorhees in *Friday the 13th*; and the final reveal of the red-coated female dwarf in *Don't Look Now*. For 1959's *The Tingler*, William Castle equipped movie theater seats with electric buzzers that vibrated during the film's jump scares, adding a touch of goofy realism. Churcher argues that audiences, especially young ones, crave this kind of adrenaline rush: "They are paying for the director to frighten them. They might even be willing to forego a great story and well-developed characters as long as they get scared out of their wits" (p. 55). The first jump scare in *Halloween* fails to contribute to the plot, but it does elicit a playful scream from the audience, and it mirrors Michael's smashing of the car window in the earlier sanitarium scene.

Loomis uses the moment of calm that follows the jump scare to provide Brackett a brief history of Michael Myers. When the doctor first met Michael fifteen years ago, the child had no understanding of "good or evil, right or wrong." Loomis adds that Michael had "the blackest eyes, the devil's eyes," reminding audiences of the children's hypnotic gaze in *The Village of the Damned* (1960) and the mutant dwarf's eyes in *The Brood* (1979). Michael's black eyes might also be connected to an urban legend of the late 1970s. According to Doyle Parker (1980), author of *The Mothman, the Jersey Devil, and Other Mystical Creatures*, "Black-eyed children are scary hybrids that look like kids and come out only at night. They will often knock on your door during a full moon, asking to use the phone, for food to eat, or a place to sleep. *Do not invite them inside.* Black-eyed children are almost certainly vampires, aliens or demons" (p. 68-69). Again, Carpenter gives Michael supernatural abilities that link him to classic genre villains (Dracula, the Mummy, the Wolfman, et al.). These abilities also mythologize Michael within the fictional boundaries of Haddonfield, and connect him to American myths that exist beyond the screen, like interdimensional beings or bogeymen.

In the next scene Laurie reads to Tommy a story about King Arthur, reinforcing the film's theme of the warfare between good and evil. Tommy's comic books—including *Tarantula Man* and *Neutron Man*—prompt the film's central question: "What's the bogeyman?" But the ringing telephone, a portent of terror in so many horror films, prevents Laurie from answering (see *Dial M for Murder*, 1954; "The Telephone" from *Black Sabbath*, 1963; *The Killer Is on the Phone*, 1972; *When a Stranger Calls*, 1979).

While talking on the phone, Annie tries to set up Laurie with Ben. Tommy spots Michael lingering near the house in a telepathic response to the possibility of Laurie taking a lover. Like Dr. Gogol and Norman Bates before him, Michael displays a sexual jealousy that propels the rest of *Halloween*'s frenetic plot and highlights the violent misogyny rooted within every move the killer makes. Michael begins a more committed and perverse descent onto Laurie and her friends, starting with an extended paraphilic observation of Annie's domestic activities around the Wallace house and the killing of the family dog.

As Michael stares at her through a window, Annie spills melted butter on her clothes in the kitchen of the house. The butter—a wink to *Last Tango in Paris* (1972) and representative of the teen's spermaphotobia—forces Annie to strip to her underwear and put on a masculine work shirt that ends just above her thighs. Outside, in a heightened state of morbid arousal, Michael knocks down a potted plant, which falls to the ground in a premature ejaculatory crash. During his refractory period—that is, the time in which it would be impossible for him to have another "orgasm"—Michael kills the family dog in a sadistic variation of post-coital *tristesse*. When the dog stops barking, Annie remarks that he just "found a hot date." We then see Michael from the waist down, clutching the dog's limp and elongated dead body to his chest in a shot that underscores Michael's sexual dysfunction.

In American culture, the bogeyman is an amorphous, mythical creature that threatens to eat and kill children if they fail to obey their parents. Predominantly male, he lurks in bedtime stories, dark fairy tales, and urban legends like "The Babysitter," "The Hook," and "The Killer in the Backseat." In a brief cutaway scene, Laurie insists to Tommy that "there's no such thing" as the nocturnal monster. The boy is unable to describe the bogeyman with any detail, but the film presents him as a mute, sexual deviant drawn compulsively toward young Caucasian females.

In the next sequence, Michael makes two ghostly appearances as Annie washes her clothes in the laundry room, located around the side of the house in an outbuilding. Annie accidentally locks herself inside, and in the film's first of two gratuitous shots, Lindsey Wallace (Kyle Richards) discovers the babysitter stuck in the laundry room window. Annie is bent over, floral-patterned panties and thigh-high yellow socks in full view, in a fetishsized, submissive, and victimized position. Michael must be watching from some vantage point, the visual reminding him of his sister sitting in her underwear before he stabbed her to death. Carpenter places Annie in the *coitus more ferarum* position, Latin for "sex in the way of beasts" (colloquially known as "doggy style"). Transgressive sex in the horror genre is not new; see

The Defiler (1965) or *Love Camp 7* (1969), not to mention Rose's mutated sexual appetite in *Rabid* (1977), or the urophiliac and sadomasochist Krug Stillo in *The Last House on the Left* (1972). But unlike the characters in those films, Michael is unable to perform sexually; his desire and inability to penetrate Annie in this animalistic position of male dominance leads him to another kind of sexual transgression: erotic asphyxiation, or the act of choking one's sexual partner.

After dropping off Lindsey at the Doyle house, Annie primps her hair in the mirror and sings impromptu lyrics about her inability to resist her boyfriend's sexual advances. The song functions as submissive foreplay, a musical lubricant before the bloodshed. Annie's search for her car keys becomes a drawn-out sequence that turns every nook in the Wallace house into a potential death trap. Once Annie is inside the car, Michael springs up from the backseat in terrifying "jack in the box" fashion, lunging for the girl's throat with one hand. Annie writhes, chokes, and gasps in the killer's grip. His mask prevents us from identifying what pleasure he receives from this "breath play," but authors Pratt and Hartwig (1981) argue that people who induce erotic asphyxiation, usually male and sexually dominant, obtain sexual gratification from the act of controlling and manipulating their partner's breath (p. 75). After this "choking game," Michael kills Annie by slashing her throat with a knife. Though he could have murdered the young woman anywhere in the Wallace house, the killer chooses to take her life from the backseat of her car—the penultimate symbol of carnality, promiscuity and, in the case of "The Hook" legend, sexual denial.

In the next scene, Tommy spots Michael carrying Annie's body into the Wallace house, but Laurie scolds him for making up scary stories just to scare Lindsey. "There's no bogeyman," Laurie insists again, employing a defense mechanism to protect her fragile ego. Freud argued that, in the act of denial, we reveal repressed truths from our unconscious mind. Throughout *Halloween*, Laurie repeatedly denies the existence of the bogeyman, despite exhaustive evidence that he *does* exist and, more alarmingly, that he wants to see her dead.

Back at the Myers house, Loomis frightens a group of kids away from the decrepit haunt. In his desire to not see the children hurt, Loomis reveals a paternal instinct that brings into question his relationship with Michael Myers. In *Father, My Guardian, My Protector,* a book that explores how fathers contribute to a healthy and safe family life, Jonathan Barrett (1972) claims that "Fathers are programmed—in their hearts, muscles, brains and perhaps even their souls—to protect their children from harm" (p. 212). In the film, Loomis makes no mention of having a wife or children of his own, but he transfers his parental instinct to Haddonfield's youth, and to Michael himself. Without question, Loomis wants to capture or kill Michael, but both would be transfigurative acts that would protect the killer from himself and his inherent sadism.

Lynda and boyfriend Bob (John Michael Graham) pull up to the Wallace house in a blue van that captures the psychedelic spirit of the "Mystery Machine" from the *Scooby-Doo, Where Are You!* cartoon series (1969-1975). In the film's third pedophiliac moment (and this one far more inexplicable than the others), Bob tells Lynda, "Then you rip my clothes off, then we rip Lindsey's clothes off." *Halloween*'s transgressivism is nowhere near as radical as in *Salo* (1975), *Suspiria*, or even *Rosemary's Baby*, but the subtext of Bob's line is disturbing, bringing to mind child sexual abuse (Lindsey Wallace is around 7 or 8-years-old in the film) and gang rape. The cans of cheap beer and Lynda's infantile giggling contribute to the abjection of the scene.

Lynda and Bob cross the metaphorical River of Styx when they step through the doorway of the house. The couple begins kissing on the couch. In *The Exorcist*, when Chris MacNeil (Ellen Burstyn) and Regan (Linda Blair) are roughhousing on the floor, the camera slowly withdraws from the living room, suggesting an invisible and evil force in the house. Carpenter employs a near-identical shot here, only the evil force is *not* invisible: Michael Myers stands in the foyer, collar turned up, waiting patiently for his time to strike.

As Laurie laments her dull night with the two kids, Lynda and Bob have sex in one of the rooms in the Wallace house. A flickering jack-o'-lantern, an omen of death in the film, leers from the bedstand. Michael's shadow—like Count Orlock in 1922's *Nosferatu*—crosses the bedroom wall to the sound of a synthesized stinger. In another macabre fusion of sex and death, Michael's shadow appears at the moment that Lynda and Bob climax. Foster argues that "Horror films are directed by men and they are almost always told from a man's perspective, and as a result they reflect a systemic fear and disdain of female sexuality" (p. 21). But here, in *Halloween*'s only sex scene, Lynda has enjoyed herself as much as Bob, smiling and indulging in a post-coital cigarette in emulation of both Mrs. Robinson in *The Graduate* (1967) and Evelyn Mulwray in *Chinatown* (1974). When Bob goes to the kitchen, Lynda nestles comfortably in the bed, clearly satisfied, her complexion dewy and bright.

In the next scene, Carpenter uses several doors to "false scare" the audience. In "The Conventions of Modern Horror," Gordon Trim (1981) states, "Unlike the jump scare, which is designed to make the audience scream, the false scare ratchets up the suspense and gets the pulse racing, forcing viewers to question just when the real scare is going to occur" (p. 9). In the darkness of the kitchen, Bob opens the refrigerator door and takes down two beers. As he puts the bottles on the counter, the back kitchen door opens on its own. Bob closes it, then opens the pantry on his left. It is empty. Convinced someone is trying to scare him, Bob turns to the closet (the bogeyman's quintessential hiding spot) across from him. In a burst of rage, Michael explodes from inside, driving Bob against the pantry door and lifting him several inches off the floor by his throat. In arguably the film's most violent scene, Michael plunges his knife into Bob's chest, pinning the teenager to the wall. Bob hangs from the rack like an interred corpse, elevated on gruesome display.

After Michael kills Bob, he gazes at the mounted corpse in silence, slowly tilting his head to the left and right. A dog will often cock its head in order to better hear human language, especially if the language is communicating an activity that the dog enjoys (Levine, 1975, p. 283). If Michael is displaying canine-like behavior in this scene, then the human language he is listening for is the sound of suffering—the loosening of the bowels, the body spasms, the death rattle. Moreover, like the scopophilic protagonist in *Peeping Tom* (1960) who likes to play back and watch his murders on film, Michael gains pleasure from observing his crime. He stands before his victim like a curator in a museum, contemplating the "art" of his bloody handiwork and deriving from it his own hellish meaning.

The archetype of the "ghost in white bedsheet"—evoking images as disparate as the regalia of the Ku Klux Klan to Charlie Brown's Halloween costume in *It's the Great Pumpkin, Charlie Brown* (1966)—appears in the fourth murder set-piece in Carpenter's film. To trick Lynda into thinking he is her boyfriend, Michael cuts two eyeholes in a white sheet, drapes it over his body, and puts on Bob's oversized glasses for spooky, comedic effect (with the addition of the glasses,

Michael is essentially wearing a piece of his victim, imitating the crossdressing Leatherface from *The Texas Chain Saw Massacre*). The killer now stands in the doorway to the bedroom. His heavy breath taunts Lynda, mocking her aftersex glow and subverting the power of her sexual release. The teen appears golden-haired and bare-breasted in the film's second gratuitous shot, while the sawing of an Emory board across her fingernails combines her femininity and impending death. As Michael remains stationary and mute, Lynda gets up from the bed to call Laurie. The phone becomes an inverted symbol of terror as the killer approaches Lynda from behind and strangles her with the telephone cord.

Like Annie before her, Lynda groans, gasps and chokes, sounds that Laurie, unaware that her friend is being killed, calls "squealing." This symbolic coding debases Lynda to a lowly animal, a hog plump for slaughter. Though Michael does not physically penetrate Lynda due to his impotence, he does attack the half-naked girl from behind, aping the rear-entry position and grunting like an animal. According to *The Behavioral Science Casebook*, "Strangulation, especially by a ligature, is common in sexual sadistic homicides" (Button, 1978, p. 411). Michael's use of the phone cord has a Freudian reading as well: the uncoiled ligature that the killer grips so tightly resembles an umbilical cord. Murdering Lynda reflects Michael's failed relationship with his mother and leaves him longing to return to an inorganic state that can only be found in the dark, amniotic comfort of the womb.

As Michael listens to Laurie's youthful voice over the phone (a sort of erotic hypnosis that bonds him to her even further), we see his mask clearly for the first time. Though Carpenter obviously modeled the disguise after the phantasmal white mask in 1960's *Eyes Without a Face*, Michael's mask is not as expressionless as the one in Georges Franju's film. As he listens to Laurie's voice on the phone, Michael has a melancholy, dysphoric look about his (masked) features, not unlike the gorilla in *King Kong* (1933) or the man-as-insect in *The Fly* (1958). Though the close-up shot is fleeting, it calls into question Michael's psychology. Does the bogeyman feel sadness or remorse? Does he have the ability to love?

The antithesis of the psycho-biddy in *Strait-Jacket* (1964), the cannibalistic matron in *Frightmare* (1974), and the deranged mother in *Mother's Day* (1980), Laurie dutifully checks on Tommy and Lindsey, who are both sleeping in an upstairs bedroom. Meanwhile, outside the Myers house, Loomis spots Michael's escape vehicle down the street and runs toward it. Cut to Laurie as she steps out onto the porch of the Doyle house. Dressed in masculine blue clothes, Laurie approaches the Wallace residence in a series of shots that mirror Michael's POV sequence at the start of the film, a cyclicality that turns the innocent into aggressor, the virgin into predator. In her open-necked shirt, the autumn wind blowing through her hair, Laurie is radiant here, a potent mix of beauty and power, about to face the manifestation of all her psychosomatic fears.

As Laurie nears the Wallace house, a dog barks in the distance, a forewarning of Michael's presence. Laurie enters the house through the back kitchen door. The low-key lighting of the scene (aided by the fact that Laurie does not turn on a single light) adds to the piano-wire tension as she ascends the stairs, searching for her friends.

In the upstairs bedroom where Lynda and Bob had sex, Laurie discovers Annie's corpse arranged on the seminal bed in a ritualistic display that hints at Ensor's *Lady in Distress* (1882). More forcibly, the scene returns us to the murder of 19-year-old Arliss Perry who, in 1974, was found murdered inside a church on a California university campus, strangled and ice-picked to death, her half-nude body adorned with votive candles in "a vicious, sickening, and depraved act of brutality and devil worship" (Hotton, 1980, p. 4). In a similar exhibition of blasphemy and human sacrifice, Michael deposits Judith Myers' headstone above Annie's head as a symbolic crown of thorns, and he poses her body in the position of crucifixion. The jack-o'-lantern flickers nearby, its wide-mouthed grin as mocking as Regan MacNeil's sexual overtures in *The Exorcist*.

Laurie stumbles against the closet, causing Bob's corpse to drop down from the ceiling, swinging back and forth like a trapeze artist. Laurie screams and stumbles again. The closet door creaks wide to reveal Lynda's body, bare-breasted, mouth open, eyes pointed to God in a Goyaesque juxtaposition of beauty and horror. Laurie runs to the hallway. There, she backs against a wall as Michael materializes from the shadows, stabbing her shoulder and causing her to topple over the stairwell in a disorienting shot lifted from *The Omen* (and one that Kubrick would later borrow for *The Shining*). The camera remains fixed in the foyer as Michael comes down the stairs to kill Laurie, thereby thrusting his groin into the audience's lap. As menstruation is a source of abjection in *Carrie*, Michael's knife-as-phallus in *Halloween* represents all that is contemptible and obscene. It is no coincidence that the killer uses another phallic object, a rake (idiomatic for "libertine" or "lecher"), to prevent Laurie's escape out the back kitchen door.

To escape the Wallace house, Laurie shatters the glass on the kitchen door, another cyclical moment that reminds us of Michael's escape from the sanitarium. Laurie runs, limping and screaming, into an empty street. She reaches a house and bangs on the front door. A porch light comes on, a man peeks out the window, and the light goes off, bathing Laurie in darkness. In her fight against Michael, Laurie remains alienated in a bloody war she must fight herself, surrounded by dark, unwelcoming houses and deserted streets.

Laurie returns to the Doyle house in an intense chase sequence that De Palma would later eroticize in *Dressed to Kill* (1980). Tommy opens the door for Laurie in fulfilled prophecy of his worst fear: *the bogeyman is real*. Laurie locks the door and orders the child upstairs. In another wasted cry for help, she discovers that the telephone has been disconnected. Carpenter lingers on the telephone-as-umbilical-cord, reminding us of Michael's shattered bond with his mother and his desire to return to the maternal womb.

Whimpering, Laurie notices that one of the windows is open, which has allowed Michael access to the house. She sits by the couch and reaches for a sewing needle. The simplicity and tenuousness of Laurie's weapon of choice clash with the repulsive, phallusized magnitude of Michael's knife, Leatherface's chainsaw, Jason's machete, Alex's penis sculpture in *A Clockwork Orange*, or Reno's electric drill in *The Driller Killer* (1979). Laurie takes a household object associated with female domesticity and motherhood and wields it in protest against the subjugation of women and the traditional gender roles subscribed to them. Though Foster argues that women in horror films "rarely defend themselves successfully against an attack by a lust murderer or control-motivated killer," Laurie confidently stabs Michael in the neck with the sewing needle after his own attempt to stab her fails (p. 12). The killer collapses, not so much from the severity of his wound but from the exhaustion of his sexual dysfunction and his failure to "penetrate" his virgin prize. Laurie takes Michael's knife (his source of virility) only to emasculate him by dropping it to the floor, disgusted by the cold-blooded denigration the knife represents.

Outside, Dr. Loomis stalks the neighborhood, an isolated figure amidst blowing October leaves. Like all authority in the film, the inept Sheriff Brackett offers little help. Upstairs in the Doyle house, Laurie tells the children that she has killed Michael. But Tommy provides *Halloween*'s most startling tagline: "You can't kill the bogeyman." The words ring out like a crazed mating call, provoking Michael's sudden appearance in the hallway. Laurie safely locks the children in the bedroom, while she hides in a nearby closet, a fitting set-piece for the film's final confrontation. Enraged, Michael smashes through the wood frame. The closet's bare bulb sways and flickers like the light fixture in Hitchcock's musty fruit cellar. Relying on another simple tool of female domesticity, Laurie lunges for a wire hanger, twists it into a sharp point, and jabs it into Michael's eye. Stunned, the killer drops his knife. Laurie picks it up and stabs Michael in the chest. He collapses out of the frame.

Halloween highlights its denouement with a brief and singular moment of terror that borrows its symbolism and hypnotic motion from German Expressionism and silent horror films like *Dr. Jekyll and Mr. Hyde* (1920) and *Nosferatu*. After Laurie sends the children next door to get help, she leans, weak and exhausted, against a doorjamb. An out-of-focus Michael lays prostrate on the floor in the background of the shot. But the imagery of the scene—the doorknob, the moulded wood, and the shadows of the windowpanes—appears as upside-down crosses, signaling the killer's resurrection. The audience knows that Michael will kill, die, and rise to kill again, and the final shots of *Halloween* reinforce this truth.

Just then, Michael sits up from the floor and turns his crude male gaze toward Laurie. The moment is startling in its silence before the piano score rushes in the climax of the film. Michael follows his quarry into the darkness of the hallway and begins to strangle her. Loomis rushes up the stairs as Laurie, in a moment that rivals the unmasking scenes in *The Phantom of the Opera* (1925) and *Mystery of the Wax Museum* (1933), dislodges Michael's mask. But unlike the grotesquely deformed men in those films, Michael looks like a normal man. Carpenter does not depict the bogeyman as an ugly creature or disfigured ghoul (e.g., Phibes in *The Abominable Dr. Phibes*, 1971; Leatherface in *The Texas Chain Saw Massacre*; Pluto in *The Hills Have*

201

Eyes, 1977); instead, Michael is a human sociopath who exists as much in the real world as onscreen. It is not teratophobia that *Halloween* fosters (as does *Rosemary's Baby* or *It's Alive*, 1974) but bogyphobia, the fear of demons, monsters, evil spirits, or the devil in physical form.

After firing six bullets into Michael, Loomis watches him topple over the second-floor balcony. Laurie says that Michael *really was* the bogeyman. With a touch of fatherly care that Laurie could have used earlier in the film from Mr. Strode, Loomis softly confirms: "As a matter of fact, it was." When Loomis looks over the railing to discover that Michael has vanished, Carpenter cements *Halloween's* depiction of the bogeyman as an indestructible and unstoppable force, capable of transmutating from an amorphous shape under the bed to a living, breathing hulk coming through the front door. *He can be anyone and anywhere*, a reality that Laurie Strode understands. The last shot of her in the film has her crying, her face buried in trembling hands, courageous and strong and alive…but doomed to an inexorable fate.

"THE BLACK NOTEBOOK": VOLUME IV

"The most loving parents and relatives commit murder with smiles on their faces. They force us to destroy the person we really are: a subtle kind of murder."

--Jim Morrison

From police interview with Shawn Cote (recorded on Nov. 5, 1981 at the Marion County Police Department, Precinct 9, Homicide Division, p. 1-3):

KENT: This interview is being tape-recorded at the Marion County police department. The time is 5:43 in the evening on the fifth of November, 1981. This is Detective Sergeant Ron Kent speaking, and in the room with me is Detective Gary Bianco.

Can you state your full name for us, please?

COTE: Shawn Lewis Cote.

KENT: Mr. Cote, you're here voluntarily, correct?

COTE: Yes.

BIANCO: We were going to bring you in for questioning, but you got to us first, kiddo.

COTE: I want to do the right thing.

BIANCO: Well, that's good, because we could use your help on this. This whole thing, you know…I don't have to tell you how bad it is.

KENT: What can you tell us, Mr. Cote?

COTE: How far back do you want me to go?

BIANCO: Take your time, son. We're here to listen to what you have to say. Detective Kent and I can decide if it's relevant or not.

KENT: Actually, if you could start this past summer. I'll let you know if we need to go back any further. And speak loudly for the tape.

COTE: Well, the school year was over, and me and Beverly were living together. She was working at Pipe Dreams. I got a job waiting tables.

KENT: And where were you living exactly?

COTE: Her place. Her apartment in Woodhurst.

KENT: That's 1775 Shreveport Drive…apartment 4?

COTE: Yes sir.

KENT: What was her mood like that summer? You two get along?

COTE: Bev was happy. She was starting to get back into film, writing, researching in the library. She was exercising too. Getting strong. Life was good.

KENT: Researching what?

COTE: I'm not sure. She just liked reading a lot. It's how she got her ideas for scripts and stories and stuff.

KENT: When was the last time you were at the apartment on Shreveport Drive?

COTE: Two days ago.

KENT: Was Beverly there at that time?

COTE: No sir.

KENT: Is she there now?

COTE: I don't know. I haven't gone back since everything happened.

BIANCO: Let me be frank, Shawn. We have no hard evidence that your girlfriend committed these murders. If we could just find her and talk to her, we could—

KENT: Excuse me. Detective Bianco, can I see you outside for a minute? Stop the tape.

[The tape is stopped. Detective Sergeant Kent and Detective Bianco exit the room. Three minutes later, Detective Sergeant Kent enters the room.]

KENT: I've restarted the tape, and the interview with Shawn Cote will now continue. It is 5:58 in the evening, and this is Detective Sergeant Kent. I am alone in the interview room with Mr. Cote.

COTE: I didn't mean to cause any trouble.

KENT: Not at all. This is a complicated case, and Detective Bianco got called away. Let's get back to why you came here today.

COTE: Okay. I'm here because I think I know what caused all of this. Or what *could* have caused all this.

KENT: I'm all ears.

COTE: I told you Bev was getting back into film. Not so much acting—she didn't want to do that anymore—but more on the writing side of things.

KENT: What was she writing?

COTE: Movie scenes, snippets of dialogue. Poetry, short stories. She kept everything in this black notebook that she had taped and stapled together. But...uh, I don't know how to explain this next part.

KENT: Just put it in your own words.

COTE: Her paper on *Halloween* was like purification, okay? A chance to start over, to wipe the slate clean.

KENT: Hold up a minute. What paper?

COTE: It was a film analysis paper for one of her classes.

KENT: And it was about Halloween? Trick or treat, dressing up like a vampire, that sort of thing?

COTE: No. It was about the *movie*—the movie is called *Halloween*.

KENT: I don't get to the movies much. You're gonna have to fill me in.

COTE: It's a horror movie, a slasher movie. Like *Friday the 13th* or *My Bloody Valentine*. Have you heard of those?

KENT: That first one, maybe. My son likes those things.

COTE: Well, *Halloween* really messed with Beverly's head. The movie made her believe in all sorts of scary stuff. But by writing about it, by breaking it down into small parts, she could see that it was only fiction. It helped her get over her fears.

KENT: I think I understand.

COTE: But it wasn't enough for Bev. She wanted to destroy him, even if it was just in her mind.

KENT: Who, exactly?

COTE: The bogeyman.

KENT: Are you fucking kidding me?

COTE: So you're familiar with the legend.

KENT: Childhood monster. Hides in your closet, under your bed, that kind of thing. Yeah, I get it.

COTE: Look, Beverly's not crazy. She knows the bogeyman isn't real. It was just her brain freaking out after years of her mother's psycho bullshit.

KENT: Speak into the tape, Mr. Cote. I want to be sure we can all hear this.

COTE: She wanted to write the next installment of *Halloween*. Like, a sequel to the first one.

KENT: You're talking about the movie again.

COLE: Uh-huh. And she was going to *kill* the bogeyman this time. We talked about all the different ways he could die in her script. He could drown or get burned in a fire. Maybe get all his limbs or even his head cut off. She wouldn't call it *Halloween II*, she didn't want to get sued, but we both knew what she was doing.

KENT: When she talked about killing this bogeyman, did she ever talk about using a knife?

COLE: Sure. How else are you gonna chop a guy's head off?

KENT: Did Beverly own a knife?

COLE: You mean like a kitchen knife?

KENT: No, not like a kitchen knife. A specialty knife. One that would stand out if you saw it.

COLE: No, not that I remember. Listen, I'm speaking metaphorically here. Beverly didn't kill anyone in real life, and she didn't own any special knives. *Writing* was her weapon.

KENT: Writing?

COTE: Yes sir.

KENT: Mr. Cote, let me ask you something. Were you and Beverly Dreger on drugs? LSD, maybe, or angel dust? Are you on drugs now?

COTE: No.

[There is a pause.]

COTE: Do you write at all, Detective?

KENT: I write reports when I put people in jail.

[There is another pause.]

COTE: What I'm saying is, writing can be therapeutic. It can ease pain and help people overcome trauma. I'm reading this book, *The Dawns of Revelation*, which says that confessional writing increases our white blood cell count, wards off disease and depression, makes us feel *alive* again—

KENT: I'm going to stop you there, Mr. Cote. Listen to me carefully. I'm on the ass-end of one of the longest days of my life and I don't have the time or the patience for this. There's a man outside this door—we call him Big Leroy—he's been to *five* interrogation schools. Would you rather he come in here and talk to you?

COTE: No.

KENT: You'd rather talk to me.

COTE: Yes sir.

KENT: Then tell me what this has to do with the murder of three girls at Woodhurst State on Halloween.

COTE: Okay, okay. Beverly wrote her sequel. Well, a treatment for it. Do you know what a film treatment is, Detective?

KENT: Enlighten me.

COTE: It's a detailed outline of the movie you want to make, written out almost like a short story.

KENT: Gotcha. So Beverly wrote one of these treatments.

COTE: Yeah. It was a fun little B-movie, and she seemed happy with it. We had a lot of nice days together after that.

KENT: And then what happened?
COTE: Then the real *Halloween II* came out.
KENT: And?
COTE: And all hell broke loose…

The Black Thing in the Dark, a treatment for a short film by Beverly Dreger (Summer, 1981):

PROLOGUE – BUDGET MOTEL SLAYINGS
TITLE CARD: HALLOWEEN NIGHT, 1981
FADE IN

Roach motel along the interstate. DR. HERMAN MUDGETT, 50, watching TV in his room. Gun and cash on the table.

From the TV: "Escaped mental patient JEREMY PARKER is suspected of killing at least three teenagers tonight in what can only be described as a psychotic frenzy of violence."

Mudgett appears onscreen: "He was my patient. I warned them this would happen. They didn't listen!"

In the motel room, Mudgett shuts off the TV and lights a cigarette.

EBONY, 20, comes out of the bathroom. Mudgett nods at the cash on the table. Ebony takes it and splits.

Later. Mudgett sleeping. He's having a nightmare. We see it in surreal flashes: A city in Germany being bombed. A cat set on fire. Jeremy Parker getting shock treatment. Jeremy in a straitjacket. A knife scraping across whetstone. A pretty BLONDE being gutted on a sacrificial altar.

Mudgett wakes with a jolt. Drenched in sweat. A KNOCK at the door. The doctor gets up. Goes to the door. The KNOCK comes again.

Ebony calls out from behind the door. She needs to use the phone. Mudgett unhooks the latch and the door swings open.

There's Ebony, her face a sudden rictus of pain and terror as she's stabbed from behind. Blood bubbles from her mouth. She drops. Mudgett looks up.

JEREMY PARKER stands there in his infamous MICKEY MOUSE GAS MASK circa 1942. A piece of his shirt has been torn off and there's blood there.

He raises his combat knife. Dr. Mudgett screams as Jeremy delivers the vicious death blow.

ACT ONE - THE WITCHES

Same night. A modest home in the suburbs. Glowing pumpkins on the porch. Windswept October leaves.

An upstairs bedroom inside the house. A shaft of moonlight through the window. In the bed, KATHIE MOORE, 18, face bandaged, sleeping peacefully.

The door opens. CECILIA MOORE, 52, walks in, dressed in black. She holds Kathie's hand, whispering a prayer that sounds vaguely witchy. Cecilia has long and pointy nails, painted a frosted purple.

Cecilia slips a sachet of herbs underneath Kathie's pillow and exits the room.

In another room in the house: BILL MOORE, 55, asleep in bed. The man is terribly ill. His hair is gone, his face is gaunt, almost skeletal. On the bedside table: jars of elixirs and oils, candles, and a book titled CANCER AND THE HEALING PROPERTIES OF HERBS.

Cecilia enters. Approaches Bill and caresses his cheek. She picks up one of the oil jars and dabs a few drops onto Bill's neck with her fingertips. She tells him she will keep their daughter safe.

In the kitchen Cecilia dials a number on the phone. We can hear it RINGING on the other end. A female voice answers and Cecilia gives quick instruction.

Cut to the exterior of a Victorian house in another neighborhood. Inside, NELLA PERRY, 45, dressed in a flowing black robe, is gathering up items from the house: candles, ceremonial plate, ritual knife, pentacle disc.

Cut to FRANCESCA SCOTT, 23, having sex with her boyfriend in bed. Francesca on top. The phone begins to ring. Francesca has an orgasm, then hops off and answers the phone. She listens to the voice on the other end, then hangs up.

In a room adorned with tapestries and magickal artifacts, Francesca opens a closet. She removes a long spear and two daggers. She then puts on an ivory cloak and a leather biker jacket with HEAD HUNTERS MOTORCYCLE CLUB stitched on the back.

Back to Nella Perry, outside, hoisting her duffel into the trunk of her car. Rain starts to fall.

Cut to Cecilia Moore, placing a piece of cloth onto her kitchen table. The cloth is actually a torn piece of shirt, spotted with blood.

Nella, soaking wet, getting into her car. She turns the keys. The car won't start.

Cecilia sprinkling a black powder onto the torn piece of shirt. She whispers a black magick spell.

Nella turning the keys again. Pumps the gas. The car starts and Nella breathes a sigh of relief. Just then, the masked Jeremy Parker rises from the backseat!

He clutches Nella's skull and slams it repeatedly into the window, shattering the glass. He keeps smashing her head on the door and broken glass until Nella's skull becomes gooey pulp in his hands.

Cecilia lights a match. She finishes her black magick spell and drops the flame onto the bloodied shirt. It catches and burns.

In Nella's car, Jeremy freezes. He tilts his head, as if listening to a faraway sound. His breathing turns heavy behind the mask. He's almost snorting. His hands ball into fists of rage.

ACT TWO - THE CONFRONTATION

Kathie Moore wakes up. She's groggy. It takes her a moment to recognize her surroundings.

Cecilia comforts her daughter. Tells her that the ritual has begun and that Jeremy is in a weakened state. Cecelia asks Kathie what happened that Halloween night.

Kathie explains that she was babysitting two children at a house in town. Two of her friends, RACHEL and KERRI, dropped by to visit. Jeremy Parker broke into the house and killed Rachel and Kerri.

After fighting Jeremy and tearing off a piece of his shirt, Kathie was able to get the two children to safety at a neighbor's house before police arrived. By then, Jeremy Parker had vanished.

Kathie begins to cry, saying all her friends are dead.

VROOM! The sound of a motorcycle. Cecilia looks out the window. Francesca has just pulled up on her Harley.

Cecilia orders Kathie to stay put. Before her mother goes, Kathie asks about her father. Cecilia tells her that she touched him with Dragon's Blood oil to keep him safe from harm.

Cut to the kitchen. Francesca lays out her weapons on the table. Cecilia adds a black-handled knife to the collection, explaining to Francesca that it is a blessed knife filled with energy and power.

While they wait, Cecilia confesses her feelings of guilt. We learn that Jeremy Parker was 8-years-old during World War II. He died in an industrial bombing. At the time, Cecilia was an American pre-teen living with her parents in the remote English countryside.

Cecilia dabbled in the occult and magick. While playing with a Ouija board, she contacted Jeremy's spirit and chanted a resurrection spell. Jeremy returned to life as the bogeyman, embarking on a lifelong killing spree while searching for Cecilia and her family.

CRASH! The sound of glass breaking. Grabbing their weapons, Cecilia and Francesca split up into different parts of the house.

Kathie sitting upright in bed. She heard the crash and is freaking out. She calls out for her mother. No answer. She hears a creaking on the stairs and begins to panic.

Cut to Bill Moore, stirring in bed. The door opens. Bill wakes up. He tries to make out the shape standing in the door.

The figure steps forward. Lightning cracks outside, and in the flash we see that the shape is Jeremy Parker. He takes his combat knife from his sheath and approaches Bill.

Bill's eyes widen in terror. With trembling hands he holds up the wooden pentacle disc around his neck.

Jeremy thrusts his blade through the wooden disc and into Bill's Adam's apple. Blood pours out over the disc, soaking the bedsheets. Bill dies.

Kathie at her bedroom door. She inches it open. Peers out into the hallway. It's empty.

Francesca is in the music room, crouching next to an old-fashioned pump organ. She holds her spear to her chest.

She peeks out the window. Through the pouring rain she sees Nella's car. Thinking Nella has arrived at the house, she creeps into the living room. She whispers Nella's name, but there's no answer.

Kathie, moving slowly down the upstairs hall. She reaches a door. Nudges it open and peers inside. It's dark. She calls out for her dad. Moves toward the bed.

Kathie sees the bloody sheet and a twisted shape underneath. Terrified, she slowly pulls the sheet back to see her emaciated father, his throat ravaged by Jeremy's combat knife. The pentacle disc has been shoved into Bill's mouth. Kathie screams.

Alerted by the scream, Cecilia runs from her hiding spot. She goes for the stairs, clutching her black-handled knife.

Cecilia reaches the foot of the stairs and freezes. Jeremy Parker stands at the top, breathing heavily in his gas mask. Cecilia holds out her knife, challenging him, as he descends.

With a flick of his wrist, Jeremy sends his combat knife spiraling into Cecilia's shoulder. She drops her own weapon, reeling back in pain.

Jeremy reaches the bottom of the stairs and wrenches the knife out of Cecilia's shoulder. He raises it to deliver the killing blow when...THWUNK!

Francesca's spear has pierced his neck. Jeremy topples to the floor, crashing into a glass curio cabinet and sending magick trinkets flying.

Francesca tells Cecilia to go help Kathie while she takes care of Jeremy. Holding her wounded shoulder, Cecilia grabs her black-handled knife and hurries up the stairs.

Francesca gets close to Jeremy, peering down at him. He's still breathing, but he looks unconscious. She removes the two daggers from the belt at her waist.

She gets close...raises the two daggers...brings them down...just as Jeremy's tree-trunk arms shoot out and his hands grab Francesca's wrists.

Using all her strength, Francesca tries to drive the daggers into Jeremy's chest. She just can't do it.

Suddenly...SNAP! The sound of Jeremy breaking both of Francesca's wrists. She wails in agony and crumples to the floor, dropping the daggers.

Jeremy stands up. He yanks the spear out of his neck. Black goo spurts from the hole. He casts the spear aside.

He looks down at the wreckage on the floor. Realizes he has three knives to choose from. He picks up ALL OF THEM.

Francesca moving worm-like on the floor, trying to get away. Jeremy kicks her so that she rolls onto her back. Francesca looks up at Jeremy and begins pleading for her life.

Jeremy silences her by driving one knife through her leg, pinning her to the floor. Jeremy drives another knife through her other leg.

Francesca's now stuck in place, an insect on a spreading board, dying...

Jeremy hammers the last knife into her heart, killing her.

ACT THREE - THE FINAL BATTLE

Upstairs, Cecilia finds Kathie shaking in the hallway. Kathie tells her that Bill is dead. Cecilia does her best to hide her sorrow and focuses on protecting her daughter.

Cecilia takes Kathie into the upstairs office. The room resembles a witchcraft museum, covered in twig pentacles and rowan crosses.

From the closet Cecilia removes a box and opens it. She takes out her Ouija board, the same one she used over 30 years ago when she raised Jeremy Parker from the dead.

Kathie argues that the board never worked for them. Cecilia explains that the reason it never worked is because Jeremy's evil spirit was trapped inside it. No other spirit entities could come through. She says they have weakened Jeremy through the cloth-burning ritual; now they are going to kill him by setting the board on fire.

They rush out into the hallway...to find Jeremy Parker waiting at the end. In one hand he holds up the body of Francesca for Cecilia and Kathie to see...then he hurls the body over the stair banister.

Jeremy comes for them. Kathie tells her mother to light the Ouija board, but the matches are where Cecilia left them on the kitchen table. Cecilia gives the board to her daughter and tells her to make a run for it while she distracts Jeremy.

As Cecilia stands off against the killer, she grips her knife firmly and begins chanting a "weakening curse." It seems to take effect, making Jeremy sluggish and disoriented.

Kathie tries to dart past for the stairs, but Jeremy lashes out, blindly. He strikes her full-force on the back, sending her reeling over the stair railing. Kathie nearly falls. She manages to hold on to the ledge, but the Ouija board crashes to the floor below.

Cecilia continues the curse, holding her knife in one hand and the pentacle around her neck in the other. As she chants, she slashes Jeremy repeatedly across his mask with the knife, stunning him further.

Kathie, shouting for Mom. Cecilia tells her she has to find the courage to drop to the floor.

Kathie, clinging to the ledge. Glances over her shoulder at the floor below. Sees the Ouija board, the destroyed room, Francesca's crumpled body. Closing her eyes, she drops.

Kathie shatters her ankle as she hits the floor, crying out. Her daughter's pain distracts Cecilia, giving Jeremy a chance to regain his focus and wrap his enormous hands around her throat. The knife falls from her hand.

Kathie grabs the Ouija board and drags herself into the kitchen. Finds the matches and the black powder on the table. She covers the board in the powder, but she can't get a match to light...

Jeremy choking the life out of Cecilia...

FLICK. FLICK. FLICK. Kathie struggling with the matches...

Jeremy strangling Cecilia. Her eyes bulge. Jeremy is crushing her windpipe.

FLICK. FLICK. Finally a match lights. Kathie drops it onto the board. It explodes into flame, scorching her face. A horrifying SCREAM echoes throughout the house as the Ouija board burns and shrivels.

Upstairs, Jeremy releases Cecilia and she collapses to the floor. The Ouija board's scream seems to pierce Jeremy's very soul. He clutches his head in great pain, stumbling backward.

Kathie has crawled out to the living room, looking up the stairs at the contorting Jeremy.

Jeremy takes hold of his Mickey Mouse gas mask, the mask that his parents gave him as a child in 1942, and rips it from his face.

Kathie looks. Jeremy's face is a charred mess of blackened and desiccated skin, burned beyond recognition. His eyes are hot, steaming coals. He falls over the stair railing onto the floor, a mass of broken bones.

Kathie reaches him. Looks down at the mangled face and the smoking eyes. Jeremy is clearly dead...

Kathie pours the rest of the black powder all over his body. FLICK. This time she is able to light a match with ease. She drops it on the body of Jeremy Parker and he begins to burn.

Kathie turns to find Cecilia at her side. They hurry out of the house and onto the street.

From the street they watch their house explode into flames. Windows shatter. The roof caves in. They're watching the front door. Waiting. Waiting. In the distance a fire engine wails...

A FIREFIGHTER approaches Cecilia and Kathie. He asks them if there is anyone alive in the house as his men begin battling the flames. Kathie tells the Firefighter, "No. Not anymore."

PARAMEDICS tend to Cecilia and Kathie.

The house collapses in a heap of ash and dust and bone, ending the bogeyman's reign of terror once and for all.

FADE TO BLACK

WOODHURST - From the payphone in the theater lobby, Tim Cooke dialed 911.

"Someone's gone crazy," he cried into the receiver. "We need your help!"

As the 17-year-old usher gave the operator the address of the Triplex movie theater in Woodhurst, he could hear people shouting from one of the theaters and saw them running for the exit doors.

It all happened late last night, during the midnight premiere of *Halloween II*. According to Cooke, the show was sold out, but people had snuck inside the auditorium playing the horror sequel.

"We were way beyond capacity, which only added to the chaos," Cooke said.

As the movie was near its end, Cooke was standing next to the entrance to Auditorium 3 when a woman burst through the doors and said there was trouble inside. The woman then bolted toward the exit and left.

"I was a little frightened," Cooke said, "but I thought it was just kids goofing around, which happens a lot at scary movies."

Halloween II continues the story of a masked killer who stalks and murders teenagers on Halloween. Cooke described a rowdy line of moviegoers that curled all the way around the block in the hours leading up to the midnight screening.

"It was the night before Halloween, everyone was pumped up, but I didn't expect this," he said, recalling the unease he felt stepping inside the theater.

Cooke heard the sounds of a scuffle coming from near the front row, but the theater was too dark to see what was happening. Some people got up from their seats and moved quickly toward the exit.

Then Cooke heard a sound he says he will never forget.

"It was the most ugly, most awful scream I've ever heard in my life," he said. "At first I didn't think it was human. It sounded like an animal, like a dog or a wolf or something, that had been shot."

Cooke turned on his flashlight and hurried down the aisle to see if someone had been injured.

"It was the scariest thing I had ever seen. People were running and pushing each other. One lady fell down," he said. "I heard crying, and a woman was screaming something like, 'He will come for you! He will come for all of you!' I pointed my flashlight in the direction of her voice."

Cooke said that his flashlight fell upon a young woman who had a terrified look in her eyes, but that she ducked out of the way before he could get a clear look. Cooke was almost certain that he saw the woman holding a knife, so he ran back into the lobby to call 911.

"In the few seconds that I saw her, I knew this was someone to be afraid of," Cooke said. "As I ran out, I heard the scream again, and I'm positive it was coming from her."

Cooke's frantic call to 911 reveals the chaos and confusion of the scene. The brave teenager crouched against the wall of the lobby as he dialed the phone.

Dispatcher: "Who has a knife, sir?"

Cooke: "Someone inside the theater. A girl."

Dispatcher: "Does she still have the knife?"

Cooke: "I don't know. I'm in the lobby now."

Dispatcher: "Deputies are on their way. I need you to stay on the line with me. Can you tell me what this person looks like?"

Cooke: "She has dark hair, that's all I could see. She's screaming and everyone's going crazy here."

Marion County Police arrived and cleared the theater, but they were unable to find the screaming woman or the knife. Chief Deputy Chris Meadows said that police would continue to investigate the incident, noting that the woman could have slipped out one of the rear exits inside the theater.

"We don't know the identity of this person, or if she is a danger to others or to herself," he said. "It was disturbing, with many people clearly shaken by the her screams and the mad rush to get out of the theater. Fortunately, no one was seriously injured at the scene."

Tim Cooke says that the manager of the theater has no plans to stop showing *Halloween II*, but that he will require his employees to undergo training on how to deal with similar crisis situations in the future.

From "Beverly and *Halloween*: A Match Made in Hell" (p. 11-13):

In Mexican folklore, *El Cucuy* is a demon or monster that feasts on naughty children who disobey their parents. In Iceland, *Gryla* is a hoary female ogress that makes soup from the flesh of misbehaving boys and girls. In northern India, the "sack man" snatches unwanted children up in his *bori*, carries them away, and eats them.

So what exactly was the bogeyman for Beverly Dreger?

We might find an answer in E.T.A. Hoffmann's *Der Sandmann* (1817), a German folktale that features the monster. In the story, the Sandman is a malevolent figure that creeps through the windows of children's bedrooms and throws sand in their eyes; he then puts their eyes in a bag and feeds them to his hungry, beak-nosed children. The inspiration behind Freud's 1919 essay "The Uncanny," Hoffmann's bogeyman is a manifestation of the nightmarish themes of childhood: punishment, abandonment, dislocation, and bodily mutilation.

In 1981's *Halloween II*—released in movie theaters one night before the murders took place at Woodhurst State—The Chordettes' version of the song "Mr. Sandman" plays over the closing credits. The tune, with its cheerful handclaps and escalating xylophone, offers a lovelorn plea for the titular character to deliver a "dream"—in other words, a handsome boy—to the female singer; the boy must have "two lips like roses in clover" and a "lonely heart like Pagliacci"—the sad clown from Leoncavallo's Italian opera.

According to Shawn Cote's interview with police, he and Beverly attended the midnight premiere of *Halloween II* at the Triplex movie theater in Woodhurst. Beverly saw the evil bogeyman cut his bloody swath of terror throughout a near-empty hospital, bludgeoning security guards with hammers and stabbing pretty nurses with hypodermic needles—a cinematic nightmare ended by an ironically optimistic coda over the end credits. Did the song "Mr. Sandman" trigger Beverly? Did it force her to emulate the imaginary figure that had haunted her for so long? In other words, did *Halloween II* make Beverly Dreger kill?

Shawn Cote told police that Beverly "freaked out" at the end of the film, "screaming her goddamn head off." The DSM-III states that psychiatric problems, especially those that involve hallucinations, can cause screaming and violent behavior. Beverly most likely suffered one of these hallucinations during the film, reliving the times when her mother threatened to kill her. But Cote also told police that Beverly was acting "on edge" from the very moment that *Halloween II* began, "scratching her skin" and acting "like it was a mistake to be there." According to some reports, Beverly may have even brought a knife once belonging to her mother inside the theater. Regardless of what exactly took place, the movie clearly plunged Beverly into the terrible depths of her childhood—but it also rejected her newfound strength and repudiated her film treatment in which she tried to destroy the bogeyman legend and eliminate its presence from her life. As she sat in the theater, as the killer rose from the burning flames that for Beverly had always been a source of beauty and pain, she must have experienced a condemnation of her entire future. Her abandonment of Shawn Cote at the scene, her disappearance into the night for parts unknown, suggest that she had finally given up…

From *My Roommate, My Friend: The Untold Story of Beverly Dreger* (unpublished manuscript):

The monster can see my boobs!

That was my first thought when an embarrassing dream about *The Creature from the Black Lagoon* jolted me awake. I had seen the movie earlier that night in Webster Hall, and images of the Gill-man and the lovely Julie Adams had obviously crept into my subconscious.

It was just a silly dream, but the absolute silence in the air as I woke told me something was wrong.

It's Halloween night…where is everybody?

I blinked the sleep from my eyes and listened. All I could hear was the rain outside, but my heart still thudded in my chest. Campus was rarely this quiet, even late at night. Wearing only a tank-top and panties, I sat up and felt an icy shiver pass through my body.

I looked across the dark room. My roommate's bed was empty, a sight that unsettled me until I remembered that Jill was visiting her parents in Clarksburg. Feeling uncomfortable in my own skin, I threw the covers aside and swung my legs off the bed.

Across the room the curtains stirred in the breeze. Had I left the window open? In this weather?

Another chill passed through the air, and my nipples hardened. My face turned hot and prickles of sweat broke out along my temples; I became self-conscious of my body, as if someone was watching me.

Thunk. Thunk, thunk.

Footsteps. Boots. Outside in the hall.

Boys snuck into our dorms all the time, but the doors on either side of the building would be locked by now. Someone would have had to let him in. But I hadn't heard the doors being opened or closed. I hadn't heard the peels of drunken laughter or the pitter-patter of slippered feet. I hadn't heard anything. Why was there no noise at all?

Get a grip, Lisa.

I crouched on the floor. My jogging shoes were propped against the sliding-door closet. I could slip them on, climb out the window, make a run for it…

Thunk, thunk.

The steps approached. Closer now. Was the door locked? Jill was good about locking it, especially at night, but Jill wasn't here…

Thunk.

Someone was on the other side of my door.

Panicking, I inched across the floor toward it, clasping the knob lock gently and turning it clockwise.

I waited. Nothing happened. No sound at all, except for the rain outside. Whoever had been walking in the hallway was gone now.

I waited another few minutes, then slipped into bed and closed my eyes, hoping for sleep. But the cold wind swept over me again, and I remembered the open window. I hopped out of bed and faced Jill's side of the room.

That was when I saw the thing inside the closet, its face black and crinkled, like a burned mask.

Screams died in my throat. Two red eyes flickered open and the thing shambled out of the closet.

I stumbled backward. My legs hit the bed and I fell, absurdly, into a sitting position. As the thing rose to its full height, I saw that it was a man, dressed in black, with enormous work boots on his feet.

"Get out of here!" I shouted.

His cold hands clutched my arms. He pulled me off the bed and toward his face, which was burned and grotesquely scarred. His lips looked like two shriveled worms.

My mind raced with questions—*how the hell did he get in here? How long had he been hiding in the closet?*

I was panicking now, kicking and clawing, trying to scratch at his disfigured face. The man batted away my hands the same way you would an insect.

"Help me!" I shouted, louder this time. "Please help me!"

But he threw me down and clamped one of his filthy hands over my mouth and nose. I couldn't scream. I couldn't breathe. I couldn't do anything but stare into his burning red eyes.

I saw the coil of rope attached to his belt. I saw the knife, tucked into his pants. He knelt between my legs, using his enormous thighs to push my knees apart.

He's going to kill you. He's going to rape you and then he's going to kill you.

I thought of my flimsy shirt and cotton panties, the icy wind on my nipples—and all the while this man had been hiding in my closet, watching me. It was humiliating. Obscene. And now I was going to die. But the man was going to fuck me first.

No!

I kicked and thrashed. With my good hand I swung at his face, lunging for those terrible eyes. I thought of my friends. I thought of my mom and dad. The man punched me in the face, twice, and still I scratched and clawed and fought. As he raised the knife high in the air, his grin stretched wide and thin like warm taffy, I closed my eyes and prayed...

"Dorm Slayings Shock College Community" by Lena Sharp (originally published in *Chicago Star*, Nov. 1981, p. 1-2):

Marion County Police will continue to enforce strict security measures, including nightly patrols and surveillance, following the murder of three students at Woodhurst State. The victims were found in their dorm rooms on Halloween night.

Dead are roommates Tracy-Ann Watkins, 21, and Cherylen Montgomery, 21; and Tamara Albright, 20. The victims lived in a senior women's dormitory on the Woodhurst State campus. On the night of the murders, another student, senior Lisa Brown, 21, was attacked in her room by a male assailant who fled the scene. Brown survived the incident and remains in stable condition at Marion Memorial Hospital.

According to police, the murders occurred sometime between midnight and 3 a.m. The victims were struck with a foreign object and stabbed with shards of glass that police believe came from a broken mirror in the building's communal bathroom. There were no signs of forced entry on either of the locked doors leading into the dormitory, but police stated that the assailant might have entered the building through an open window.

Officials from Woodhurst State and local police agencies have openly communicated with students and parents about the murders, stressing the importance of maintaining order on campus, respecting the victims, and helping students feel comforted and safe. A letter from college president Warren Pennell to the Woodhurst community asked that students stay in groups at night, keep their rooms locked, and report any suspicious activity or persons to campus police.

The letter also warned students against spreading rumors about the crimes, which can often derail a murder investigation.

"This is a tragedy of the highest magnitude, an unimaginable assault on four young lives and Woodhurst State as a whole," wrote Pennell in the letter. "We grieve and pray along with the families of Lisa, Tracy-Ann, Cherylen, and Tamara."

Herbert Cardoza, a campus security officer and one of the first to respond to the scene, said that he had never seen violence on this scale before. "I don't understand how one human being could do this to another, not to mention young women," Cardoza said. "We will do everything we can, doubling shifts, 24-hour patrols, whatever it takes, to prevent this kind of tragedy from ever happening again."

In addition to studying and collecting evidence from the crime scene, interviewing students and faculty, and gathering witness statements, police are arranging a timeline of the events leading up to the murders, but Cardoza admits it has not been an easy task. "There is a lot of confusion about how the suspect entered a building that was locked, and not only that, how no one saw him go in or out. And then there's the issue of the knife found outside the building. Police haven't said a word about it."

Cardoza is referring to a knife that was found in the bushes near the crime scene. Investigators have yet to determine how the knife ended up there, or if it was used in the murders.

Cardoza hopes that Lisa Brown might be able to clear up some of the mystery, as soon as the young woman recovers from her injuries.

"Lisa could be the missing link," he said. "She's a very brave girl. If she hadn't fought back, she might not be with us."

The bodies were found inside a two-story dormitory for female senior students. Though all of the victims lived on the first floor, their rooms were not adjacent to each other. Police believe that the suspect wandered the corridor and tested the doors to see which ones were unlocked.

All residence halls at Woodhurst are locked from 11 p.m. until 6:30 a.m., during which time residents must use their key to gain access to the building. Detectives are investigating whether any residents lost their key or gave their key to someone else. There is also the possibility that the suspect was allowed into the building by a resident.

In the days since the slayings, the college campus has remained relatively calm. Classes resume next week, while a memorial service is being planned for the victims and their friends and families.

However, some students are speaking out at a time when others are calling for peace and quiet.

Gerda Ostrander, a senior and president of Living in Freedom Everyday (LIFE), a feminist organization at Woodhurst State, has provided a report to the school administration and student body that summarizes a number of violent incidents that have occurred on campus since 1978. The incidents include:

A female sophomore filed two complaints with campus security about a strange man who was following her on Oct. 6 and Oct. 8 of 1978. There was no follow-up record to indicate that campus police had investigated the complaints.

In May of 1979, a female senior was battered in the parking lot behind the swimming pool. Despite countless tips and an eyewitness identification, the case was never solved.

On the evening of Jan. 1, 1980, a fire broke out at the Cressman Center for Health on College Drive. The blaze, which investigators determined was caused by arson, caused extensive damage to school property. No one was arrested or charged with the crime.

A male junior was beaten with an unidentified object on Sept. 21, 1981, and left nearly for dead on the outskirts of the softball field. The student was hospitalized for three weeks and did not return to Woodhurst State upon his release. No one was arrested or charged with the crime.

"I am a senior on this campus, and for four years I have walked knee-deep in the spilled blood of my brothers and sisters," Ostrander announced before a small gathering of students outside Blaney Hall. "With this latest incident, I am now drowning in it. The murder of these poor girls has ripped the soul right out of the world."

From initial crime scene report at Woodhurst State (Marion County Police Department, Homicide Division, Precinct 9, Nov. 1981):

Tracy-Ann Watkins lies on her back in a northeast to northwest orientation, right arm bent and pressed against the north wall, her left arm outstretched. Her left hand hangs over the edge of the bed, fingers slightly curled. The bed-cover is bunched up on the floor and her feet are nearest the door. Her head faces the opposite side of the bed where the bed presses against the northeast wall. Her chin is tilted so that her jaw and neck area are exposed. Her left leg lies flat while her right leg is at a 180-degree angle with the foot tucked under the left thigh. Watkins is wearing a white camisole top that is soaked in blood that is red-brown in color. She is wearing turquoise blue cotton shorts. Her throat has been slashed. Her right earlobe has been cut with a laceration that has split the lobe in half, and there are flecks of blood in her hair and on the lower portion of the northeast wall above her head. The sheet underneath the torso of the body is also soaked in blood, red-brown in color. The sheet is covered in what appears to be patches of peeled-away skin that is red and scaly. No other stab marks are observed on the body and the victim appears to have no defensive wounds...

Cherylen Montgomery lies on her right side facing the wall in a northeast to southeast position. She is on the bed perpendicular to Watkins. Bedsheets are bunched up at the foot of the bed, covering her feet. Flakes of burned skin are observed on top of the bedsheets. Cherylen is wearing a silver necklace around her neck with a horse pendant, a white jersey-type shirt hiked up at the waist and yellow cotton underwear. The shirt is drenched in blood and there are blood smears on her abdomen (blood is red-brown in color). Her navel is pierced with a small silver ring, also covered in blood. Her underwear has blood drops on the waistband. Another smear of blood noted on the back of the underwear on the left of the decedent's posterior. Her throat has been cut in a jagged manner, and there is a large hole in the middle of the throat. Inside the hole is a jagged piece of glass. Blood has soaked through the right side of the bed and there is blood on the east wall where the bed touches it. No other stab marks are observed on the body. The victim has defensive wounds on her hands and lacerations on the fingers of left hand. Post-mortem lividity on right side of the body is consistent with the position in which it was found...

Like the other two victims, Tamara Albright is found in her bed inside her dorm room. Tamara lived in a "single" room that has only one bed, which is positioned near the window on the south side of the room. Albright is on her left side, arms outstretched over her head, in a northeast to northwest orientation. She is wearing a white bra that is drenched in blood. The right strap and cup of the bra have been pulled off the body, exposing the right breast. Her right breast has been stabbed to the point of disfiguration. Several stab wounds noted on her hands, arms, and face. A contusion, red in color, noted on her forehead and extending to right temple. Laceration noted on her right cheek, exposing her jawbone. A large piece of glass is embedded in the laceration. The right side of her hair is swept back across her head and covered in blood. White flakes of skin are visible throughout the hair. Albright is wearing pink cotton shorts that have dried blood on them. She has a thin copper-colored band on her left ring finger. She has been stabbed multiple times in the abdomen and thighs, and her abdominal region is smeared with blood in a circular pattern. No defensive wounds were observed on the victim. Post-mortem lividity was noted on left side of the back and left posterior...

From "Night of the Devil" by Scooter Smith (originally published in *The National Buzz*, July 1982, p. 3):

An analysis of the gruesome crime scene at Woodhurst State reveals chilling possibilities about the killer who butchered three girls while they slept in their rooms. As police continue to hunt for fugitive Beverly Dreger, who was spotted near the murder site by at least two eyewitnesses, The BUZZ can provide a startling hypothesis about the inspiration behind these unsettling crimes.

Tracy-Ann Watkins and Cherylen Montgomery were found with their throats slashed, not unlike the teenage beauties in recent horror movies *Friday the 13th* and *Halloween*. The girls were attacked in bed, evoking scenes from *The Hills Have Eyes*, a twisted cannibal movie from 1977. And the murders happened on a school campus, echoing the sick plots of *Graduation Day* and *Black Christmas*. Investigators must be wondering if the Woodhurst killer was trying to send them a message inspired by Hollywood's love of the bloody and macabre!

Each of the victims in the slayings was stabbed with shards of a broken mirror, but Cherylen Montgomery and Tamara Albright were also mutilated, sustaining lacerations all over their bodies. Horribly, Albright had a jagged piece of the glass lodged in her own cheek.

Mirrors, especially broken ones, have long been a source of disgust and warped psychosis in horror flicks like *The Shining* and *The Boogey Man*, the latter telling the perverse story of an evil spirit trapped in broken shards of glass. A psychiatrist who is connected to the case told The BUZZ that the Woodhurst killer "looks in the mirror and is disgusted by what he sees. So he takes the mirror, a symbol of his ugliness, shatters it, and turns it into a murder weapon."

The doctor added that using pieces of glass to kill someone is guaranteed to create an extremely violent and sickening crime scene. "It's a way to put the body on gruesome display, to create a spectacle, and to scare the hell out of people. The killer is showing off," he said.

Police reports also indicate that a strange-looking knife with a black handle was discovered near the crime scene. Even more bizarre is that the genetic material on the blade of the knife is reportedly not blood, but a foreign substance that forensic scientists have not been able to identify.

Big knives have long been the weapon of choice for movie-killers of all kinds, including those in *Psycho*, *Friday the 13th*, and Beverly Dreger's personal favorite, *Halloween*. Is the knife found at Woodhurst State a red herring for police, or was the weapon used in the murders? And, if not blood, what is the material on the knife, and why haven't police spoken about it?

Slasher movies, especially the ones revered by rabid fans like Beverly Dreger, feature graphic murder tableaus similar to what was discovered at Woodhurst. Was the killer paying homage to these movies by imitating the gory climaxes of shockers like *Maniac!*, *Happy Birthday to Me*, and *Prom Night*?

"With murders this brutal, this senseless, it's impossible to say what the killer's intentions were," says the psychiatrist. "But there's no denying that the crime scene looked like something from one of these sick drive-in movies. It was that awful."

The witness statements of Stephanie Mansfield, Stephen Bainsley, Rachel Palmer, Helena Boxer, Matt Griffin, Brandon Kendrick, and Charles Hollis (written on Nov. 3-5, 1981 at the Marion County Police Department, Precinct 9, Homicide Division):

My name is Stephanie Mansfield. I am a senior at Woodhurst. In my freshman year, I lived on the first floor in the Tupper Dorms. Cherylen Montgomery and Beverly Dreger also lived on my floor. I don't want to write anything bad about someone who died, but a few weeks after the year started, Cherylen was saying all these nasty things about Beverly, calling her "ghost-face" and "Vampirella" and saying that Beverly would put a spell on you if you crossed her. She said other mean things too, like Beverly would dig up bodies from the cemetery and perform Satanic acts on them and have sex with them. Nobody took it seriously, but there was this one night when Beverly approached Cherylen in the hallway and they started arguing. I don't remember who hit who first, but they started slapping each other and Cherylen grabbed Beverly's hair and nearly threw her to the ground. Our R.A. had to break up the fight, and I remember the campus cops showed up and took a report. As far as I know Beverly and Cherylen didn't get in any more fights after that, but they definitely hated each other's guts.

My name is Stephen Bainsley and I am a senior at Woodhurst State. I have been asked by Detective G. Bianco to write about my encounter with Beverly Dreger on the night of October 31st, 1981.

I was at the Spooktacular costume party in the Webster Hall lounge. Beverly walked in around 11:30 or 11:45. She stood to the side without getting a beer or talking to anyone. She was wearing all black, jeans, boots, and a coat with a fur hood. She had on purple lipstick that kind of glowed in the dark. I noticed her right away.

I felt bad she was standing by herself, so I went over to talk to her (we had taken a few classes together and sort of knew each other). I said hello and joked that it looked like her date wasn't going to show up, and Beverly said something like, "He always shows up," but I had a hard time hearing her because the DJ was playing "The Monster Mash" crazy loud. I said something dumb then. I said I was surprised to see her out at the party, which probably sounded rude. Beverly said that she came to the party to be around other people—I heard her clearly because the DJ was in between songs at that point. I asked her if she had seen any good movies lately and that I saw *Halloween II* and liked it. She didn't answer and she looked pretty miserable, so I left and went to the other side of the lounge and started dancing.

A few minutes later I saw Beverly leave the party. It was around midnight. I didn't see her again after that.

My name is Rachel Palmer. I am a senior at Woodhurst. On the evening of October 31st of this year, I was walking back to my room inside Belltower Dorms. The time was around 1:30 in the morning, so technically what I saw took place on the morning of November 1st.

I was walking alone from the "haunted house" that the Spanish Club had put on in the Ceramic Center. Belltower is on the opposite end of the campus from there, so it was a long walk in the freezing cold. I was drunk but not to where I was falling down or not in control in any way. I walked into the library plaza and saw Beverly Dreger and Lisa Brown sitting on one of the benches underneath the awning. Beverly was wearing a dark-colored coat with a furry hood. Lisa was wearing a dark jacket and had a scarf wrapped around her neck. The three of us had worked on a science project in our sophomore year, and we were decent friends back then, so I know it was them. They were talking and Beverly seemed upset. As I walked past I could tell that she was crying and I heard Lisa say, "I'll help you, it's going to be all right," or something close to that. I don't think they really noticed me as I went by.

I reached the end of the plaza and heard footsteps behind me. I looked over my shoulder and saw Lisa Brown walking in the direction of Belltower. I assumed she was going to her room, just like I was. She was alone. I did not see Beverly with her, and I do not know where Beverly went after I saw her in the library plaza.

When I got to Belltower I used my key to get inside because the doors are locked at night. I turned to see if Lisa was behind me and to hold the door open for her if she was, but she was pretty far back from me, so I didn't wait. The hallway was empty and quiet. I went straight to my room. I washed my face and changed clothes. I got into bed and looked at the clock before going to sleep. It was 2:05 in the morning.

My name is Helena Boxer. I am a senior at Woodhurst State and I live in a single room on the second floor of the Belltower Dorms. At approximately 2:45 in the morning on November 1ˢᵗ of this year, I was startled awake by someone shouting. I thought someone had gotten in a fight outside, which happens all the time on weekends. I listened closely and thought I heard the shouts again, but I can't be sure. I still do not know if the shouting came from the first floor or from outside.

I did not hear any other noises that night and I slept until being woken up by police the next morning.

My name is Matt Griffin. I am a junior at Woodhurst and I have been asked to provide this written statement by Detective Gary Bianco of the Marion County Police Department. On Halloween night of this year, I was walking to my room from a party in Cornett Dorms, up on the hill. I live in Compton Hall, which is across campus. I'm not sure of the time because I don't wear a watch, but I'm estimating it was close to around 3 in the morning. I was walking the path between Belltower Dorms and the art lounge when this girl ran into me. It was dark as hell out, and freezing, and she had a big coat covering her face and most of her head, but I could see her long hair spilling out everywhere. She was running so hard she nearly knocked me down. She stumbled a little, and I tried helping her up, but she just kept going, running toward the baseball field. At the time I figured she was drunk and maybe needed to throw up, but after I heard about the murders I wondered if there might be some kind of connection. I have been shown several pictures by Detective Bianco but I have not been able to indentify the girl who ran into me. It was too dark and I never got a clear look at her face.

My name is Brandon Kendrick. I recently transferred as a junior to Woodhurst State, where I am studying English. On November 1ˢᵗ I was driving onto campus after having gone to a Halloween party in Bartlett. It was almost 3 in the morning when I drove through the security gate. There was no one in the office there, and the barrier was up, so I just drove on through.

To get to Compton Hall where I live, you turn right once you get past the security gate. After you make the turn, the baseball field is on the right, and you can see Belltower Dorms behind that big grove of trees there. As I drove past the field, I saw a girl running across the baseball field from the direction of Belltower. The big lights above the bleachers were on, and I could see her pretty clearly. She had brown hair and she was dressed in black clothes. She was wearing boots and a coat with a furry hood that kept flapping behind her as she ran. She was running pretty hard. There was something dark smeared across her face. I thought maybe it was face paint from a Halloween party or something. I turned to look again as I was making the left turn past Belltower, but by then she was out of sight.

Detective Ron Kent has shown me three photographs of Beverly Dreger, and the picture of her in the coat with the fur hood looks just like the girl I saw running across the baseball field on the morning of November 1st.

My name is Charles Hollis. Everyone calls me Chip. I'm a junior at Woodhust State. On the morning of November 1st I was walking from my room at Compton Hall to the cafeteria to get some breakfast (I am in training for a weightlifting competition, and I eat a protein breakfast every day). It was early in the morning, a little after 7, and the campus was quiet. Most students were probably still sleeping. The walk from Compton to the cafeteria takes you past Belltower Dorms, which is a residence hall for all the hot senior girls, just over the hill behind the new student lounge.

When I got past the hill, Belltower was on my left. I noticed that the door on the left side of the building was closed and there was no one around anywhere (the silence was kind of creepy, actually). There is a bench and a little path with some trees outside the doorway, and just as I was walking past I saw something that looked off in the dirt underneath the trees. It was kind of shiny. When I got closer to the trees I could see that it was a knife. A big knife, with a thick black handle. I didn't touch it and I continued my walk to the cafeteria.

WILLOW CREEK - Police have combined forces with Chicago law enforcement agencies after receiving information that the suspect in a grisly triple homicide may be hiding somewhere in the Kentucky foothills.

The Willow Creek County Sheriff's Office announced yesterday that the manhunt for suspect Beverly Dreger has intensified after a jogger reported seeing a woman who looked like Dreger near a hiking trail on the Willow Creek River.

Dreger, 21, is the primary suspect in the murder of three women that occurred in October of last year at Woodhurst State, where Dreger and the victims were students. The victims were mutilated and stabbed to death with shards of broken glass. Despite a police search that has lasted over four months, Dreger remains at large.

"Based on new pieces of information that have come in, along with reports from Chicago, we are currently searching for the suspect at this time," Lt. Paul Becker of the Kentucky Police Department said.

State police have learned that Dreger was familiar with the geography of the Willow Creek area and had spent time at a nearby ranch in Wasawillow. Becker stated that detectives are investigating the ranch and its residents in an effort to determine if Dreger has been in contact with any of them.

Becker refused to comment on recent speculation that Chicago law enforcement has bungled the case, but he did acknowledge that the exhaustive legwork and inordinate number of detectives pursuing various leads have stalled the investigation.

"There are a number of dead-ends and conflicting stories about the suspect and the murders in question, all of which have pulled the investigation in different directions," Becker said.

Chicago police have reported that Dreger suffers from a mental disorder, but would not indicate a motive for the killings in October or point to specific evidence linking Dreger to the crime.

Becker also made clear that the recent rash of unusual crime activity in the Willow Creek area—including two burglarized homes and the murder of a local teenage girl—is not linked to Dreger.

Police are urging anyone with information about the suspect to call their local law enforcement agency immediately...

From transcript of CNT-TV's "Dorm Massacre Survivor Speaks Out" (originally aired July 13, 1983 – 20:00 ET):

THIS IS A RUSH TRANSCRIPT FROM "UP CLOSE AND PERSONAL WITH GAVIN TRACE." THIS COPY MAY NOT BE IN ITS FINAL FORM AND MAY BE UPDATED.

GAVIN TRACE, HOST: Tonight, the lone survivor of the Woodhurst State Slayings reveals the shocking truth about that tragic Halloween night almost two years ago.

(BEGIN ARCHIVAL FOOTAGE)

TERRENCE MORTIMER, NEWSCASTER: In what police are calling a sickening display of homicidal rage, three Woodhurst State seniors were found dead this morning, killed in their beds as they slept.

(END ARCHIVAL FOOTAGE)

TRACE: You'll hear about the disfigured man dressed in black who hid in her closet for hours, waiting for his chance to strike. Could he be the one responsible for these terrible crimes?

(BEGIN ARCHIVAL FOOTAGE)

HELENA BOXER, FORMER WOODHURST STUDENT: I woke up to the sound of someone shouting, like they were in a fight.
MORTIMER: Tracy-Ann Watkins, Cherylen Montgomery, and Tamara Albright—each one found brutally beaten and stabbed after police responded to an emergency phone call.
LISA BROWN, SURVIVOR OF WOODHURST STATE SLAYINGS (voice-over of 911 call): "I'm calling from Belltower Dorms at Woodhurst...you need to send someone...please! I've just been attacked!"

(END ARCHIVAL FOOTAGE)

TRACE: Tonight you'll learn what the public never knew about that terrible night, and why their hunt for primary suspect Beverly Dreger might be a wild goose chase after all. That's tonight on UP CLOSE AND PERSONAL WITH GAVIN TRACE.

(MUSIC AND TITLES)

TRACE: This is going to be a wild ride, folks, as we uncover new information about the brutal slayings that rocked a little college town in Illinois to its core. Before we begin, let's take a look back at that Halloween night of terror in 1981.

(BEGIN ARCHIVAL FOOTAGE)

HERBERT CARDOZA, CAMPUS SECURITY OFFICER: It was horrible. For the rest of my life I will never forget what I saw that morning.

GERDA OSTRANDER, STUDENT: Wake up, parents of America! It's Manson all over again! Your children are being killed in their beds and no place is safe anymore! And these are just the victims we know about! Who's to say how many more are out there!

DETECTIVE SERGEANT RON KENT, MARION COUNTY POLICE DEPARTMENT: It was a very brutal homicide. The victims were killed without mercy. There's no sense of compassion or human decency in any murder scene, but this was beyond the pale.

DETECTIVE GARY BIANCO, MARION COUNTY POLICE DEPARTMENT (voice-over with crime scene photos): Whoever did this had access to the building. The front doors were locked. Except in Lisa Brown's room, the windows were shut and locked. There were no signs of forced entry. The killer probably knew the victims. We believe that he or she is connected to this campus in some way.

EUGENE STONE, STUDENT: They were sweet girls. Smart and beautiful. From what I could tell, they didn't have any enemies.

RACHEL PALMER, STUDENT: I lived just a few doors down from where my best friends were killed. Why didn't I hear anything? Why didn't I do something?

(END ARCHIVAL FOOTAGE)

TRACE: On the night of October 31st, 1981, someone entered a women's residence hall at Woodhurst State and killed three girls: Tracy-Ann Watkins, an aspiring musician; Cherylen Montgomery, a competitive equestrian who loved animals; and Tamara Albright, a softball player and honors student. Also attacked that night in her room was Lisa Brown, but her life was spared. The victims were not merely killed; they were slaughtered, their lives cut short by the hands of a true psychopath.

(PHOTOS OF BEVERLY DREGER)

TRACE (voiceover): Marion County Police focused their investigation on this woman: Beverly Dreger, 21-years-old and a film student at Woodhurst when the murders took place. Dreger was known around campus as "Goth Girl" and "Vampirella," but far more relevant to police was the fact that a bloody knife found near the crime scene resembled one that Lisa Brown, Dreger's former roommate, had seen in the girl's possession. Dreger was also seen late that night, fleeing the campus from the direction of the crime scene with blood on her hands and face.

(CRIME SCENE PHOTOS)

TRACE (voice-over): The killer treated the victims mercilessly. Their bodies were stabbed and beaten, their clothes and beds soaked in blood. And police believe that this was the murder weapon—these shards of glass taken from a broken mirror inside the residence hall's bathroom.

(END OF ARCHIVAL FOOTAGE)

TRACE: Though police suspected Beverly Dreger was tied to the murders, they had no motive—and more importantly, they had no Beverly. She disappeared that night, and despite a manhunt that has lasted nearly two years, remains at large. Other persons of interest came and went—a drifter with a record for battery, a custodian with keys to all the buildings on campus—but police could find no evidence connecting them to the murders. By the start of the new year, the case had gone nowhere.

(PHOTOGRAPHS OF LISA BROWN)

Equally perplexing to law enforcement was Lisa Brown's violent encounter that Halloween night. Brown also lived in Belltower Dorms, and it was her 911 call, after she was attacked by a man hiding in her closet, that alerted police to the violent scene inside the residence hall. But who was this man and how did he end up inside Belltower that night? If he was the perpetrator of the murders, how did he move from room to room, undetected? And why could police find no evidence that he had been there, or that he even existed?

Lisa Brown is our special guest tonight, now 23-years-old and a graduate student at Seattle Pacific University. She is currently writing a book about her relationship with Beverly Dreger, and the events of that fateful night in 1981.

We are also joined by Gabriel Lumpkin, a general practice attorney and Ms. Brown's lawyer. Welcome, both of you.

BROWN: Thank you for having me.

GABRIEL LUMPKIN, GENERAL PRACTICE LAWYER: Thank you, Gavin.

TRACE: So, Lisa, where to start—first, let me say that I've read the reports, I've seen some of the pictures…Thank God you made it through what must have been the worst night of your life.

BROWN: Thank you. It definitely was.

TRACE: Did you know the other girls?

BROWN: I knew them all in passing, we lived on the same floor and Woodhurst is a pretty small school. But I was closest to Cherylen because we were both into horseback riding. They were all nice girls, very outgoing and friendly.

TRACE: Okay, take me through that night.

BROWN: Well, it was a mellow night for me. I met some friends and we went to a showing of *The Creature of the Black Lagoon* that was playing on campus.

TRACE: Now, at this point, you haven't seen Beverly.

BROWN: That night? No, not yet.

TRACE: She was living off-campus, correct?

BROWN: Right. She had left school for a while near the end of our sophomore year. We were roommates then. When she came back, she rented this cute little apartment close to school.

TRACE: Why did she leave school?

BROWN: For personal reasons.

TRACE: Was she drinking, taking drugs, in a bad relationship—what was it?

LUMPKIN: Whatever it was, Gavin, it had nothing to do with the murders.

TRACE: But we don't really know that, do we? There's so much we don't know about this case. Lisa, that's why you're here tonight, right? To tell us what we don't know.

BROWN: That is why I'm here, but I'm not going to hurt other people in the process. The tabloids have already printed so much crap about this case and about Beverly.

TRACE: That Beverly worshipped the devil, that she slept with her psychiatrist, her mother was a witch, that sort of thing?

BROWN: All that crap. I'm here to talk about what happened to me that night. The police don't want to listen, they don't believe me, fine. But maybe your audience will.

TRACE: Okay, let's get into it. What happened after you saw the movie?

BROWN: I went back to my room and found Bev sitting outside my door.

TRACE: How did she get into the building? Wasn't it locked by that time?

BROWN: Yes, it was. I don't know how she got in. But remember, Beverly was back at school by that time. Someone probably recognized her and let her in.

TRACE: And what did you say to her?

BROWN: Well, I was a bit surprised. We usually met up at her place or at this pinball joint near school. I rarely saw her on campus, especially at night.

TRACE: How did she look? What—why did she come see you at that time, late at night?

BROWN: That was the funny thing, because, that night, she was dressed like her old self. Very Gothic, punk style, with black raccoon eyes and purple lipstick. We hugged, you know, just the usual thing you do when you say hello to a friend...and then she started to cry.

TRACE: Now, Beverly struggled with depression for most of her life, right? She had a pretty rough childhood, from what I gather, her mother committed suicide—

BROWN: Beverly did suffer from depression, but we had a lot of good times too. It wasn't all doom and gloom.

TRACE: Why was she crying?

BROWN: To really understand this, you have to know about the movie *Halloween*.

TRACE: That's a horror movie, if I'm not mistaken.

LUMPKIN: A very popular one, Gavin.

BROWN: Most people know that Beverly loved horror movies, and she loved *Halloween*, despite how it made her feel.

(BEGIN FILM CLIP FROM *HALLOWEEN*, COURTESY FALCON INTERNATIONAL)

(END FILM CLIP)

TRACE: Scary stuff. Lisa, you said this movie, *Halloween*, made Beverly feel a certain way.

BROWN: Well, it scared her, for one, just like it scared me and everybody else who's seen it. But Bev had grown up in a very paranoid household, an abusive household. Not just physically sometimes, but psychologically. Her mother convinced her that there was a man out there who was trying to kill her.

TRACE: The bogeyman.

BROWN: That's right. Beverly had seen *Halloween II* the night before she came to see me, and she was a wreck.

TRACE: And there was trouble at the theater, wasn't there? It was reported that a woman went crazy in the audience, that she had a knife and was threatening to stab people with it?

BROWN: No one has ever been able to prove that the woman inside the theater was Beverly.

TRACE: Okay. I want to ask something because I'm confused. If the original movie scared Beverly so much, if it made her think the bogeyman was a real person, why did she go see the second one?

BROWN: She said she hoped they'd kill him off in the sequel. And that his death would bring her peace. Or something like that.

TRACE: Lisa, you don't sound convinced yourself.

BROWN: I'm not denying that it sounds strange, but you have to understand, this was Beverly's way of looking at the world.

TRACE: In horror movies, don't the bad guys always win?

BROWN: Usually. But I guess Beverly was hoping for a different outcome.

TRACE: Wow. Okay, there's so much more to uncover when we come back. Lisa will take us to the scene of the crime, into that dark dormitory where a murderer struck down three innocent lives. We'll be right back.

(COMMERCIAL BREAK)

(BEGIN SECOND FILM CLIP FROM *HALLOWEEN*, COURTESY FALCON INTERNATIONAL)

(END FILM CLIP)

TRACE: Another terrifying scene from *Halloween*, a movie that our guest says gets to the heart of the murders at Woodhurst State in 1981. We are back with Lisa Brown, who was attacked that night by a man police have yet to catch or identify.

Lisa, you were telling us—Beverly Dreger came to see you, she was upset about this horror movie. The two of you went for a walk around campus, is that right?

BROWN: We did. It was late, about one in the morning, and we bundled up and started walking.

TRACE: Was Beverly wearing a coat with a rabbit-fur hood?

BROWN: I have no idea what it was made out of, but yes, she was wearing that coat.

TRACE: And where did the two of you go?

BROWN: We went to the plaza, which is this nice area outside the library. And we just talked. She told me about a movie script she was writing, and we talked about her boyfriend.

TRACE: Was she still upset?

BROWN: No, she had calmed down by that time.

TRACE: She didn't give you any indication that she was angry, that she might have had plans to hurt someone that night?

BROWN: Not at all.

TRACE: But wasn't there an altercation between Beverly and Cherylen Montgomery? Didn't they hate each other?

BROWN: That happened *three* years before the murders took place. And they didn't hate each other. They just stayed out of each other's way.

TRACE: What about the knife? Police reports say that you told them Beverly had a knife that looked just like the one they found near the crime scene?

LUMPKIN: You don't have to answer that, Lisa.

TRACE: I'm not trying to cause—I've got the report here in front of me.

BROWN: That was a misunderstanding. Either that, or the cops just want to pin this on Beverly so they can wipe their hands clean of it. I told them that Beverly used to steal knives from the cafeteria, for protection at night, but I never said that the knife they found in the bushes belonged to Beverly.

TRACE: So you never saw Beverly with a large knife with a thick black handle?

BROWN: No.

TRACE: Police say the knife belonged to Beverly's mother, who was quite a dangerous person herself.

LUMPKIN: Gavin, if I could interrupt—the police don't think the knife they found is the murder weapon. The blade on that knife is not consistent with the types of cuts found on the three victims.

TRACE: But was there blood on the knife?

LUMPKIN: I heard there was a substance on the knife, but that police determined it wasn't blood.

TRACE: So the knife might not be relevant to the case after all. Okay. So, Lisa, you're in the library plaza. Then what?

BROWN: We finished talking around 1:30 in the morning. Bev said she was going to catch a ride with her boyfriend. He was going to pick her up at the main gate.

TRACE: But according to her boyfriend, he hadn't spoken to Beverly since they went to the movies together the night before.

BROWN: All I know is what Beverly told me. She thanked me, and we hugged again, and then we both left.

TRACE: You go back to your room at this point?

BROWN: Yes. I used the bathroom in the hall, then went to my room.

TRACE: And the doors to the building were locked when you got there?

BROWN: The door I used, on the east side, was locked. I used my key to get in.

TRACE: Was the mirror in the bathroom broken at that time?

BROWN: No.

TRACE: And your room was empty when you got there. Your roommate was gone.

BROWN: It was empty. Or at least I thought it was. I got into my bed clothes and went to sleep.

TRACE: Lisa, before we go on, I want to show—these are some photos you gave our producer, and we have your permission to show these, is that right?

BROWN: Yes.

(BEGIN PHOTO MONTAGE)

TRACE: These are pictures of you. Now—these are very hard to look at. Your left eye is swollen shut here, there are bruises on your face. And your lip is torn open—now these injuries happened during the attack?

(END PHOTO MONTAGE)

BROWN: Yes. I wanted to show them tonight because—well, not everyone—the police, and others—not everyone thinks I'm telling the truth. Obviously I got those injuries from somewhere. I didn't do that to myself.

TRACE: I need to ask you—and I want to apologize in advance before I do—but this man tried to rape you, is that correct?

BROWN: Well, I thought he was going to rape me, but he…I'm not sure how to say this on national television.

TRACE: Go ahead. We can bleep it if we need to.

BROWN: He had knocked me on the ground. He had forced my legs apart, and I thought he was going to…but he stopped. He got this confused look on his face. I don't think…I don't think he was able to perform.

TRACE: I see.

LUMPKIN: It's not as uncommon as you might think. There are many rapists out there who suffer from sexual dysfunction, including impotence. He cares more about inflicting punishment and asserting his power than he does his own sexual gratification.

TRACE: Lisa, tell us what happened in your room.

BROWN: Like I said, I went to sleep. And then, around 2:30 in the morning, I woke up from a bad dream. That was when I heard footsteps outside my door. Heavy footsteps, like a big person walking in boots.

TRACE: All right.

BROWN: I quickly got up and locked my door.

LUMPKIN: Now, at this point, Gavin, according to the coroner's report, Tracy-Ann, Cherylen, and Tamara are all already dead.

TRACE: So he's moving from room to room. But Lisa, you said you locked your door, so—

BROWN: I did. And I got back into bed after that. I could sense something was wrong. I looked across the room and saw that the window was open. When I got up to shut it, I saw the man inside the closet.

TRACE: Now, before we—how much time had passed between when you heard his footsteps outside your door and when you saw him in the closet?

BROWN: Maybe two minutes. Two or three minutes.

TRACE: So there was not enough time for the man to exit the building, find your open window, climb through it, and hide in your closet—all without you noticing or hearing him?

BROWN: Correct. That would be impossible.

TRACE: But there he was, regardless, waiting for you. Now was he standing behind the clothes, or—?

BROWN: He was crouching at first. Then his eyes opened. They were red, or very bloodshot—he looked right at me, and then he came out of the closet.

TRACE: Did you scream?

BROWN: I couldn't. Not yet. I was in absolute shock.

TRACE: And what did he look like?

BROWN: He didn't look real. I thought he was wearing a mask at first. Like a Halloween mask turned inside out. But then when he got closer I saw that his face was horribly burned all over.

TRACE: And he attacked you.

BROWN: Yes. He knocked me down. He got between my legs, forcing them apart. He had rope on his belt and he wanted to tie me up, but I resisted. I started screaming and fighting back as hard as I could.

TRACE: Did he say anything while he was doing this?

BROWN: No.

TRACE: Was there blood on his clothes, or on his face?

BROWN: I didn't see any blood.

TRACE: And this is what has police confused. If the other girls were already dead, and if this man killed them, he would have been covered in blood.

BROWN: Probably.

TRACE: And how he moved between the rooms—it just doesn't make sense. First you hear him outside your door, then he's inside your closet.

BROWN: I admit, it's peculiar.

TRACE: It sounds almost supernatural, like he was in two places at once.

BROWN: I'll remember that you said that.

TRACE: He must have come in through the window, don't you think, when you were out with Beverly?

BROWN: At the time, that's what I believed.

TRACE: You don't believe that now?

BROWN: Well…I believe there are other forces at work here.

TRACE: Well, now, wait, let's be logical—how long was he there, waiting for you to come in? And if he was, when did he kill the others?

LUMPKIN: We can't answer those questions, Gavin.

TRACE: Well, somebody needs to answer them, the police, a private detective, or somebody. Or else this case is never going to get solved. Lisa, this man almost killed you.

BROWN: Yes, he did.

TRACE: He had a knife, correct?

BROWN: Yes. It was attached to his belt, I think. And he took it out and raised it above his shoulder. He had punched me in the face a few times—

TRACE: He broke your nose.

BROWN: I didn't know it at the time, but yes. After he hit me, I couldn't focus. The room was spinning. I couldn't breathe. My body was shutting down.

TRACE: How did you manage to escape?

BROWN: Beverly.

TRACE: You—excuse me?

BROWN: She must have climbed in through the window. I don't know exactly what happened. I might have passed out for a second or two. But I saw her, in the room, standing behind the man.

TRACE: Wait a minute, wait a minute. I want to make sure I'm hearing you correctly—Beverly Dreger was in your dorm room the night you were attacked?

BROWN: Yes.

TRACE: And you told the police this?

BROWN: Of course. But they kept it out of the press because—

LUMPKIN: I don't think you want to get into all—

BROWN: It's why I'm here, Gabriel. This is my story, not yours, not theirs. Beverly saved my life.

TRACE: This really is extraordinary. I'm not trying to push you, and Mr. Lumpkin, if you want us to take a break while you talk with your client—

BROWN: Just let me finish.

TRACE: Lisa, go ahead.

BROWN: The police are waiting to find Beverly and see if her story gels with mine. I'm not afraid to say this—they want to catch us both in a lie. That's why you've never heard this before.

TRACE: And you said Beverly saved your life?

BROWN: Yes. Absolutely.

TRACE: This is unbelievable. What did she do?

BROWN: I couldn't see too well, but she came up behind him. Beverly was a strong girl, and she grabbed the guy around his neck.

TRACE: She was trying to strangle him?

BROWN: I think so, yes.

TRACE: And then what happened?

BROWN: He broke free and lunged for her. I could only see him from behind but his skin was...*flaking* off. Drifting through the air like...like ashes. He tried for Beverly's throat but she sidestepped him.

TRACE: My god.

BROWN: Then she hit him. Or stabbed him. I don't know, but he went down *hard*. That's the last clear thing I remember seeing, the man falling onto the floor.

TRACE: Could she have stabbed him with the knife that was found in the bushes?

BROWN: I don't know. Maybe.

TRACE: Okay, keep going, Lisa.

BROWN: My vision was blurry. Hazy, almost like smoke in my eyes. Green smoke. Beverly checked on me, making sure I was okay. Then I passed out. I don't know for how long, but the 911 call was recorded at 3:01, so it could only have been for a few minutes.

TRACE: You said you saw green smoke?

BROWN: Yes. And it smelled terrible.

TRACE: Did the smoke alarm go off?

BROWN: There are no smoke alarms in the dorm rooms. Only in the hallway. But no, it didn't go off.

TRACE: You made the 911 call from your room?

BROWN: Yes.

TRACE: And where was Beverly? Where was the man who attacked you?

BROWN: When I woke up, they were gone.

TRACE: Gone?

BROWN: Yes.

TRACE: And when the police came to your room—later, when you told them your story and they searched your room for clues—did they find his blood, or the rope he brought, or maybe his bootprints outside your window, I don't know—did they find anything like that?

BROWN: That's just it—they didn't even bother to check. They thought they had their killer in Beverly, but they're wrong.

LUMPKIN: It's called tunnel vision, and it's one of the leading causes of wrongful convictions in the United States.

TRACE: But, Lisa, as far as we know—there was no evidence at all of this man in your room?

BROWN: There was one thing. A burn mark on the floor.

TRACE: A burn mark?

BROWN: A black circle burned right into the carpet. And before you ask—no, it wasn't there before.

TRACE: But you don't know how it got there?

BROWN: I haven't quite wrapped my head around that yet.

TRACE: Did the police investigate the burn mark?

LUMPKIN: I've been told they cut out pieces of the rug to study, but I've never seen any evidence that this is true. And since then, the entire room has been torn up and remodeled.

TRACE: So, at this point, we really don't know what evidence was preserved from the crime scene and what was lost in the demolition of the room?

LUMPKIN: You'd have to ask one of the investigating detectives about that.

TRACE: And, Lisa, you said the man's skin was flaking off, that it looked like ashes in the air. Did police confirm this in any way by the evidence collected at the scene?

BROWN: If they did, they've never shared that information with me.

TRACE: I see. This is just so bizarre. Lisa, let me ask you, and I'm sure our viewers are wondering—why come forward now, almost two years after the murders, with this story?

BROWN: Because, like a fool, I trusted the police. I figured they would find Beverly and learn for themselves that she saved my life. Then they'd go after the man who broke into my room and attacked me and killed those poor girls. But they've failed on every level since then. Frankly, I don't blame Bev for hiding out. I would have done the same thing. When everyone wants to crucify you, sometimes you have no choice but to run.

TRACE: Lisa, I've got a lot more questions and not enough time to ask them, but—given all that we know, all that you experienced that night, the confusion with the timeline, Beverly's disappearance, the man who vanished from your room—what I want to know is, what is your take on all this? Who was that man in your room?

BROWN: I think the best way to answer that question is to say that some things can't be explained.

TRACE: But that doesn't help to solve crimes, does it?

BROWN: No, probably not.

TRACE: Do you know where Beverly is hiding, Lisa?

BROWN: I only know what the police have chosen to disclose.

TRACE: They thought she was in Kentucky somewhere, right? That she had gone off the grid somehow.

BROWN: It's just another in a long line of stories the police want the public to believe.

TRACE: Would you tell me if you knew where she was?

BROWN: I'm not sure.

TRACE: If you're in contact with Beverly, would you encourage her to turn herself in?

BROWN: I'm not in contact with her.

TRACE: But you just told me you wouldn't tell me if you were.

BROWN: No. I said I'm not *sure* if I would tell you.

TRACE: I want to thank you both for being our guests tonight.

BROWN: Thank you.

LUMPKIN: Thank you, Gavin.

From "No Stone Uncovered in Beverly Dreger's Tragic *Halloween*" by Gustavo Carrillo (originally published in *Monsters & Mayhem*, Aug. 1984, p. 6):

Intrepid reporter and horror ranconteur Gustavo Carrillo reunites with *Monsters & Mayhem* favorite Eugene Stone to discuss his wild promotional tour for his first full-length feature, *Squatters*. Stone also gives us the latest scoop on the Beverly Dreger saga with news that is sure to titilate. Carrillo spoke with Stone during the 25-year-old director's appearance at the Ghosts and Gravestones Film Festival in Los Angeles, where *Squatters* took home the prestigious Audience Award...

M&M: First things first—are you okay? You looked a little wiped out at the press conference.

STONE: I'm exhausted. But I love this town, and people have been so nice to us. *Squatters* premiered last night at Ghosts and Gravestones and got a standing ovation, so life is pretty good right now.

M&M: While on this junket, you've continued pumping out your 'zine, "The Black Notebook," which collects pieces of the Beverly Dreger story and the Woodhurst Slayings of 1981. How's that been going?

STONE: Honestly, it's been tough. With *Squatters*, we wanted to make you laugh and scare you at the same time. But there's not much laughter in Beverly's story. I've read her paper on *Halloween* and there is a real sadness there that's come to represent her entire life.

M&M: You've published a lot of sensitive material that has never been available to the public before. How did you manage that?

STONE: In this crazy line of work, it's all about who you know. I think you get the gist of what I'm saying.

M&M: But I've heard rumors that you've run into legal trouble with some of the documents you've published in "The Black Notebook." Will that stop you from working on the project?

STONE: We live in a litigious society, with everyone and their brother trying to make a buck off someone else. But until a judge orders me to stop, or I'm hauled off to jail, I'll keep telling the Beverly Dreger story in the way I see fit.

M&M: So there will be a final installment of the 'zine?

STONE: Yes, quite a big one, actually! Near the end of the project, I contacted one of Beverly's college professors, Lauren Reid, hoping to score an interview. Beverly had written the *Halloween* paper for her class. We ended up talking for hours about everything, and we came to the decision to make a movie based on Beverly's story. Lauren and I are going to write the script, and I'm going to direct.

M&M: That's exciting news! Are you officially announcing it as your next project?

STONE: Yes. I've got some research to do before we start up, but this will definitely be my second feature film. I want to go back to her childhood, to the Ouija board, to when Beverly first started believing in the bogeyman, and try to capture her innocence and naïvete in the script. Then juxtapose those feelings with the murders that happened later.

M&M: Have you seen *The Exorcist* or *Amityville 3-D*? Playing with a Ouija board is not a good idea!

STONE: Well, to really bring Beverly's experience to the big screen, to understand her fears and pain, I need to walk in her footsteps. I can't just gather the materials of her life; I need to live them. Besides, have you seen the disaster that was *Amityville 3-D*? I think I'll be okay!

M&M: Speaking of movies, are you nervous about making one about a suspected killer who hasn't been caught by police yet?

STONE: You know me, Gustavo. I've never been nervous about doing *anything* in my career…

JOHNSON - Original Story (8:30 a.m. on Sept. 1, 1984):

Johnson County Police are investigating a suspicious death reported on Saturday morning at the Southwest Motor Motel on Bush Road in South Hill.

Two uniformed officers responded just before noon to a frantic call from the motel manager, who said there was an unconscious male bleeding in his room. Paramedics were dispatched to the scene and arrived shortly after police.

Officers found the deceased man covered in blood on the floor of the motel room. The JCPD did not release an official statement, but said that due to the nature of the deceased's injuries, a homicide investigation would most likely be underway. The Medical Examiner's Office arrived at the scene as investigators began collecting evidence and interviewing possible witnesses.

The victim's identity was not released to the media at the time of this writing.

Update (9:00 a.m.):

Police are treating the death of a man at the Southwest Motor Motel on Bush Road as a homicide. Though the exact cause of the man's death remains unknown, his jugular vein had been cut with a sharp instrument, an injury that resulted in major blood loss, according to Assistant Coroner Lee Hardner.

The Johnson County Medical Examiner's Office left the scene with the body at 8:35 a.m. Several police officers were at the motel to canvass the area while two detectives began logging and removing items from the decedent's room, including several legal pads and a typewriter.

Update (4:30 p.m.):

Police have identified the body that was found in a South Hill motel room on Saturday morning as Eugene Stone, 26, of Evanston.

Stone, a graduate of Woodhurst State and an independent filmmaker, had his throat slashed and sustained other severe bodily injuries, including lacerations to his hands and face, according to a press release from the Johnson County Police Department.

Though investigators could not confirm, it appeared that Stone was in South Hill doing research for his next film project. His motel room was covered in old police files, interview transcripts, and photographs of young women, possibly actresses.

Police also found several used candles and a Ouija board in the room, suggesting that the victim was involved in some kind of occult practice or was gathering props for his film.

Stone's motel room showed no signs of forced entry, though police noted unusual scratches on the door of the closet.

Assistant Coroner for the Johnson County Medical Examiner's Office Lee Hardner identified the cause of death as severe blood loss due to a penetrating injury to the throat.

From "Gruesome Murder Sparks New Interest in Homicide Case" by Scooter Smith (originally published in *The National Buzz*, Oct. 1984, p. 8-9):

After the grisly motel-room murder of Eugene Stone, shocking new insights have shed light into the world of murder suspect Beverly Dreger, The BUZZ can reveal in this exclusive story.

Three years after the Woodhurst Slayings of 1981, in which three women were found slaughtered in their beds, Beverly remains a fugitive, eluding capture and frustrating Chicago police.

But the death of Stone, a filmmaker and writer who published several "indie" magazines dedicated to Beverly and the killings, has deepened the mystery behind this bizarre story.

As part of an in-depth investigation, The BUZZ contacted 22-year-old Charlene Duncan, a bartender at Sparky's Bar and Lounge in South Hill, Beverly's hometown.

"I met Eugene one night at the bar," Charlene explains. "He said he was doing research into his movie about the Woodhurst murders. I went to high school with Beverly, so he wanted to interview me. We talked until closing, and then I joined him at his motel for some beers. Eugene was a nice guy, cute in a nerdy way, and easy to talk to."

But it was inside Stone's motel room that Charlene said the fun night took a turn for the worse.

"He took out a Ouija board from his suitcase and put candles all over the room. He held my hand and told me he wanted to have a séance," Charlene said. "But I'm Christian and I didn't want anything to do with it.

"I warned him to not mess around with all that demonic stuff, and then I left," Charlene added.

Wanting to know more, The BUZZ contacted Lauren Reid, a film professor at Woodhurst State who had been working with Stone on a screenplay about Beverly Dreger and the brutal slayings of 1981.

"It's been three years since this tragedy happened," Reid says, "and most people don't seem to care anymore. But I care. That's why I'm doing this."

In an exclusive interview with The BUZZ, the professor revealed that she and Stone were also in the process of writing a screenplay based on the life and times of Beverly Dreger.

The script was to include all of Beverly's morbid obsessions, including her twisted love for the horror flick *Halloween*, and climax with the gruesome slayings at Woodhurst State.

"Beverly Dreger was born into a world of paranoid delusion, but in reality the monster was right there in front of her, scribbling in her little black book and playing with Ouija boards," Reid said, referring to Susan Dreger, Beverly's mentally ill mother who killed herself in 1976.

"This woman made a holy mess of her daughter. It was child neglect, child abuse. Beverly was a psychologically battered kid, a fact that Eugene and I hoped to capture in our screenplay."

Eugene Stone was just 26 when his body was found in the tiny motel room in South Hill. His throat had been cut nearly ear to ear.

Scattered about Stone's motel room were pages from Beverly's paper on *Halloween*, as well as police reports, books on directing and screenwriting, and several photographs of young actresses.

Lauren Reid says that the screenplay she was writing with Stone would have been the crucial link to understanding Beverly's entire psychology.

"We were going to call it *The Girls of October*," the raven-haired professor said, a touching tribute to the three beautiful young women who died tragically in October of 1981.

"We had finished about twenty pages of the script when Eugene left to do some research in Beverly's hometown," Reid said. "I didn't hear from him for weeks. Then I got the call that he was dead. And before the police told me, for some reason I knew that he had been murdered."

After media outlets revealed what was found in Stone's room— including the Ouija board and unusual scratches on the closet door— Reid has grown more alarmed by Beverly Dreger's obsession with "the bogeyman," an infamous nocturnal creature that the professor now believes may be more than just an urban legend.

"After what happened to Eugene, I could no longer dimiss it as some silly superstition," she told The BUZZ. "He went down the rabbit hole and met someone there who killed him."

Reid said that Stone's murder has brought her understanding of Beverly Dreger to a harrowing climax.

"Beverly is suspected of killing three people. And if you count Eugene, which some people are, that makes four," Reid said. "If she's guilty, she should be punished under state law.

"But here's the thing—the police can't explain the burn mark in Lisa Brown's dorm room. They can't identify the weird substance on the knife found in the bushes. And though they won't admit it, they have no idea who killed Eugene.

"I don't believe in fairy tales, spooky legends, or magic," Reid concluded. "But I lock all my doors and windows at night now, and I check to make sure my closet's empty before going to bed."

CHICAGO - Detectives have relaunched their investigation into a murder case that has haunted a quiet Chicago community for three years—and the results are truly shocking.

An eyewitness interview on *Gavin Trace Up Close and Personal* led police to return to the home of Jack Dreger in South Hill, hoping to spark new leads in the case of a triple homicide that occurred on the Woodhurst State campus in 1981.

Dreger, 51, is the father of the primary suspect in the murders, Beverly Dreger, now 24, who has been missing since the night of the slayings.

In the televised interview aired in July of last year, Lisa Brown placed her former roommate near the scene of the murders, but adamantly denied that Beverly had anything to do with them.

Instead, Brown told host Gavin Trace that Beverly rescued her from being killed by an intruder who had broken into her dorm room.

Brown added that police were so focused on Beverly as the killer that they believed Brown was lying to protect her friend.

Police now say they want to find Beverly to hear her side of the story and possibly eliminate her as a suspect in the college slayings.

In an interview conducted at his home, Jack Dreger told police that his daughter has been troubled all her life, but that he has tried to get her the help she needed. According to the police report, Dreger stated that he feels partially responsible for any crimes Beverly may have committed.

"Mr. Dreger was very emotional at the time, but I won't get into the specifics of all that was said," said Detective Clayton Brewer of the South Hill Police Department.

During the interview, Dreger denied rumors that he has been in communication with his daughter since the murders.

"We addressed that issue, and we did have some concerns based on what we observed in the residence, but it was not enough to move forward legally at that time," Det. Brewer said.

Two days later, when investigators returned to the Dreger home with a search warrant, they found the house empty.

Det. Brewer said that clothes and other personal items appeared to be missing from the residence, and that Jack Dreger's car was not parked in the driveway.

"We are going on the assumption that Mr. Dreger either went in search of his daughter, or that he knows right where she is.

"We found evidence pointing toward their whereabouts, but I'm not willing to disclose anything major right now," Det. Brewer said.

Det. Brewer hopes to organize a more concentrated task force devoted to the investigation of the murders and to remedy some of the errors that law enforcement has made since the slayings occurred.

"We should have kept watch on Mr. Dreger's house, and I take full responsibility for that mistake," he said.

The detective explained that he has a personal connection to the case that has made him a driving factor in the investigation.

"Tracy-Ann Watkins was my niece. She was a loving girl and she suffered horribly," he said, referring to one of the three victims in the slayings. "And I'm convinced that Beverly Dreger has the answers we need.

"We're going to find her. It's just a matter of time."

From "Nebraska's News of the Weird" by Samantha P. Newton (originally published in *The Curtis Gazette*, July 1984, p. 5):

A maid at the Country Western Motel on Center Avenue made a curious discovery on Sunday morning when she found the closet door nailed shut in one of the guest rooms she was cleaning.

The manager of the motel, Garth Tejada, told *The Gazette* that the maid was vacuuming the room when she noticed a strange pattern of marks along the outer frame of the closet door. Upon inspection, the maid realized the marks were actually nails that had been twisted and hammered into the jamb of the door.

Unnerved by what she saw, the maid hurried to the front office and alerted Tejada. Rather than pry the nails from the closet door and open it, the manager contacted the Frontier County police.

"An officer arrived and used one of my hammers to remove the nails. It took a while because the nails were bent at odd angles. There was nothing else unusual in the room, but we were all a little freaked out by what might have been inside the closet," said Tejada.

When the officer removed the last nail and opened the door, the manager breathed a sigh of relief. Aside from the usual wire hangers and a bag of mothballs, the closet was empty.

Tejada said that a man and a woman had checked into the room the previous evening around midnight.

"They might've been father and daughter. She was a lot younger than him, with hair cut down real short, like a boy's," said Tejada. "They didn't have a car, and they paid in cash, so I have no way of billing them for the damages."

Tejada told *The Gazette* that his cleaning staff has made plenty of unusual discoveries while cleaning rooms over the years, including vintage stamps, a prosthetic leg, and a pair of used dentures.

"But this was creepy," the manager said. "Why did they nail the closet door shut? What were they trying to keep inside?"

Though the Country Western Motel does receive some regular guests, Tejada doubts that he will see the duo again.

"Roadside motels like this, people just pop in and out," he said. "With the bus depot right across the street, I have a feeling these two are long gone."

ABOUT THE AUTHOR

Josh Hancock is a teacher, author, and documentary filmmaker. His two non-fiction films, *Cabin 28: The Keddie Murders Part I* and *Part II*, reignited interest in one of Northern California's most bizarre unsolved murders. His first novel, *The Girls of October*, is inspired by his love of all things horror--especially John Carpenter's *Halloween*, Tobe Hooper's *The Texas Chain Saw Massacre*, and William Friedkin's *The Exorcist*. To unlock all of the mysteries within *The Girls of October*, please visit thegirlsofoctober.tumblr.com.

OTHER GREAT TITLES FROM

Burning Bulb

PUBLISHING

WWW.BURNINGBULBPUBLISHING.COM

GARY LEE VINCENT'S
DARKENED
THE WEST VIRGINIA VAMPIRE SERIES

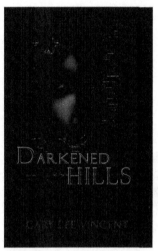

DARKENED HILLS

When evil descends on a small West Virginia town, who will survive?

Jonathan did not start out his life to become a rambler, it just worked out that way. William was a troubled youth with something to hide. Both were from Melas, a small town tucked away in the West Virginia hills... a town where disappearances are happening more and more frequently.

After the suicide of a wanted serial killer, the townsfolk thought the nightmare was over. But when a centuries-old vampire is discovered they find out the hard way it's just getting started. Dark secrets can only stay hidden for so long and when the devil comes to collect, there will be hell to pay. Can Jonathan and William find a way to stop the vampire before it's too late? Find out in *Darkened Hills!*

DARKENED HOLLOWS

In the heart-stopping sequel to the award-winning *Darkened Hills*, Jonathan and William must return to West Virginia to face possible criminal charges stemming from their last visit to the damned town of Melas, where both had narrowly escaped the clutches of a vampire seethe.

And as livestock start mysteriously getting murdered with all of their blood drained, worried farmers are searching for answers - leaving the local Sheriff and his deputy racing against time to learn the cause before a more violent crime is committed.

Burning Bulb
PUBLISHING

WWW.DARKENEDHILLS.COM

GARY LEE VINCENT'S
DARKENED
THE WEST VIRGINIA VAMPIRE SERIES

DARKENED WATERS

When the world goes to hell, the chosen must arise!

As Talman Cane orchestrates a flood of epic proportions in this third installment of the *Darkened* series the towns of Melas and Tarklin are caught completely off guard by the deluge. Hell-bent on finishing what they started, the evil brothers return to the lunatic asylum to take care of the witnesses and add to the ever-growing army of the undead.

Aided by Lucifer himself and the insane vampire demon Legion, the stage is set to channel all of the forces of hell to come forth. In an all-out race to survive, Jonathan, William, and Amanda soon discover they are up against impossible odds as Lucifer opens the Gateway to Hell, ushering in the zombie apocalypse and the End Times.

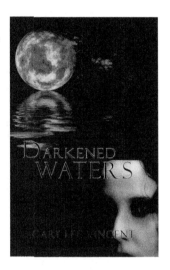

DARKENED SOULS

Melas and the Madison House are about to be rebuilt. True evil is about to be reborne!

Young ex-priest and vampire-killer William is drawn back to the West Virginian town that almost killed him, where his vampire arch-enemy Victor Rothenstein still stalks the earth.

The town of Melas lies destroyed after the battle of the End of Days. But why is wealthy Jackie Nixon so eager to rebuild it using the bone dust of murdered souls?

Terrible evil has visited before, but the Gateway to Hell is about to be reopened in a horrific climax. And this time – it's personal.

WWW. DARKENEDHILLS.COM

Burning Bulb
PUBLISHING

ANTHOLOGIES
BIZARRO AND TRANSGRESSIVE FICTION

THE BIG BOOK OF BIZARRO

The Big Book of Bizarro brings together the peculiar prose of an international cast of the most grotesquely-gonzo, genre-grinding modern writers who ever put pen to paper (or mouse to pad), including:

NIGHT OF THE LIVING DEAD *horror writers John Russo & George Kosana;* HUSTLER MAGAZINE *erotica contributors Eva Hore, Andrée Lachapelle, & J. Troy Seate and established Bizarro genre authors D. Harlan Wilson, William Pauley III, Wol-vriey, Laird Long, Richard Godwin and so many more!*

From Alien abductions to Zombie sex, *The Big Book of Bizarro* contains OVER FIFTY STORIES *of the most outrélandish transgressive fiction that you'll ever lay your capricious and curious hands upon!*

WARNING: *This book may be one of the most controversial and dangerous books you'll ever read.*

WESTWARD HOES

Nine outlaw writers rode into town from obscurity to pen nine tantalizing tales of horror and fantasy, and leaving once they branded their own personal marks on the weird western genre and became living legends of the American Frontier experience.

Like drunken Indian scouts, the writers fervidly tracked down and captured the Western genre, tore off its fashionable veneer and ravished its exposed essence.

So belly up to the bar with your favorite soiled dove and enjoy perusing these thrilling tales of Old West debauchery, danger and desire; compiled by the publisher of The Big Book of Bizarro and featuring the bizarro novella *Big Trouble in Little Ass* by Wol-vriey.

Burning Bulb
PUBLISHING

ANTHOLOGIES
BIZARRO AND TRANSGRESSIVE FICTION

THE BIG BOOK OF BIZARRO SPECIAL KINDLE EDITIONS

OTHER AWESOME COLLECTIONS

WOL-VRIEY
BIZARRO AND TRANSGRESSIVE FICTION

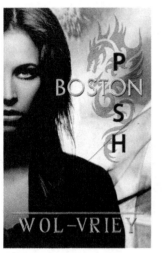

BOSTON POSH

In 2028 AD, the USA is a nation ravaged by hungry dragons and dinosaurs. In Boston, Massachusetts, private eye Bud Malone is hired to rescue a kidnapped heiress. But nothing is as it seems.

Malone works to unravel a tangled web involving Boston Chinatown, a 200-year-old woman with a 9-year-old body, white robots, a human-liver-eating psychopath, a golem, a porcelain dragon, and a snake goddess with a crush on him. There's also a woman obsessed with chicken sex. Then Malone meets Posh Lane, a gorgeous call girl who's desperate to quit her pimp.

Romantic sparks ignite between Posh and Malone, but Posh's past suddenly catches up with her in a BIG way. To save Posh, Malone agrees to run a quest for Earth's new rulers, the Forks. But, Malone has no idea that agreeing to the Fork's odd request will send him on the weirdest trip he's ever been on in his life.

VAGINA MUNDI

Rachel Risk is a professional thief with super-strong hair that can stretch like tentacles to manipulate objects. Ashley Status has both a digitally augmented brain, and 'muscle-purses' in her arms and leg in which she stores inflatable objects—cars, guns, rocket launchers, etc.

When Raye is framed as the fall girl in a jewel robbery, the pair flee Chicago's vengeful robot gangsters and take refuge in the Hotel Bizarre, where the gorgeous 'vagina singer,' Femina, is performing for a week.

But the Hotel Bizarre is even stranger than its name suggests, and very soon Raye and Ash are involved in an deadly adventure, a struggle for survival the likes of which they'd never imagined possible—with loads of deviant sex, drugs, music, and violence at every turn. And just what is the old woman in the skin desert really doing with all those cats glued to her walls?

Vagina Mundi—a Bizarro Hymn in praise of WOMAN!

Burning Bulb
PUBLISHING

WOL-VRIEY
BIZARRO AND TRANSGRESSIVE FICTION

VEGAN VAMPIRE VAGINAS

The biggest bank heist in US history. And Tom Palmer can't remember pulling it off. And no, this isn't your standard case of amnesia. After a one-night-stand gone horribly wrong, Boston salesman Tom Palmer wakes up with a vagina implanted in his left hand. Then his day gets worse.

Tom is transported across space-time to a nightmare version of Boston, one where the Bizarro virus has transformed half the population into cannibals. Worst of all, Tom discovers that in this new Boston, he's the infamous gangster Pussypalm, wanted for robbing the Federal Reserve Bank of Boston a year ago. He also learns that the vagina in his hand is prophetic, i.e. it talks . . . after sex.

With 130 people left dead during his bank heist and six billion dollars missing, Tom knows he's living on borrowed time. It is in his best interests not to remember anything. Because once he does . . .

VEGAN ZOMBIE APOCALYPSE

In the post-apocalypse worlderness, zombies rule the earth. They're allergic to meat, and brains literally make them explode. Zombies now eat blood potatoes, parasitic tubers grown in the flesh of humancows corralled in maximum security farms. Two fugitives meet in the ancient ruins of Texas. The first is Soil 15-f, a woman-cow who's escaped her farm a week before she's due to be killed and her blood potato crop harvested. The second fugitive is Able Kane, former head necros food technician, now sentenced to death for heresy. But Soil is no ordinary humancow.

Unknown to herself, she's the vegan zombie agricultural revolution, and the zombies desperately want her back. And the necros equally desperately want Able Kane dead. He's fled with a forbidden discovery which will reshape the world for the worse if used. And Able is just hardheaded/misguided enough to use it.

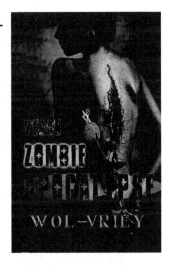

Burning Bulb
PUBLISHING

WOL-VRIEY
BIZARRO AND TRANSGRESSIVE FICTION

MELANIE NEMESIS CATCHPOLE

In Springfield, Massachusetts, Melanie Catchpole is hired to fetch back a magic teddy bear worth millions of dollars from warehouse across town. Problem is, the warehouse is down in Springfield's O-Zone—that totally weird sector of the city where Bizarro fell to Earth. The 'O' is a fairytale land, a place where dreams and nightmares literally live and breathe. Worse still, the gingers—mutant cannibals—prowl the O. The gingers have already eaten everyone else Melanie's employer sent to get back the magic teddy bear.

Accompanied by the handsome but ruthless Doug Fisher (who she finds sexy but doesn't dare entrust her heart to), Melanie enters the O-Zone. Melanie and Doug are instantly caught up in an adventure they'd never have believed credible even if written as fiction . . . and Melanie's used to experiencing the very weird as the norm.

And now, additionally, there's a mystery to unravel: What does the dark, freezing-cold being called The Fixer want with Mary, the barkeep's daughter?

BIZARRO 101 (A BASIC PRIMER)

Welcome to the strange place:

A collection of 37 flash fiction stories designed to introduce one to the Bizarro/New Weird Genre.

Weird, dreamy, nightmarish, absurd, sad, surreal, humorous . . . this collection of tales is all this and more.

***

"This primer is the very essence of any and all styles and types of Bizarro writing. Wol-vriey collects, distills, and bottles up these 37 tiny stories for your sensory enjoyment. This is an absolute must-read for anyone new to the genre, because it demonstrates the scope of what Bizarro is, and what it can be."
—Teresa Pollack, Bizarro commentator and blogger

Burning Bulb
PUBLISHING

ZAKARY MCGAHA
BIZARRO AND TRANSGRESSIVE FICTION

SEA OF MEDIUM-TO-HIGH PITCHED NOISES

The zombie apocalypse is changing; the world is coming to an odd demise; and a serial killer tries to change his ways and redeem himself before it all goes away. Now, Crabby has entered the world he left behind; the world of the undead. And things are changing. Everything will come to an end. In this new wave of the apocalypse, everything changes every five minutes. And death would be an absolute luxury. Psychological torment meets physical bloodletting in Sea of Medium-to-High Pitched Noises.

PARK MASTERS

Bad breakups, Bigfoot costumes, ghost bears, and more. Park Masters is a wacky, intelligent, quirky comedy about the power relationships have on people, good or bad. Also, it's just plain fun!

Burning Bulb
PUBLISHING

WEST VIRGINIA-THEMED *HUMORROROTICA*

BY RICH BOTTLES JR.

HELLHOLE WEST VIRGINIA

From the heights of Mothman's perch high atop the Silver Bridge in Point Pleasant to the depths of Hellhole Cavern in Pendleton County, evil lurks within the shadows as the sun sets upon the haunted hills and hollows of West Virginia.

Bizarro author Rich Bottles Jr. blows the coffin lid off horror genre clichés with this tour de force cast of Eco-friendly vampires, beach-yearning zombies and sex-starved she-devils.

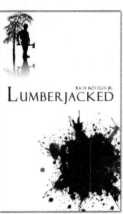

LUMBERJACKED

If you are easily offended or do not possess a truly depraved sense of humor, this story may not be the light summer reading fare you desire. As for the four feisty female freshmen stranded on top of West Virginia's third highest mountain, they have no choice but to experience the sick, twisted debauchery and perverted mayhem described deep inside the tight unbroken bindings of this horrific missive.

Lumberjacked takes the reader to a nightmarish world where character development and aesthetic integrity are prematurely cut short by the swinging axes of maniacal lumberjacks, who are hell bent on death and destruction in the remote forests of Appalachia. And at the climax, when paranoia crosses over to the paranormal, Lumberjacked makes Deliverance look like a family raft trip down the Lower Gauley.

THE MANACLED

What happens when twin brothers lease out the former West Virginia State Penitentiary with the false purpose of filming a documentary on supernatural phenomena, but their true intention is to make a pornographic movie?

Chaos ensues as the disturbed spirits of murdered convicts, along with the reanimated dead from the neighboring Indian Burial Mound, take their vengeance on the unwary and undressed trespassers.

Zombies, ghosts, mobsters and porn collide in this bizarre tale from horror author Rich Bottles Jr.

Burning Bulb
PUBLISHING

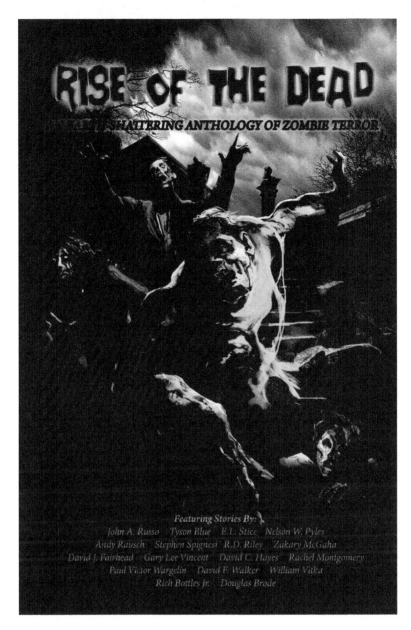

RISE OF THE DEAD - a collection of seventeen tales of unspeakable zombie terror. Featuring a foreword and short story by John A. Russo!

www.TheJohnRusso.com

Burning Bulb
PUBLISHING

NIGHT OF THE LIVING DEAD

Why does **Night of the Living Dead** hit with such chilling impact?
Is it because everyday people in a commonplace house are suddenly the
victims of a monstrous invasion? Or is it because the ghouls who surround
the house with grasping claws were once ordinary people, too?

Decide for yourself as you read, and the horror grips you. All the
cannibalism, suspense and frenzy of the smash-hit move are here in the
novel.

www.TheJohnRusso.com

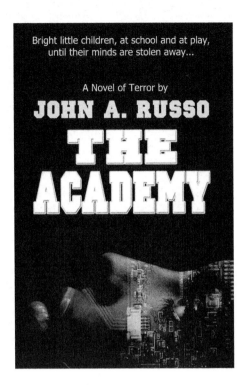

Bright little children, at school and at play,
until their minds are stolen away...

A Novel of Terror by

JOHN A. RUSSO

THE ACADEMY

THE ACADEMY

The Academy. It's every parent's dream, turning their little darlings into geniuses, superachievers, perfect little children.

And if there's a problem, the Academy fixes that too. It's a simple operation. Just a little device. Then a teeny pink scar on a tender little skull . . .

One boy knows the secret. Now he wants his mind back. But it's much, much too late. Too late for anything but the ugly feelings. The bad feelings. The messy sexy feelings. The knife-cold hatred, the murderous rage, for total, screaming, blood-drenching revenge . . .

www.TheJohnRusso.com

Burning Bulb
PUBLISHING

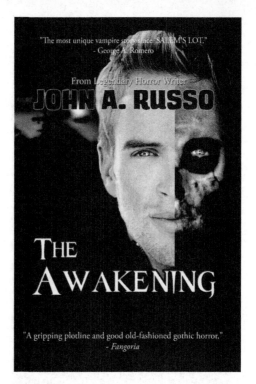

"The most unique vampire story since 'SALEM'S LOT."
- George A. Romero

From Legendary Horror Writer
JOHN A. RUSSO

THE AWAKENING

"A gripping plotline and good old-fashioned gothic horror."
- *Fangoria*

THE AWAKENING

For two hundred years, he has rested. Now he rises. Now he will be satisfied. Nothing can stop him. No one can resist him.

Benjamin Latham is young and handsome, his eighteenth-century mind wakened to a bizarre twentieth-century world. And there is the need deep within . . . an animal need, frightening, murderous, unholy . . . a vital need that must be fed.

And with his need comes a power over men and women to do his bidding, to quiet his dark craving . . .

Until the murders begin. And the inquiries. All suggesting the same hideous truth.

Now Benjamin must find a sanctuary: a lover, a partner, a friend. Someone who can share his darkness. Someone he can lead to . . . The Awakening.

www.TheJohnRusso.com

Burning Bulb
PUBLISHING

THE BOOBY HATCH

With NIGHT OF THE LIVING DEAD, John Russo helped blaze a path in the horror genre that has never been equalled. In this hillarious erotic novel, he blazes a path through the wild, zany Sex Revolution of the 1970s.

Sweet, innocent Cherry Jankowski works for Joyful Novelties, where she tests sex toys ranging from the ridiculous to the sublime. But she can't find love or peace of mind and her efforts are hampered by a Peeping Tom, an exhibitionist, a cross-dressing boyfriend, a quack psychiatrist, and even her own product-testing partner, Marcello Fettucini, who can't get it up anymore and is scared of losing his job!

www.TheJohnRusso.com

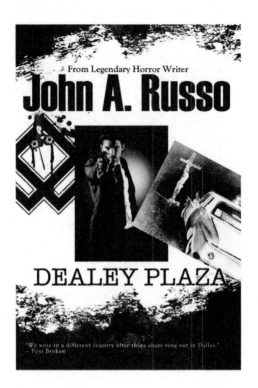

From Legendary Horror Writer John A. Russo

DEALEY PLAZA

"We were in a different country after those shots rang out in Dallas." — Tom Brokaw

DEALEY PLAZA

From legendary horror and suspense writer JOHN RUSSO comes a harrowing tale where no one is safe!

Dealey Plaza is one of the most notorious places in America, and when youthful conspiracy buffs go there in 1964 to stage their own reenactment of the Kennedy Assassination, four of them are brutally murdered ~ the first victims of a hate-filled legacy that continues for four more decades.

The survivors of that long-ago Dallas trip, each of them now icons of the American way of life, are about to be honored ~ or killed.

Who will live and who will die? Will it be country-western star Lori McCoy? Her loving husband? Her scheming ex-husband? Or the case-hardened FBI agent and longtime friend who risks his life trying to protect them?

www.DealeyPlazaBook.com

Burning Bulb
PUBLISHING

From Legendary Horror Writer
JOHN A. RUSSO
LIMB to LIMB

LIMB TO LIMB

SUCH A PRETTY GIRL . . .
Tiffany Blake was a beautiful long-limbed dancer with a glorious future and the backing of a rich benefactor. Then a monstrous accident severed her leg at the hip.

SUCH A COLD, CRUEL KNIFE . . .
And now her fellow dancers are disappearing without a trace. One by one they fall victim to a dark and deadly pattern of evil – caught by the bloody, brutal logic that would have them pay with their lovely bodies for the cruel fate of another . . .victims of the sadistic madman whose flashing knife will make them writhe a gruesome new dance.

www.TheJohnRusso.com

Burning Bulb
PUBLISHING

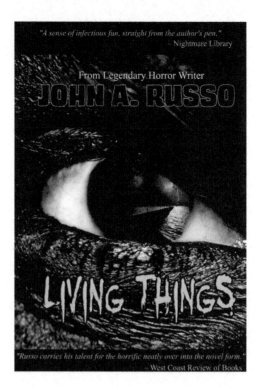

LIVING THINGS

Beneath the shimmering Miami sun sprawls one of the Mafia's biggest empires, a glittering worldof lavish beachfront mansions, neon-painted nightclubs, beautiful women, expensive cars—and absolute control over the state's billion-dollar drug trade. But, one by one, its ganglords and henchmen are falling prey to a new rival. His powers are fueled by monstrous ancient rituals; his hellish undead legions slaughter mobsters and innocent citizens alike, his unholylust for power is virtually unstoppable.

Now a burned-out ex-detective and a brilliant anthropologist must enter a gruesome, nightmare world to fight this master of malevolence and illusion. Their time is short, their weapons few, and they face an ultimate, terrifying choice - annihilation or the loss of their souls to the eternal torment of those who never die. . .

www.TheJohnRusso.com

Burning Bulb
PUBLISHING

MAD WORLD BY ANDY RAUSCH

"*Mad World* is dark, twisted, no-holds-barred fun."
—Jason Starr, author of *Bust*, *Slide*, and *The Max*

EVERYONE'S PLAYING AN ANGLE IN THE CITY OF ANGELS

Mad World tells the stories of a black hitman who doubles as a university professor, a Catholic priest who longs to be a gangster, a would-be author from Kansas, a gay phone sex operator who claims he's straight, a group of rich twentysomethings playing a deadly game of life and death, a vicious Mafia boss, and a sleazy Hollywood movie director. As each of their stories intersect, the body count piles up and the action comes nonstop in this tense, white-knuckle thriller by first-time author Andy Rausch.

"A wild ride. If you like it gangster, *Mad World* delivers."
—Daniel Birch, author of *Get Some*

Burning Bulb
PUBLISHING

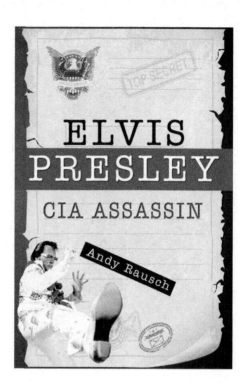

ELVIS PRESLEY, CIA ASSASSIN

"I can guarantee you. Read this book and you'll never look at Elvis the same way again!"
~ Douglas Brode, author of ELVIS CINEMA AND POPULAR CULTURE

SOON TO BE A MAJOR MOTION PICTURE

In 1970, singer Elvis Presley secretly met with President Richard Nixon. This new comedic novel imagines that Presley became a Central Intelligence Agency operative, eventually moving up through the ranks to become a skilled assassin.

Presented in an oral history fashion, the book tells us about Presley's secret transformation by the people who knew him best.

Did he fake his death in 1977? Was Presley involved with the Watergate scandal? The Iran hostage crisis? Communicating with aliens?

Read this book to find out the answers to these and many more questions.

Burning Bulb
PUBLISHING

BLOODLETTING: A TALE OF REVENGE BY ANDY RAUSCH

"Relentless… Addictive… The kind of nightmare you don't want
to wake up from."
—Heywood Gould, screenwriter of *Rolling Thunder*

He was just an average Joe. But when he finds his family held at
gunpoint by merciless thugs, he's told he must murder a Mafia
chieftain if he ever wishes to see his loved ones again.

Against all odds, Joe keeps his end of the bargain, but the criminals
don't. Now at his wits end, Joe is pushed beyond his breaking point
and forced to exact bloody revenge against those who've done him
and his family wrong in this powerful and violent novella by author
Andy Rausch (*Mad World*).

"Andy Rausch has a tight noir style that combines gritty, realistic drama
with a cinematic flair that makes for a powerful, compelling (somewhat
Stephen Kingesque), authentically visual reading experience."
—Stephen Spignesi, author of *Dialogues*

Burning Bulb
PUBLISHING

THE FALL OF TOMORROW

Hopelessness... How do you protect your loved ones when Hell itself opens its insidious mouth?
Horror... Nightmarish Creatures invade your world and there is nowhere to hide.
Blood... How long can you hold out before they come for you?
Pain... Where do you run to avoid being eaten alive by monsters with a voracious appetite for your flesh?
Screams... While you selfishly run for your own life.
Questions... Who is to blame? Where did they come from? How many people survived...and how does the human race find the means to fight back?

THE FALL OF TOMORROW is man's last tale of desperation told by those that are striving to salvage some hope against a ravenous bastion of evil beasts bent on ruling our world.

"David Fairhead writes compelling stories that offer very human characters and very inhuman monsters. There is no subtlety in Fairhead's imagination - he is simply dying to scare the hell out of you."
      - Nelson W Pyles - author of DEMONS, DOLLS AND MILKSHAKES

Burning Bulb
PUBLISHING

THE TAILSMAN

BURNING BULB

COMICS

From the creators of *The Big Book of Bizarro* and *Westward Hoes* comes a new comic unlike anything you have ever seen!

He's hot on the trail, looking for some *tail...*

Sly Franko was a man of the West, a forger of the wild frontier. Like the Country Western song that would be written years after he died, the words, "Faster horses, younger women, and more money," seemed to be the anthem of this horn dog cowboy.

Franko would ride into town on a blazing saddle, find the closest saloon to wet the whistle, belly up to a good card game, and find him a hot-loving hussy to get his cowpoke on with.

However, Sly might have met his match when a visit to bathroom leads to terror and death. Can Sly and his poker buddies solve the mystery before more of the townsfolk are murdered? Find out in this exciting premier issue of *The Tailsman*!

WWW.BURNINGBULBCOMICS.COM

THE HAGS OF BLACK COUNTY

by Michelle Bowser

Ruled by a committee of Hags, and fueled by toothless rivalries, Black County lurks just far enough out of the way to be completely unnoticed by the rest of civilization. Its inhabitants have been mentally warped for generations and the land itself seems to have the power to drive anyone unlucky enough to visit into ridiculous hillbilly madness. When a construction Company needs to bury a pipeline through its ludicrous hills and valleys, a twisted charm goes to work and every aspect of already bizarre Black County life takes a gory turn for the hysterical. Take a preposterous trip along with its citizens, both native and new, through escapades such as the Hag parade, the grand opening of Madame Skunk's House of Ill Repute, the demolition derby riot and the rabid, zombie clown apocalypse.

THE ABANDONED SOUL

by Daniel Sellers

After spending most of his 20s in a drug and alcohol fueled daze, a young man finally hits rock bottom. Having used up his friends and their good graces, he ends up squatting in an abandoned house. Forcibly sobering he begins to realize that he is not alone in this abandoned house. Left with one last friend and a mountain of regrets, he must decide if this presence is a guilty conscience, or a malicious hunter.

WE WISH YOU A HAPPY KILLDAY

by Jason Heroux

"We Wish You a Happy Killday" is the story of an international b eloved holiday called "Killday" where one day a year everyone over the age of fifteen is permitted to register for a license allowing them to kill one other person. But this year Chad Ovenstock doesn't feel like killing anyone. His friends and family urge him to participate in the festivities, but he can't seem to get into the holiday spirit. On the day before Killday Chad comes in contact with Ambrose, an old friend who suffered a nervous breakdown and is now part of The One Ant Army, a mysterious cult dedicated to making the future disappear. When the holiday finally arrives Chad refuses to participate and tries to survive on his own, surrounded by constant gunfire, countless corpses, and the nagging suspicion that Ambrose may have secretly brainwashed him into becoming a member of The One Ant Army cult.

Burning Bulb
PUBLISHING

Printed in Great Britain
by Amazon

31540958R00165